They'd made a blood vow and swore to take it to the grave

Tyler watched as Nick pulled a white candle out of his pocket, then knelt to anchor the taper in the black soil with a piece of driftwood.

Goose bumps peppered his skin as Jules lit the candle and the white flame flickered to life, rising like a ghost into the humid darkness.

Brushing off his pants, Nick stood and removed the pocket knife strapped to his leg. Teeth clenched, he dragged the blade across the inside of his knuckles. The pain was a swift stroke of fire to his nerve endings, but he made no sound. Neither did his friends as they cut their own flesh.

Standing there in the darkness, the faces of the other boys illuminated by the flickering candlelight, Nick knew something basic in his life had changed. "From now on, we're brothers by blood. No matter what happens or where we are," he vowed, "we'll be there for one another—always."

Dear Harlequin Intrigue Reader,

We have another outstanding title selection this month chock-full of great romantic suspense, starting with the next installment in our TOP SECRET BABIES promotion. In *The Hunt for Hawke's Daughter* (#605) by Jean Barrett, Devlin Hawke had never expected to see Karen Ramey once she'd left his bed—let alone have her tell him his secret child had been kidnapped by a madman. Whether a blessing or a curse, Devlin was dead set on reclaiming his child—and his woman....

To further turn up the heat, three of your favorite authors take you down to the steamy bayou with *three* of the sexiest bad boys you'll ever meet: Tyler, Nick and Jules—in *one value-packed volume!* A bond of blood tied them to each other since youth, but as men, their boyhood vow is tested. Find out all about *Bayou Blood Brothers* (#606) with Ruth Glick—writing as Rebecca York—Metsy Hingle and Joanna Wayne.

Amanda Stevens concludes our ON THE EDGE promotion with *Nighttime Guardian* (#607), a chilling tale of mystery and monsters set in the simmering South. To round out the month, Sheryl Lynn launches a new series with *To Protect Their Child* (#608). Welcome to McCLINTOCK COUNTRY, a Rocky Mountain town where everyone has a secret and love is for keeps.

More action and excitement you'll be hard-pressed to find. So pick up all four books and keep the midnight oil burning....

Sincerely,

Denise O'Sullivan
Associate Senior Editor
Harlequin Intrigue

BAYOU BLOOD BROTHERS

REBECCA YORK, METSY HINGLE AND JOANNA WAYNE

RUTH GLICK WRITING AS REBECCA YORK

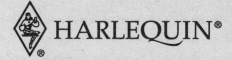

HARLEQUIN®

TORONTO • NEW YORK • LONDON
AMSTERDAM • PARIS • SYDNEY • HAMBURG
STOCKHOLM • ATHENS • TOKYO • MILAN • MADRID
PRAGUE • WARSAW • BUDAPEST • AUCKLAND

ISBN 0-373-22606-3

BAYOU BLOOD BROTHERS

Copyright © 2001 by Harlequin Books S.A.

The publisher acknowledges the copyright holders of the individual works as follows:

TYLER
Copyright © 2001 by Ruth Glick

NICK
Copyright © 2001 by Metsy Hingle

JULES
Copyright © 2001 by Jo Ann Vest

ABOUT THE AUTHORS

Award-winning, bestselling novelist Ruth Glick, who writes as Rebecca York, is the author of close to eighty books, including her popular 43 LIGHT STREET series for Harlequin Intrigue. Ruth says she has the best job in the world. Not only does she get paid for telling stories, she's also the author of twelve cookbooks. Ruth and her husband, Norman, travel frequently, researching locales for her novels and searching out new dishes for her cookbooks.

Metsy Hingle is an award-winning, bestselling author of romance who resides across the lake from her native New Orleans. Married for more than twenty years to her own hero, she is the busy mother of four children. She recently traded in her business suits and a fast-paced life in the hotel and public relations arena to pursue writing full-time. Metsy has a strong belief in the power of love and romance. She also believes in happy endings, which she continues to demonstrate with each new story she writes. She loves hearing from readers. For a free door-knob hanger or bookmark, write to Metsy at P.O. Box 3224, Covington, LA 70433.

Joanna Wayne lives with her husband just a few miles from steamy, exciting New Orleans, but her home is the perfect writer's hideaway. A lazy bayou, complete with graceful herons, colorful wood ducks and an occasional alligator, winds just below her back garden. When not creating tales of spine-tingling suspense and heartwarming romance, she enjoys reading, golfing or playing with her grandchildren, and, of course, researching and plotting out her next novel. Joanna loves to hear from readers. You can request a newsletter by writing her at P.O. Box 2851, Harvey, LA 70059-2851.

GLOSSARY

chère dear

fais-dodo a big party

galerie a front porch

grandmaman grandmother

Laissez les bon temps rouler. Let the good times roll.

loup-garou werewolf

mais non but no; of course not

mais oui but yes; of course

pirogue a flat-bottom boat similar to a dugout canoe

TYLER
REBECCA YORK

RUTH GLICK WRITING AS REBECCA YORK

To Norman, first, last and always.

Prologue

A hot breeze floated through the gnarled gray fingers of Spanish moss hanging from the dark branches over Tyler Belton's head, stirring the hair on the back of his neck. He was from the streets of New Orleans, and this midnight stretch of cypress and oak trees leading down the bayou made his skin crawl. But then, so did almost everything about Peltier Point, the Louisiana boot camp for boys who'd gotten into trouble with the law.

In the moonlight he scanned the cypress knees jutting out of the dark like gravestones. When he thought he heard the sound of some nocturnal animal slithering through the underbrush, he stiffened.

"That you?" a voice demanded in the darkness. The voice was Nick's, and Tyler breathed a little sigh of relief.

"It's about time you got here, city boy," another voice chimed in. Jules.

They were all present and accounted for.

"Any problem getting past the hall monitors?" Tyler asked.

Jules snorted. "I grew up out here, remember? A Duquette never has trouble giving anyone the slip." His eyes searched Tyler's. "Were you able to get a call out to Dave's family?"

Tyler's throat tightened as he flashed back to the conversation. Gabby, Dave's little sister, had answered the phone. And so he'd had to tell her in a trembling voice that her brother was dead—killed by a rich kid named Sincard who thought he could pass murder off as a boating accident.

He and Dave had arrived at the boot camp together a few months ago after being convicted of auto theft—two scared kids who had vowed to protect each other's backs. They'd hooked up with Nick and Jules. And the four of them had tried to stick together, for all the good it had done Dave.

"Yeah. I told his sister that the DA, LeBlanc, was threatening to call the governor if the sheriff doesn't arrest Sincard for Dave's murder."

"Good," Nick said, his voice gritty, his expression fierce. "But we still go ahead with our own defensive plans."

Tyler's heart began pounding wildly in his chest. It was really going to happen—this secret ceremony they'd discussed. Tensely he watched as Nick pulled a white candle out of his back pocket, then knelt to anchor the taper in the black soil with a piece of driftwood.

Goose bumps peppered his skin as Jules lit the candle and the flame flickered to life, rising like a ghost into the humid darkness.

Brushing off his pants, Nick stood and removed the pocket knife he'd strapped to his leg. Teeth clenched, Tyler snatched the knife from Nick and dragged the blade across his palm. The pain was a swift stroke of fire to his nerve endings, but he made no sound. Neither did his friends as they cut their own flesh.

Standing there in the darkness, the faces of the other two boys illuminated by the flickering candlelight, he knew that something basic in his life had changed. And he knew the others felt it, too. "From now on, we're brothers by blood. No matter what happens or where we are, we'll be there for one another."

"Always," they intoned together, their voices strong in

the midnight swamp as they clasped hands and mingled their blood.

It was official now. Three boys who had met by chance were brothers. Nick, from an old-money family. Jules, whose people scraped by on what they could wrest from the bayou. And Tyler himself, from the city streets.

The pledge had barely faded when another figure stepped from the darkness. My God, Tyler realized, it was Sincard. He must have followed them from the dorms. But where the hell had he gotten the shiny little pistol in his hand?

"What a touching scene," he taunted. "And now, since you three are brothers, I don't guess you'll object to dying together, will you?"

"What are you doing here?" Nick demanded, almost successful in keeping his voice steady.

"Eliminating the DA's witnesses."

Tyler pressed his hands to his sides to keep them from shaking. "If you shoot us, everyone will put two and two together."

Sincard's lip curled. "I'm not that stupid. I'm not going to kill you. You're going into the bayou, where the gators will get you. So drop the knife now," he ordered Nick, "and kick it over here."

"Whatever you say." In one fluid motion Nick dropped the weapon, kicking hard, sending dirt and leaves flying into their enemy's face.

Sincard screamed as the grit blinded him, then swiped at his eyes to clear them, but Jules and Tyler were already on him. Acting on raw nerve and blind instinct, Tyler knocked the pistol from his hand. Jules wrestled him to the ground and grabbed the gun. Handling the weapon like an extension from himself, he held the barrel to one side of Sincard's head while Tyler pointed the tip of Nick's knife at his throat.

"Kill me," Sincard sneered. "If you've got the guts."

"That would be stooping to your level," Nick answered,

giving him a shove in the direction of the camp. "The law will take care of you. They're going to lock you up. For a long, long time."

"Yeah. But not forever. Someday I'm going to get out. When I do, I'm going to come looking for you. All three of you. And when I find you, you're going to wish you'd died tonight in this swamp."

Chapter One

As the gates of the federal penitentiary at Texarkana clanged behind him, Tyler Belton threw back his dark head and took a deep breath of clean untainted air. Flexing muscles he'd kept in shape doing sit-ups and push-ups in his cell, he looked around at the rolling Texas countryside.

As he shifted the cheap suitcase in his hand, he cursed the eighteen months he'd just served for a bank robbery he hadn't committed. The old Tyler Belton might have done it. He'd certainly been headed for a life of crime when he'd been sent to juvenile boot camp at Peltier Point thirteen years ago. That was before he'd faced the reality of his friend Dave Lanier's death. Learned how much the friendship of Nick Ryan and Jules Duquette meant. And vowed he'd never end up in a place like Peltier Point again.

Nick and Jules. Lord, they thought he was dead! Courtesy of the FBI. One of the hardest things about taking an undercover assignment in prison had been letting his two best friends think he'd dropped off the face of the earth. Then when Jules had started madly beating the bushes for him, the bureau had come up with a cover story to tell his friends—that he'd died in a plane crash in Alaska during a hush-hush assignment.

The bureau's solution to the problem had made him damn

mad. But by that time he was stuck in Texarkana, working to get the goods on some punk suspected of several murders.

Tyler had nailed him. Now he was taking the long bus ride to New Orleans, where he would fade into the back alleys of the city. Then the bureau would whisk him off to another city, another assignment—this time chasing criminals, instead of pretending to be one.

His first stop was a men's clothing store, where he bought a couple of shirts, a pair of jeans and some underwear. Then, still using his prison alias of Troy Burns, he rented a cheap room near the levee. After stuffing his prison-issue clothing into the trash, he stepped under the shower, letting the hot water sluice down his broad chest and narrow hips. When he'd washed off the smell of incarceration, he wiped the steam from the mirror and peered at his face. His cheeks were leaner. His features harder. His jaw tighter. And his dark eyes had the watchful look of a man who expected trouble.

"Who the hell are you?" he asked. He might have been in Texarkana under false pretenses, but he knew that living inside the system had stripped away part of his soul. Each minute, each hour behind bars had been an eternity. He wasn't the same man who'd heard the metal gate clank shut behind him and endured his first strip search. And it was going to take a long time to get back the part of himself he'd lost.

Flopping onto the bed, he propped his hands behind his head, enjoying the simple luxury of feeling the air-conditioning blowing on his skin. There was nobody to tell him when he had to get up, when he had to eat, nobody crowding his personal space. He could even go down to one of the restaurants in the French Quarter and buy a bucket of steamed crawfish if he wanted.

He might have rejoiced in the freedom; instead, he fought a sudden stab of panic. Later, as he sat alone in a bar off

Bourbon Street, sipping his beer and listening to the conversation swirling around him, he felt cut off from the rest of humanity. The irony of his life didn't escape him. He'd gone straight after Peltier Point. Worked hard in school and gotten a part-time job at the gas station down the street from his house. Then he'd won a scholarship to college, aced the FBI training and thought he'd escaped from his low-life beginnings to something better. Now he was sitting in a seedy bar feeling as if he'd lost ground, rather than gained any.

He looked toward the phone at the back of the bar, thinking how much he wanted to call Jules or Nick. But how do you make a cold call like that? *Hey, buddy, I'm not dead, after all?*

After half an hour he left, shoulders hunched, hands in his pockets. He was making his way up a darkened street when he caught the sound of stealthy footsteps behind him. He didn't look around; he simply ducked into a garbage-strewn alley. When the guy behind him hurried to keep up, he let him pass, then grabbed the bastard, twisting his arm behind him in a grip that brought a yowl of pain.

"You don't have to take my arm off, Belton," the would-be assailant gasped.

Tyler cursed. "Swenson, are you trying to get yourself killed?" he asked, loosening his hold on the man's arm.

Special Agent Swenson moved his shoulder to ease the pain. "I know you're not armed."

"You can do a pat-down from fifty feet away?"

"I know you got here a couple of hours ago. I know you haven't bought a piece."

"So you've had me followed."

"Standard operating procedure." Swenson turned his palms upward. "You did such a good job on your last assignment, we'd like you to stay in character for a while longer. That's why I don't want you anywhere near headquarters."

"I'm not going back to prison—for you or anyone else," Tyler said, punching out each word for emphasis. "I've had enough of bad food and guarding my back every minute to last me a lifetime." What he didn't say was that another few months inside would destroy him.

The agent shifted from one foot to the other. "We're just asking for a few weeks of additional undercover work. With your prison background and your special computer skills, you're perfect for the job. And we'll double the money you got for the last assignment."

Tyler kept his face neutral while he did a rapid calculation. "That's over ten thousand dollars a week. What do you want me to do—rob a federal depository?"

"Not quite. At least hear our proposition."

"HOLD THE LIGHT a little closer," Tyler ordered as he loosened the screws on the control panel, knowing that removing all of them at once would trigger the alarm. "And stop breathing down my neck!"

He was speaking to one of his new partners in crime, a petty crook named Lex Robey. Lex was a real charmer, a tall cadaverous guy whose spare frame concealed a considerable amount of tensile strength. His twice-broken nose and cauliflower ear were testaments to his fondness for settling disputes with physical force.

"You want the light, or you want me across the room?"

Tyler clamped his teeth together, hoping he and Lex didn't end up killing each other before this job was finished. Quickly he removed one fastener and handed it to the rotund balding Benny Vaughn, his other cohort.

In the beam from the flashlight, he studied the guts of the office building's security system. Then, methodically, using skills he'd learned from a master burglar who was now in the witness protection program, he hooked two leads from his portable computer to the control box. "We're in," he announced after a tense few minutes.

"The alarm's off in the whole building, not just the Blankenship Corporation?" Lex asked as they made their way quietly up the stairway to the third-floor offices of the investment firm.

"Yeah."

"So we could, um, stop off at some other places if we got the time? Like the jewelry store in the front of the building."

"Forget it. Our instructions are to copy the computer files without anybody knowing." The marching orders had come from a guy named Harris Framingham, supposedly a legitimate businessman. But he wasn't choosy about the way he acquired inside information that let him get the drop on his competitors. At the moment he was out of town, with an excellent alibi.

Lex clenched his fists, and Tyler tensed, prepared for a fight. After several moments of charged silence, the other man shrugged, turned away and started up the stairs. Two minutes later they stepped into a plush reception area, furnished with comfortable couches and illuminated by only a few dim overhead lights recessed behind discreet ceiling panels.

Sucking in a breath of the cool air, Tyler fought the feeling that something was wrong.

"Nice layout," Benny said. He had once had a legitimate job as an accountant in an investment firm before starting to siphon off company funds for personal use.

They passed closed office doors, then Lex strode ahead, around the corner and toward the computer area.

Tyler and Benny were still in the hallway when they heard a sharp exclamation, then scuffling footsteps and something metallic thunking to the floor, followed by the sound of plastic skittering over tile.

Springing forward, Tyler charged around the corner, his breath freezing in his lungs at the sight before him. A box of floppy disks lay scattered across the corridor. Behind it stood Lex—and a young woman dressed in an aqua blouse and navy skirt that exposed several inches of shapely thigh. Holding her close with one arm, Lex pressed a gun to her temple with his free hand.

In that charged instant, impressions assaulted Tyler so fast his brain spun. Her deep blue eyes wide with terror. Her rich brown hair swinging around her face. Her pale lips open in a soundless scream.

When her eyes focused on him, her features changed from terror to hope as recognition hit her—in the same instant her name socked him in the gut. Gabriella Lanier. Dave's sister, Gabriella. Of all people. Grown up from the skinny little girl he remembered into a woman who would have been attractive if she hadn't been scared out of her mind.

"Ty—"

Before she could finish, he shouted a curse that he hoped drowned out the rest of his name.

Beside him Benny shifted his bulk uneasily from one foot to the other. "The place is supposed to be empty. What the hell is she doing here?"

Tyler's eyes bored into Gabriella's, willing her not to speak his name.

"Want me to get rid of her?" Lex asked with a kind of casual excitement that tied Tyler's stomach into barbed-wire knots.

"No. Please," Gabriella gasped, trying to wrench herself away. But Lex held her fast.

Tyler's own denial rang out with more force. "Don't do anything stupid. We've got to think about the implications."

"She's a complication we don't need," Benny pointed out.

"*Murder* is a complication we don't need," Tyler answered, his tone steely. "Besides, she may come in handy."

Lex's narrow mouth broke into a broad grin. "Good thinking, Troy," he agreed, using the cover name Tyler had hoped to shed when he'd walked through the Texarkana gates.

Desperate plans clicked through Tyler's brain as his gaze flicked from Lex to Gabriella and back again. Of all the women fate could have thrown in his path, this was the last one he wanted to deal with now. Dave's sister. The sister of his best friend, the guy he'd sworn to protect. Only he'd let Dave down all those years ago at Peltier Point.

"You're supposed to help Benny with the computer files," he said. "I already did my job. So I'll take the hostage."

The other man regarded him with narrowed eyes.

Tyler stood there, listening to the sound of his own blood roaring in his ears, wondering if Lex was going to protest. Instead, he stepped abruptly away from Gabriella, leaving her swaying on her feet.

Tyler caught her from behind, his chest tightening painfully as her back settled against his front. He could feel the fine tremors coursing through her, sense the questions bubbling inside her.

"You don't give us any trouble, and we won't hurt you," he said, trying for the right note in his voice—a compromise between the harsh order his partners expected and the reassurance Gabriella needed to keep them both from getting killed.

God, what a freaking mess. He'd been in tight spots, but this was the worst he could remember because it wasn't just his life on the line. Now an innocent bystander was involved. Gabriella Lanier.

Mentally he measured the paces to the front door. For a split second, he conjured up a picture of himself waiting till they were alone, then abandoning the whole charade, dragging Gabriella down the hall with him and out the way they'd come. There were several flaws to the plan. He'd need Gabriella's absolute cooperation—which she might not be willing to give him. And if Benny and Lex suspected he wasn't on the up-and-up, they'd shoot him—then do God knows what to Gabriella before they killed her, too.

Apparently his mortal panic didn't show on his face. With a shrug Benny pushed past them, moving toward the computer room. When Lex followed, Tyler slowly exhaled the breath clogging his lungs.

As the goon squad's footsteps receded into the distance, his focus abruptly shifted. He was vividly aware of the woman in his arms, of every feminine curve of her body, of her long legs pressed to his and her sweetly rounded backside jammed against his groin. Of the enticing feminine aroma he'd craved during the long months in prison.

It had been an eternity since he'd held a woman. Felt her body pressed intimately against him. Damn. He swallowed hard, fighting the inevitable response.

He waited agonizing seconds to make sure the two thugs were really out of the way. His lips close to her ear, he whispered, "I won't let anything happen to you."

THROUGH THE FOG of fear clogging her brain cells, Gabriella heard the words, but she didn't believe them. Not after the way Tyler had spoken to his friends. For a wild joyful moment she'd thought he'd come to rescue her. But this man couldn't be the Tyler Belton she remembered. When she felt her knees threatening to buckle, she locked them in place and concentrated on taking deep breaths, concentrated on banishing the black dots dancing before her eyes.

"Gabriella."

He spoke again, and the reality of his voice made her stomach flip up to her throat and back again.

"Tyler?"

"Don't use that name! I'm Troy Burns. We don't know each other. Understand?"

She understood nothing. But somehow she managed a tight nod as she stood there picturing the hard unforgiving planes of his face.

Tyler's face. The same, but altered almost beyond recognition.

If you took each feature individually, you might not see the transformation. He had the same blade of a nose. The same sensual lips. The same high cheekbones and dark eyes. But the effect was different, as if someone had shoved him unprotected into a cold arctic wasteland where the wind tore at his flesh, tore at his soul.

The image made her shudder, and his arm tightened around her, lending her a smidgen of support. In another lifetime Tyler had been her brother's best friend. And after Dave had died, even after he'd graduated from high school, Tyler had come around to watch out for her, letting all the tough guys know that if they messed with her, they'd have to deal with him. She'd tried to keep up with him after he'd left the neighborhood. But when his mom died, her only source of information had been cut off.

Tyler had always been tough, closed off, except with his best buddies, Jules and Nick. Yet she'd thought she sensed the tender side of him that he managed to hide from everyone. He'd figured in so many of her adolescent fantasies. She'd imagined what it would be like to lie in his arms, talk softly to him, touch his face, melt her way through his granite exterior.

Now he was holding her, but the reality was a parody of those fond dreams. Her eyes darted to the doorway where the other two men had disappeared. "Tyler, if you have any shred of honor, any decency left, let me go," she whispered.

"You don't know how much I want to. But I can't." His voice sounded so full of genuine pain that for a treacherous moment she honestly believed him. Then she reminded herself that he was only feeding her a line—to keep her under control.

His hold on her tightened. "Gabby, listen to me," he whispered, using the childhood name Dave had used. "You've got to play this cool. You've got to pretend you've never seen me before in your life."

Her mouth was so dry she wasn't sure she could speak. Glad now that she wasn't facing him, she moistened her lips. "Why are you here? What's happening?"

"That's my line. What the hell are you doing here this late at night?"

"I work here."

"Not at midnight. You should be home in bed."

Lord, she wished she was. She wished this was simply a bad dream, and she'd wake up shivering from the aftereffects. Before she could say she'd been working overtime all week on a rush project, the skinny guy with the pockmarked face came ambling back down the hallway, the gun still in his hand.

"You want this?" he asked, gesturing toward Tyler—or was it Troy?—with the weapon.

"I don't need it," he answered in his hateful tough-as-nails voice. "She's so scared she's shaking in her shoes."

Reassured, the man gave him an appreciative laugh before disappearing again.

Gathering every once of courage, Gabriella turned to look Tyler straight in the eye. "Please, I'm begging you," she heard herself plead. "In the name of God, let me go."

"I'd like nothing better," he said. "But I can't."

Chapter Two

Tyler's fingers flexed where they gripped her arm. The part of him that was still decent and honorable wanted to tell her he wasn't like the scumbag Lex who had pressed a gun to her temple for the sheer enjoyment of hearing her gasp. But he couldn't. Because Gabriella's life depended on his acting ability.

"Gabby, you have to trust me to get you out of this," was all he could say.

She made a sound that told him she trusted him about as far as she could pitch a full-grown alligator. "How can I?"

His dark eyes looked into her blue ones. "Because I'm trying to save your life. But I need your help."

He saw her swallow hard as she considered the words. She might not trust him, but he was praying she was smart enough to play along.

Before he could say more, his partners in crime reappeared. Benny was carrying a manila envelope. The nervous expression on his face suggested that everything still wasn't proceeding according to plan. "You got the stuff?" Tyler asked.

"Uh, yeah…"

"But?"

There was a subtle shift in Benny's eyes, something Tyler

wished he could read. It was gone as quickly as it had appeared. "The files are encrypted," the portly man said.

"And what else?"

"Nothing."

Tyler watched the former accountant move toward the door, wondering what he was missing.

Before he could ask Benny another question, Lex gestured toward Gabriella. "So what about her?"

Tyler had been frantically considering and discarding possibilities. Tie her up and leave her in a closet? Nobody would find her until morning, but then she'd talk to the police. Blankenship would know the offices had been burglarized, and she could identify the guys who'd done it. Dump her on some deserted road deep in the bayou? Either she'd end up in an alligator's belly or she'd get back to town and start describing the trio who'd held her captive.

"I figure the best thing is to take her with us, then ask the boss what he wants us to do." At least that would buy him some time.

A slow smile spread across Lex's face. "Yeah, excellent idea," he agreed. "See if there's some packing tape in the supply closet to tie her hands."

Benny trotted off to find the tape. In less than two minutes he was back with a thick roll.

Before Lex could touch Gabriella again, Tyler turned her toward the wall, pulled her hands behind her and wound the tape around her wrists, feeling her body tremble as he worked. Aching with the need to tell her that everything was going to be all right, he silently vowed he would get her out of this.

When he was finished, they reversed their course, moving back toward the front office, with Tyler bringing up the rear, his hand clamped firmly on their unwanted hostage's arm.

"Please," she whispered. "Please. Let me go."

The fear swimming in her eyes tore at his heart. All he could say was, "Quiet! Or I'll tape your mouth."

They filed down to the first-floor utility room, where they'd disabled the controls for the alarm.

This time Tyler let Lex close the panel, reversing the procedure he'd initially used. As the tall man fastened the last screw into place, the alarm began to ring.

Lex jumped back like a dog who'd trampled on a nest of fire ants.

"Come on!" Tyler shouted, leading the way out the back door, feeling the hot night air slap him in the face like a wet towel as he emerged from the building.

The utility van they'd acquired for the operation was parked fifty feet away, next to the Dumpster.

"I'll take her in the back," Tyler said, opening the rear door and lifting Gabriella into a cargo area that was empty except for several large blankets used for wrapping furniture.

Benny slid behind the wheel. Lex barely had time to set his skinny bottom in the passenger seat before the van roared away.

"Slow down before the cops see you speeding," Tyler shouted above the vibration from the engine as they rounded a corner like a raft in whitewater rapids, slamming Gabriella's body against his. Cradling her close, he tried to shield her from the worst of the jolting ride.

Benny growled something unintelligible but slowed to a more moderate pace.

Little light came in through the van's back windows, and it was impossible to see Gabriella's face. But Tyler could feel the terrible tension radiating from her.

In the dark cargo compartment, he rubbed his hand up and down her arm, over the goose bumps peppering her flesh. Figuring nobody in front could see what he was doing, he turned and skimmed her hair with his lips, rubbed the tense muscles at the base of her neck. He felt her stiffen, then heard a rush of breath as she relaxed against him. Was she really comforted by the reassuring gestures—or was she only trying to make him think so while she figured out how to make a break for it?

BECAUSE HE WAS her only hope of survival, Gabriella clung to Tyler in the darkness. If it hadn't been for him, that piece of work named Lex would have killed her—or worse.

Tyler moved his lips to her ear, pitched his voice so low that the words were little more than a vibration. "The men up front are dangerous, and unpredictable. I can protect you from them. But you have to follow my lead. Do you understand?"

Seconds ticked by. Trusting him was an act of insanity. Yet playing along for the moment seemed to be her best chance of staying alive until she could escape. Because she *was* going to get herself out of this, she silently vowed.

When she gave an almost imperceptible nod, she felt some of the tension seep out of his clenched muscles.

He shifted her body, worked at her bonds. When the tape pulled at her skin, she tried to stifle a wince. But he felt it and pressed his cheek against hers. "Sorry."

She gave him the barest shrug and kept her face turned toward the small windows in the van's back door. She couldn't see much, but she kept scanning the darkness, watching for some clue to their location.

When she could move her hands again, she allowed herself a small sigh as she pushed her hair back from her face. "Thank you," she whispered, feeling her breath fanning his ear.

"You two having a good time back there?" a voice called from the front seat.

Her body jerked involuntarily. It was the one called Lex, the one who liked terrorizing her.

"We're fine," Tyler answered.

When there were no more comments from the front, he leaned back against the metal wall of the van, stretched out his legs and pulled her into a more comfortable position, his hand stroking her chilled flesh.

The soothing gesture couldn't dissipate the charged atmosphere between them. The weak vulnerable part of her desperately wanted to believe he wasn't like the other two men, but the tough part forbade her to trust him. Testing him, she asked, "Why are you working with men like that?"

TYLER'S GAZE shot to the forward area as he racked his brain for something he could say, something that would reassure Gabriella but wouldn't give him away. If he told her he was working for the FBI and she let that slip, they'd both be headed for the morgue.

"It's too dangerous for me to tell you what's going on," he said. "The less you know, the better."

Maybe she believed him, because she let her head sink to his shoulder.

Tyler had dragged her along so Lex wouldn't put a bullet in her brain. Now he had to keep the bastard's hands off her.

He stoked her hair. Long ago he had dreamed of holding this woman close, of feeling the heat from her body warm the chill of his. But he'd always known it couldn't be. Not when he and her brother had gone away to Peltier Point together—and he was the only one who had come back alive. He and Dave had been best friends. Two scared kids thrown into the juvenile justice system. They'd teamed up with Nick and Jules. And the four of them had sworn to protect one another. But it hadn't worked out that way. Not for Dave.

Lord, why had the hotheaded Dave thought he had to prove something to that Sincard kid? Why had he gotten in that boat with him alone when the four of them had vowed to stick together? He'd been bound and determined that no snotty rich kid who'd gotten sent to Peltier Point for knifing a guy in school was going to act superior to him. Really, Sincard should have been in reform school, but his dad had pulled strings to get him into Peltier Point, instead. So when the jerk had egged him into a hair-raising speedboat ride, Dave had climbed aboard. Sincard had pushed him over the side, then refused to pull him out when it was obvious he couldn't swim.

Sincard was dead now, too. Ironically he'd also died on the water—when his fishing boat had sunk a couple of years ago. Tyler squeezed his eyes shut. There was no point in focusing on anything in the past. What mattered now was saving Gabriella.

Again he moved so that his lips were close to her ear. Again he began to speak, feeling her go rigid, hearing her gasp of protest as he explained what they were going to have to do.

When the van slid to a stop, he felt his heart lurch. They were at the hideout—the weathered house, miles from nowhere, deep in the bayou country where the snake and gator population far outnumbered the people.

Gabriella made a muffled sound.

"Show time," Tyler whispered as Benny cut the engine.

Pushing open the back door of the van, he felt hot sultry air rush into the cargo area and breathed in the musty scent of damp earth and decaying vegetation. As he helped Gabriella toward the exit, he peered at the trees crowding the road, their trunks layered with lichens, their limbs covered with trailing fingers of Spanish moss.

Despite the temperature, a shudder traveled over his skin as he reevaluated the isolated location. Last time he'd been here, he'd seen the place as a great hideout. Now he thought you could scream your head off and nobody would hear you but the gators.

He kept hold of Gabriella's hand as she descended to the ground, steadying her after the long ride, watching her take in the desolate surroundings. Lex ambled over, stretched lazily and eyed their captive with renewed interest.

"Your idea of bringing this sweet little lady along is looking real good," he said, rubbing his hands together.

Tyler felt Gabriella try to duck behind him, saw her eyes dart to the swamp. Lord, was she thinking about making a break for it? Lex would put a bullet in her back before she got fifty feet.

Pretending every muscle in his body wasn't wired with tension, he slung his arm around her shoulder and wedged her against his side.

"A good idea for me," Tyler responded. "I've got dibs on her."

"I say we draw straws," Lex countered.

"Yeah," Benny agreed.

"No." Tyler snapped, his dark eyes narrowing and his jaw thrusting for emphasis. "Unless you want to fight me for her."

For a frozen moment Tyler was sure he was going to have to prove his superiority in the only way Lex understood. Then the tall man took a step back. "Aw, come on. I don't want to mix it up with you."

Tyler hardened his voice to conceal the relief coursing through him. "Then lay off the woman. She and I bonded on the ride here, didn't we, sweetheart?" To demonstrate, he pulled her around to face him, then wrapped her securely in his arms. His gaze locked with hers just before he took her mouth in a kiss that was meant to impress their audience.

For a tense terrible moment, he thought she was going to put up a fight, instead of cooperating with the plan he'd outlined in the van. Then her eyes drifted closed, either to shut him out or to shut out their audience. Whichever it was, she gave him a measure of acquiescence as his lips settled more fully on hers, staking a claim he had no right to stake. Unless you considered that searing her with his brand was the only way to keep her safe.

Somewhere in his mind he knew Lex and Benny were taking in every subtle move the two of them made. But as his mouth fused with Gabriella's, it felt as if he'd stepped out of the dark bayou country and into some private world created for the two of them. There was only the pressure of his mouth on hers, her body wedged to his, her hands desperately gripping his shoulders.

He tasted the fear on her lips, yet below the surface turmoil there was something else, something sweet and haunting that sparked a response deep in his soul.

He felt her sway against him, heard her make a small sound as he deepened the kiss; he was aware that he was taking as much as he was giving. Yet once he'd gotten a taste of her, no power on earth could have stopped him from plundering her sweetness, could have fought the surge of desire that raced through him as his body turned itself to hers. The response was as primitive as their surroundings, as elemental as a force of nature. He wanted her, needed her with a kind of desperation that went beyond the physical, to the core of what he was and what he might be if only he had this woman at his side.

Harsh laughter in his ears brought him back to real life with a jolt.

"Yeah! Go for it!" Lex urged.

His eyes opened as the woman in his arms stiffened, and the shapes of water oaks and cypress hung with moss snapped back into focus. Had she felt the flames licking at her, too, or had the reaction been all on his side? Dragging in a ragged breath, he fought his way back to harsh reality.

"You got yourself a live one, baby," Lex chortled, addressing Gabriella. "A horny guy who's been in prison for the past eighteen months. So don't be surprised if he comes on fast and furious when he gets you in the bedroom.''

He heard Gabriella make a small frightened sound as her hands shoved against his shoulders.

''Looks like she changed her mind about getting down and dirty with you,'' Benny observed.

''I think she just realized she doesn't need a cheering section,'' Tyler countered, slinging his arm around her shoulder and leading her toward the house.

After a moment of stiffness she fell into step beside him as they climbed the sagging flight of stairs to the raised first floor. Quickly he ushered her up more steps to the bedroom on the right and firmly closed the door behind them. As he turned on the lamp beside the double bed, he uttered a silent prayer of thanks that Lex hadn't followed them.

The room was sparsely furnished. As well as a double bed, there was a rickety chair, a small dresser, a night table and a small sink with a rust stain around the drain.

He expected Gabriella to cower as far away from him as she could get. Instead, she whirled to face him with what must have been a desperate show of bravado.

''Ty—''

Before she could utter his name, he surged forward and clamped his hand over her mouth.

''My name is Troy,'' he hissed, his hand tightening over her lips. ''Try and remember that, dammit!''

He regretted the curse when he loosened his hold. Her eyes were wide, and the starch had gone out of her.

''Did you bring me here to rape me?'' she gasped.

''I'm no rapist.''

''They said you were in prison. What for? Robbery? Murder?'' She stared at him as if he'd slithered out from under the floorboards.

''Robbery,'' he bit out, hating the look of contempt that settled more deeply onto her face.

Eyes narrowed, she hit him with her next question. "Why should I believe you're not going hurt me?"

He pitched his voice almost as low as it had been in the van. "First, because I don't hurt innocent people. Second, because your brother and I had a bond. I can't help him now, but I can help you."

"I don't believe you."

"It would be better if you did."

"So I'll cooperate and let you do what you want?"

"So I can figure out how to keep the two of us from ending up in a sanitary landfill."

"Us? I thought you were friends with those guys."

"That's what they think. That's what they *have* to keep thinking."

Hands clenched in front of her, she stared at him, silently demanding that he explain. But there was nothing he could say to her. And no way he could cope with the needs she'd kindled when he'd taken her in his arms and kissed her.

Seeing her standing beside the bed in this tiny room was simply too much for him to handle. Not when the feel of her was imprinted on his body. He'd told himself that reacting to her wasn't allowed, but his body wasn't listening to his brain.

"I'll be back," he said, making for the door, which had a metal bolt fixed to the outside. It made him wonder who else had been held captive here. After sliding the bolt home, he stood for a moment in the darkened hallway, breathing hard, feeling his blood pounding and his nerves zinging. Cursing under his breath, he strode across the hall to the bathroom. After giving himself a few moments to calm down, he used the facilities, then washed his hands and splashed cold water on his heated cheeks.

When he raised his face to the mirror, he saw his haunted eyes. From below he heard the sound of voices and wondered if Benny and Lex were working on the computer files—or maybe talking about how to take the woman away from him.

The thought was enough to send him hurrying back to the bedroom to make sure that Gabriella was still all right.

Unlocking the door, he stepped into the room. Panic surged through him when he didn't immediately see her. Then a flicker of movement from the wall beside the door caught his eye. Before he had time to dodge aside, Gabriella leaped forward. Hands above her head, she brought a chair leg crashing down toward his skull.

Chapter Three

Tyler dodged to the right. Instead of hitting him squarely on the head, the makeshift club landed on his shoulder, sending a jolt of hot pain through muscle and bone. He would have shouted a curse, but that would have brought the men from downstairs running to his rescue.

Gabriella was raising her arm again, trying for a more lethal blow, when he caught the club and wrenched it out of her hands, sending it spinning across the room, where it clunked against the wall.

Without a weapon, she was no match for him. But she kept fighting, kicking and flailing, her nails raking deep scratches into his cheek. Ignoring the pain, he struggled to subdue her without doing bodily harm. "Stop it. Are you crazy? Stop it."

Clamping his arms around her torso, he wrestled her to the bed. His body pressed over hers, his fingers twined around her wrists, his legs splayed to keep her from kicking the daylights out of him.

He lay there dragging in lungfuls of air, his face bleeding, anger warring with admiration. She'd made the decision to get away from him, and he gave her credit for guts.

"Don't," he panted, vividly aware of the intimacy of their positions, the feel of her breasts pressing against his chest, her hips cradling his, her long legs. Every point of contact brought him exquisite torture. It didn't matter how he'd ended up on top of her on the bed. All that mattered was the way it brought every cell of his body to life.

Her eyes bored into his, shooting sparks.

"I don't want to knock you out," he panted. "But I will if it's the only way I can keep you from killing me." When she said nothing, he continued, "Gabby, don't make me hurt you."

"It's your choice. It was your choice to drag me along with you and those goons downstairs," she spat at him, but she had stopped fighting for the moment.

"Because they were going to kill you and dump your body in the swamp."

"Is that worse than what's going to happen here?"

"Yes."

She shifted slightly under him, enough to increase the torture. He stared down at her, his nerve endings aroused by the intimate contact.

He struggled to think, struggled to frame the right words. But every speech he started made his throat clog. Closing his eyes, he pressed his cheek—the one that wasn't bleeding—against hers. "Gabby, what the hell do you want me to do?"

"Tell me the truth for a change."

He dragged in a breath and let it out slowly. "All right, I'm working for the government. On an undercover assignment. And if the lowlifes downstairs find out about it, we're both dead. That's the truth. And it's more than I should tell you."

He raised his head again, his eyes locking with hers.

"They said you were in prison," she whispered.

"That was part of my assignment. Well, the previous assignment. This is an added bonus." He punctuated the explanation with a harsh laugh.

"You expect me to believe all that?"

"I hope to hell you do, because I can't take much more of this particular method of restraining you."

Without waiting for a response, he let go of her hands, lifted his weight off of her and flopped onto his back. He lay on the bed with his hands raised in a gesture of surrender.

For long moments she remained where she was, her back pressed to the mattress. Then she rolled to her side, raising herself enough to stare down at him, her blue eyes searching his face. He kept his body very still and his features neutral under her intense scrutiny. She gazed at him as if she could read the truth or falsehood of his words by studying his eyes.

He lay beside her, breathing shallowly, waiting for the verdict. He saw her expression change. When she lifted her hand toward his face, his muscles tensed.

"I scratched you," she whispered. "You're bleeding."

"At least you didn't get me in the eye."

"That's what I was trying for."

He winced as she levered herself off the bed. Moving to the sink, she turned on the water, then reached toward the towel hanging to the right of the basin. When she saw it was grimy, she drew her hand back. After a moment's hesitation she bent and reached under her skirt, pulling off the half-slip she was wearing.

"What are you doing?"

Without answering, she thrust the fabric under the faucet, soaked it with water, then returned to the bed.

Gently, her hand not quite steady, she dabbed at his cheek, washing away the blood.

"I'm sorry," she whispered, her eyes downcast.

"Does that mean you've changed your mind about trying to knock me unconscious or claw my eyes out?"

Her face contorted. "Yes."

"Why?" he asked, watching her face carefully.

"Because of what you said. Because you let me go. You

could have done anything you wanted with me—but you didn't.''

He couldn't deal with the last part, so he only muttered, "I didn't say much."

"I guess you can't." The statement came out as a sort of gulp. Then, "You really went to prison on an assignment?"

"To get a confession out of a murderer."

"Wasn't that pretty rough on you?"

"I survived."

"Did you?"

He changed the subject by asking, "How did you end up working at Blankenship?"

She sighed. "After high school I took a computer course. I was really good at it. I've got a talent for organizing material. Blankenship hired me away from another company about six months ago. Too bad for me." Her voice went high and quivery on the last sentence.

He reached to stroke back a lock of her hair. She'd held herself together until now, but as his hand caressed her hair, he watched her face crumple, watched tears collect in her eyes.

"Oh, God, Tyler, I'm so scared."

His heart squeezed painfully in his chest. He'd listened to her crying over the phone the night he'd had to tell her Dave was dead. And he'd ached to hold her and comfort her. Then she'd been miles away in the city; now the two of them were trapped together in a room, which was as much a prison as a refuge.

He pulled her down beside him on the hard mattress and folded her close, rocking her in his arms as if she'd just awoken from a nightmare and come to him for comfort. Only they were both awake, and the nightmare was real.

Her shoulders shook as all the fear and anguish she'd held inside came pouring out of her. His lips skimmed her hair, her cheek, the line of her jaw, as his hands moved up and down her back, kneading her tense muscles. The contact was as much to comfort himself as her.

"It's all right. We're going to be all right," he crooned, the words running together in singsong, because that was all he could offer her now—words.

GABRIELLA LISTENED to the sound of his voice, felt his lips move against her hair, her cheek. By slow degrees she mastered the tears that had poured out of her. But the only way she could drive the awful fear out of her mind was by focusing on the man who held her in his arms so tenderly as he whispered words of comfort.

Alone in her bed at night, she had dreamed of kissing Tyler, had felt her body responding to the fantasy. Suddenly, against all odds, fantasy had turned into reality. And reality was far more potent than anything she could have imagined with this man. Without giving herself time to think about what she was doing, she silently slid closer to him, put her arms around his neck and brought her lips to his.

When he started to pull away, her fingers threaded through his hair, cupping the back of his head, holding his mouth to hers. She knew he could have wrenched himself from her grasp. Instead, his hands curved over her shoulders, and his lips fused to hers. Liquid heat surged through her, driving out any thought but how good it felt to be in his arms like this.

He groaned, the sound welling up from his chest as he plundered her mouth, his tongue and lips hot and urgent— as hot and urgent as her own. Angling his upper body away from hers, he moved his hands between them, finding her breasts, cupping, stroking, raising her nipples to aching peaks of sensation that stabbed against his palms.

"Gabby," he breathed as he pulled her blouse from the waistband of her skirt, then undid the buttons with shaking fingers. Next he worked the clasp of her bra so he could push it out of the way and lower his mouth to one aching breast.

The feel of his lips and teeth on her was exquisite. Yet when his hips began to thrust urgently against her, she felt a stab of doubt. She had wanted this. She was the one who had reached for him. Only now everything was moving at lightning speed.

"Tyler, slow down," she whispered, her hands pushing against shoulders as solid as andirons.

He didn't seem to hear her, and she felt a surge of pure panic.

"Tyler, please!"

He lifted his head, and his eyes blinked open. For a frozen moment he stared down at her, looking dazed. Then he made a strangled sound and rolled away from her, his body rigid, his breath coming in harsh panting gasps. She saw his fingers gather a clump of the blanket into a ball, his knuckles white as he clung to the fabric.

It was several moments before he spoke. "God, Gabby, I'm so sorry. I should never have done that."

She laid a hand on his shoulder. "I asked you to do it. Just not so fast. Could we…could we slow down a little?" she whispered, then held out her arms toward him again.

But he shook his head. "Don't."

"Come back here. I want you."

"You want to forget about the killers downstairs! So do I. But we can't. Now button your blouse before I do something we'll both be sorry about later."

The harsh words pierced her, clogged the breath in her lungs. Head bowed, she refastened her bra and blouse. When she looked up, she saw him sitting with his back against the wooden headboard.

She looked around the room, wishing there were someplace to hide. What a mess she'd just made of things. She'd let him know she wanted him to make love to her, then she'd panicked because it wasn't following the script she'd made up in her head.

TYLER SAW THE REMORSE in her eyes. She was blaming herself for what had happened, when clearly he was the one who was out of line. He hadn't made love with a woman since before he'd gone to prison, and when one had offered herself to him, he'd lost every shred of control he'd thought he possessed. At least she'd brought him to his senses before any real damage was done. "It wasn't your fault," he said.

"Of course it was. I was the one who started kissing you."

His dark eyes burned into hers. "You were using me as an escape. That's perfectly understandable. And it was perfectly understandable for me to respond. It's been a long time since I've had sex."

"Tyler, I remember when you came home from Peltier Point. You held me. And kissed me. You must have felt something for me back then. Did you stop?"

At his sides his hands clenched and unclenched. "It doesn't matter what I feel for you. We can't...be lovers," he managed.

"Why?"

All these years the truth had been locked inside him. He'd assumed he'd never see her again. But fate had given her into his care, and now it was better not to hide the truth from her, because they both needed to understand where things stood between them. Climbing off the bed, he stood facing her.

"Because I let your brother die."

"You can't believe his death was your fault."

He took a ragged breath and then another. "He and I got in trouble together. We were sent to Peltier Point together. We swore we were going to protect each other. I let him down."

Her face twisted, and he braced for her anger. Instead, she dragged in several breaths and let them out in a rush. "You were just a kid."

"I was old enough to watch my best friend's back. And I didn't do my job."

She shook her head. "No. My brother was wild. He took risks. That's why the two of you got in trouble in the first place."

He stared at her, wide-eyed. "How do you know?"

"I wasn't deaf and blind. Your father was out of the picture when you were just a baby. But my dad left us when Dave was thirteen, and I knew my brother was really angry at him, and angry at Mom, because she was working all the time and never home to take care of us. I knew Dave turned to you for support, and that he got you into stuff that was bad for the two of you."

He opened his mouth to protest, but she plowed on.

"He got you to start smoking. You all used to go out in back of the gas station down the street where you thought nobody would find you."

"You knew about that?"

"Yes. And I knew the two of you started stealing cars and going for joyrides. I know the wild ideas were coming from him, because I used to listen in. You'd try to talk him out of stuff, and he'd keep at it until you agreed. That night, when you called from Peltier Point, you told me you'd tried to keep him out of the boat with that guy named Sincard, but he wouldn't listen to you."

"I said that?"

"Yes."

He remembered watching the small craft glide away from the dock, feeling a sense of doom, knowing that his buddy Dave had really gotten himself in trouble this time. He'd run along the path beside the bayou, gasping for breath, slipping in the mud, trying to keep up. And Nick and Jules had been there with him. He didn't remember telling Gabby about any of that.

Now it all came slamming back at him. His own trembling sense of failure. His anger. And the blood pact he'd sworn with Nick and Jules. He'd lost Dave at Peltier Point, but he'd forged a bond with two friends who had helped him through the terrible weeks that followed, then helped to fill the gap in his life.

He and Nick and Jules had been there for one another. Not just at Peltier Point. Over the years. Like the summer he and Jules had visited Nick in his big house and found out that a couple of guys from the neighborhood were giving Nick a hard time because he wouldn't let them sneak into his family's swimming pool at night. They'd turned tail and run when they discovered he had two tough friends to back him up.

The bayou blood brothers had prevailed.

There were other times, too. A lot of them good times. Like the night they'd all sat around chugging beer and watching the Fourth of July fireworks from a riverboat on the Mississippi.

The memory was sliced off when he heard a stair tread creak.

Gabriella's eyes shot to the door, then to him. He strode across the room, then came back to the bed, sitting and slinging his arm around her as he heard footsteps pause in front of the door.

"You alive in there?"

Before he could answer, the knob turned and the door swung open. Lex took a step into the room, a smirk on his face as his eyes zeroed in on the couple on the bed.

Gabriella gasped and moved closer to Tyler. He pulled her tightly against his side. "What the hell's the idea of barging in on us?"

Lex's eyes raked over Gabby. "The door wasn't locked."

Tyler nodded tightly, remembering he'd been a little busy just after entering. "What do you want?" he asked, his hand stroking up and down Gabby's arm possessively.

"Benny can't do nothin' with the disk. He wants the woman to have a crack at it."

Tyler's grip on Gabby tightened. "All right. We'll be down in a few minutes."

"He says to hurry up."

Lex peered more closely at Tyler. "What happened to your face?"

"Nothing."

"It looks like you had to tame your little wildcat."

Silently Tyler stared at the other man. "Get out of here and close the door after you."

Lex's eyes narrowed, but he did as he was told.

When his footsteps had receded, Gabriella gave Tyler a panicked look. "Why did you say I'd do it?"

He brought his mouth close to her ear, lowered his voice to a harsh whisper. "Because that's what Troy Burns would do."

She gulped. "I have to go down there—with them?"

The fear in her eyes made his voice calm and steady. "I'll be with you. I won't let them hurt you, but this might be an opportunity to figure out how to get you away from here."

She nodded, then stood and tucked her blouse into her skirt.

He came up behind her, settled his hands against her ribs, holding her lightly. "Gabriella, we'd better be clear about what's supposed to have happened in here."

A flush spread across her cheeks. "You know what happened."

"I'm not talking about the truth. I'm talking about what I want them to think. They'll both be watching us—just like Lex was doing—trying to figure out if I—" He stopped, roughly cleared his throat. "If I had you."

She raised her chin. "All right, what's the official story?"

His hands dropped away from her body, balled into fists at his sides. "I brought you up here and forced you to have sex with me."

She stared back at him in the mirror, unblinking. "How did I like it?"

He wasn't prepared for the question. "You tolerated it."

"Why?"

That part was easier. "You think of me as your protector. You think that if you cooperate with me, I'll let you go. But you're not dumb enough to make a break on your own."

"You mean like I tried to do a while ago?"

"Yeah. Like that. What were you thinking? You don't even know where you are."

"Actually I think I do."

"What?" The question rushed out of him. "I don't even know this part of the bayou country and you're telling me you do?"

"My grandmother lived around here. I used to stay with her in the summers. I recognized some stuff on the way down."

"In the dark through a couple of little windows?"

"The Southland Sugar Processing plant is hard to mistake for something else. So is the entrance to Bardow Plantation with that big wrought-iron gateway. I used to look for them on the trip down here when I was a kid, because when I saw them, I knew we were getting close to Grandma's."

"So if I could get us out of here, you could..."

"Get us to the bayou. I think," she added in a low voice. Then she went on with more force, "There's a lot of traffic up and down the water. We could catch a boat."

Before he could question her further, a loud exclamation from the floor below reverberated in the room. "I guess we'd better get down there. What I want you to do is stall. Pretend you're having trouble opening the files."

Her fingers closed around his arm, and she nodded. They descended the steps together, and when they stepped into the dining room, he swiftly took in the details of the room. Lex was nowhere in sight. Benny was seated at a table in front of the portable computer, his face tight with concentration—and something else. Something Tyler wished he could read.

He'd been eating a pizza, and the box was sitting on the floor near the kitchen door. Tyler's eyes were drawn to the box. Pizza? Where had they gotten that in the middle of the bayou? He didn't realize anyone had gone out.

He stared at the box. It looked old and kind of gray. There was something white just showing under the corner. While Benny focused on Gabriella, he edged closer to the box and nudged it with his foot. The white was a thin stack of papers that looked as if they'd come from the printer sitting next to the computer.

Had Benny been printing something? But what, if he wasn't able to access the computer disk?

Benny got up from the chair. Gabriella sat down, and the fat man hunched over her. "Nobody said nothin' about these files being password protected," he complained, jiggling from one foot to the other.

"I may not be able to do anything," Gabby murmured.

"It's to your advantage to help us," Tyler said, adding a touch of menace to his voice.

Suddenly the sound of running water erupted from the kitchen, followed by a loud exclamation from Lex. "Get in here and help me!" he shouted.

As Tyler stepped toward the kitchen, he reached down and in a quick motion scooped up the papers from under the pizza box and shoved them under his shirt into the waistband of his jeans.

Catching Gabby's apprehensive look, he said, "I'll be right back." As he stepped through the door, he saw water gushing out of the faucet assembly, spilling into the sink and onto the kitchen floor.

"What the hell happened?"

"I tried to get a drink of water, and the faucet came off in my hand," Lex grated. "The cutoff must be outside. Go shut it."

"You do it."

Lex raised his head, gesturing with the cup in his hand. "I'm tired of you telling me what to do. You're not running this show."

"I didn't say I was."

"Then how come you got to screw our houseguest while we had to work?"

"I needed female companionship more than you do."

"So you've had yours. And now it's our turn." As he spoke, Lex swung the cup upward, splashing water into Tyler's face.

Tyler sputtered as cold water hit him in the nose and mouth. Blinking droplets out of his eyes, he saw an automatic pistol materialize in Lex's hand.

Chapter Four

With no time to think, Tyler ducked low, throwing himself forward. He hit Lex in the stomach with enough force to send them both crashing to the floor, then propel them across the wet surface, slamming into the wall.

Tyler landed on top of Lex, and the thug heaved upward. Somehow Tyler maintained his position, ramming his knee over the man's gun hand.

He was shifting to the side, trying to wrest the weapon away, when he heard a muffled scream from the other room. Gabriella.

His concentration lapsed long enough for Lex to bring the gun up and pull the trigger. A bullet whizzed over Tyler's right shoulder and bored into the wall.

Seeing the shot had gone wild, Lex corrected his aim. Even as Tyler ducked, he braced for the impact of a bullet. At the same time he rammed a fist into Lex's chin, putting everything he had into the blow.

Under him Lex went slack. Tyler wrenched the gun away and staggered through the doorway.

Horror clawed at his insides when he saw Benny pressing Gabriella to the floor. She was struggling, pounding her fists against his back, but the blows seemed to have no effect.

Tyler lifted the gun, but he couldn't shoot, not at such close range. The bullet would plow right through Benny and into Gabriella. Charging across the room, he brought the butt of the gun down on the big man's head.

With a wheezing sound, Benny went slack, and Tyler shoved the gun into the waistband of his slacks so he could grab the dead weight with both hands and heave him away. Benny landed with a thud against one of the fifties-era tubular metal chairs, his arms flailing out, catching the portable computer and sending it flying across the room.

Her breath coming in gasping sobs, Gabriella pushed herself up. Looking down at her gaping blouse, she tried to fasten the front, but most of the buttons were gone.

For a frozen moment all Tyler could do was stand there and stare at her. Then he saw her eyes widen in terror as they flicked to the doorway behind him.

He whirled in time to see Lex lunge through the door, a murderous glint in his eye and an eight-inch kitchen knife in his hand.

Yanking the gun from his waistband, Tyler aimed and pulled the trigger. But nothing happened. With a curse he hurled the weapon at Lex, who grunted when it hit his shoulder but kept coming.

Benny's head must have been made of cast iron. Somehow he was on his feet, as well, charging from the other direction. As he passed Gabriella, her foot shot out, and she sent him toppling forward, in time to crash into Lex. Seizing the opportunity, Tyler picked up a chair and brought it down across Lex's bony shoulders. The man fell forward, taking Benny with him. Springing around them, Tyler bent over Gabriella, clutched her hand and pulled her to her feet.

"Come on," he shouted as he linked his hand with hers and pulled her out the door. In the humid darkness they ducked under moss-shrouded trees, then splashed through water as shots rang out behind them.

Apparently one of the thugs had found a weapon that worked.

Still holding tightly to Gabby's hand, Tyler pulled her across the soggy ground, hoping they were making enough noise to alarm any bears or gators in their path. He was passing under a low-hanging branch when a clump of Spanish moss hit him in the face hard enough to sting. But it didn't slow his steps. Not when he could hear two sets of footsteps behind them.

"Which way?" Tyler said as he dodged behind a gnarled tree, taking Gabby with him.

She stared up at him, then at the moonlight filtering through the trees. "I don't know."

"You said you knew where we were."

"Not out here in the swamp. Not in the dark. I'm sorry, but I don't even know which way we ran."

He bit back a curse. "Okay, but we've got to put as much distance as we can between us and them."

Praying that they didn't stumble over a gator or into a quicksand pit, Tyler led her farther into the treacherous bog. They sloshed ankle deep through mud, then stumbled into a trench full of water. It rose rapidly, covering their ankles, their knees, their thighs.

He was wondering if they were going to have to swim for it when the ground rose again. To his relief they emerged from the water and onto relatively solid ground. Gabriella clung to him, panting.

Not far away, he heard a large animal moving stealthily through the underbrush, then a splash as something else slithered into the water they had just vacated.

The sounds of the night set his teeth on edge. Wedging his back against the rough bark of a tree, he wrapped his arms around Gabby, feeling the fine tremors of her body as he listened for signs of a predator—human or otherwise.

The last time he'd been in the swamp at night was when he, Nick and Jules had sworn their blood oath. Fresh from the streets of New Orleans, he'd been spooked by the confrontation with raw nature out at Peltier Point. He didn't feel any better in the writhing darkness now. But at least there was some good news: He couldn't detect any sounds of pursuit.

His hands stroked up and down Gabby's arms. "I think they're afraid to follow us," he whispered.

"With good reason." Her tone was low, but he could still hear the quiver in her voice.

"Are you all right?" he asked.

Although she answered yes, her head drooped to his shoulder and her hands clutched his arms.

He made small circles on her back with his fingers. "I shouldn't have left you alone with that bastard Benny. I thought Lex was the real threat. But they must have planned it together—first to get you down there. Then to get me out of the way. I'm sorry."

Her breath hitched. "Almost as soon as you went into the kitchen, he clapped his hand over my mouth and pulled me down on the floor."

Tyler uttered a strangled imprecation, then gathered her closer. Her whole body had began to shake, and he gave her what comfort he could, his stomach knotting as he thought of what had happened in his absence—and what might have happened if he hadn't gotten away from Lex.

He wanted to keep her in the circle of his arms, to never let her go. But staying where they were wasn't an option.

"We have to keep moving."

"I know." She pushed away from him, and he saw her fumbling at the front of her blouse. When she couldn't find enough buttons to make herself look decent, she pulled the shirttails up and tied them under her breasts to hold the garment closed. Again his stomach clenched to think where the bastard had had his hands on her.

He ground his teeth to keep from screaming, then started

off, hoping he was still moving away from the house, hoping he wasn't going to blunder into a nest of gators.

When he spotted a light in the distance, he froze. "Damn, maybe we circled back the way we came."

"I don't think so. We didn't cross that water again."

He'd been so focused on other details that he hadn't thought of that. Still, he walked with caution as they approached the light.

They emerged from the trees to find themselves facing a clearing. Ahead of them were three wooden houses built on stilts.

"Wait here," Tyler said again. "I want to find out what's what."

He had crossed fifty feet of open ground when he heard the unmistakable click of a gun being cocked.

"Hold it right there and put your hands in the air," a high quavery voice demanded.

Tyler froze and raised his hands above his head as a flashlight beam hit him in the eye, making him blink.

"What are you doin' sneaking up on this camp?" the voice demanded.

"I'm running from a gang of thugs."

"Or you're one of the thugs."

"No."

"So you say."

"We—"

Before he could finish the sentence, Gabriella stepped into the light. "My God, get back!" he shouted, making a grab for her, thrusting her body behind his.

"Mrs. Chaisson?" Gabriella called out, a note of hope ringing in her voice. "Is that you?"

"You know me, *chère?*"

The light lowered and Gabriella stepped to Tyler's side, but he kept his arm firmly around her. Blinking, he made out a tiny white-haired woman hovering over Gabby. She tucked the pistol she was holding into the belt of her flowered dress.

"I'm Gabriella Lanier. I used to come down here when I was a little girl. You knew my grandmother, Heddy Lafore."

Mrs. Chaisson peered at her. "The skinny girl from the city? Heddy used to feed you fried toast with thick syrup to fatten you up. Her?"

"Yes!"

"What are you doing here now? Looking like that?"

Gabriella folded her arms across her breasts. "We were attacked by men who tried to rape me. Tyler got me away from them, and we ran for our lives into the swamp."

"Dear Lord, *chère 'tit chou*. You poor little thing," she translated in case Gabby didn't understand the Cajun phrase. Gesturing toward the house, she added, "Come inside, both of you."

"Thank you."

"You are the one named Tyler, the hero who saved her?"

"Yeah, I'm Tyler," he answered with a grimace. He wasn't feeling particularly heroic at the moment.

"I should not keep you standing out here in the dark."

Mrs. Chaisson led them up a ladder onto a narrow porch. "Take your shoes off. I don't want mud in my house."

She ushered them into a sparsely furnished room, lit by a kerosene lamp. Turning to Gabby, she gave her a closer look, inspecting her ruined blouse. "They didn't hurt you, *chère?*"

"No. Well, only a little."

"The question is, can they find us here?" Tyler interjected.

"Where did you come from?"

Tyler described the house.

"That sounds like the old Honore place," Mrs. Chaisson answered. "Men from the city come there. They know nothing of the land here. If they can cross the swamp to find you, then they have God on their side."

"They don't!" Gabriella answered.

The old woman swept her hand toward the darkness. "You must be blessed to have made it across that stretch of ground. There are bears out there. Bobcats, gators, snakes, quicksand. A thousand dangers."

The way she enumerated the perils raised goose bumps on Tyler's skin.

Mrs. Chaisson looked at his wet mud-spattered clothing, then crossed to a painted wooden chest, poked in a drawer and pulled out some clean clothing for them. "You're a mess," she declared. "The bathroom is through there." She waved him toward a door at the back of the house. "Take a shower. And put your dirty clothes in the hamper. There are towels on the shelf."

He did as he was told, surprised when he took off his shirt to find a wad of papers plastered to his stomach. Lord, he'd forgotten all about snatching them from under the pizza box. Now he smoothed them out, thinking he should find out what Benny had been hiding.

They looked like some kind of computer listing. But the light was dim and he was too punchy to read them now. So he folded them into his shirt and stepped into the shower, grateful for the hot spray.

He was back in the sitting room in less than ten minutes, his hair damp, the baggy pants rolled up at the cuffs, and the papers folded in his back pocket.

When the old woman sent Gabriella to clean up, she turned to him. "Your woman is brave."

"She's not my woman."

The old lady shook her head. "I have eyes. I saw you pull her behind you when you didn't know who held a gun in the dark. I saw the way you look at her. But I want to know, why did you put her in danger? She says it's not your fault, but I want to hear it from you.''

He swallowed, feeling his face heat, wishing he could make his role in this mess sound better.

''Speak up, boy.''

It was a long time since anyone had called him that. He considered his options and decided that this savvy old woman would only trust him if he was honest with her. And it was imperative that she trust him, that she shelter Gabby. Still, he spoke carefully as he explained, ''I'm a federal agent on an undercover assignment. Gabby inadvertently got involved. I need to get her back to the city. And I need to go back for the stolen property at the Honore place.''

''You'd be tempting fate to try the swamp in the dark again. And as for Gabriella, you can't get her to the city until the men come back in their boats. The only safe way out of here is on the water.''

When the shower cut off, she gave him a stern look. ''Stay here.'' Turning, she stepped through the door to the bedroom. Some time later he heard low female voices, probably talking about him. Walking barefoot onto the porch, he stood leaning against the railing, staring into the inky blackness of the swamp, trying not to think about the mess he'd made of this assignment.

Mrs. Chaisson was in the bedroom a long time. As soon as he heard the door open again, he stepped back into the house.

The old woman gave him a considering look. ''She needs you.''

''For what?''

''To help her forget that a heavy man with rough hands had her down on the floor, ripping at her clothing. Touching her in places where only a lover should touch.''

Chapter Five

Tyler felt as if the old woman had shoved an ice pick into his chest and probed around for his heart.

"Go in there to her. I will be in the house next door if you need anything."

Before he could answer, she stepped into the night, leaving him standing in the middle of the room.

His hands clenched and unclenched at his sides. Finally he knocked at the bedroom door. "Can I come in?"

"Yes."

In the soft light from the kerosene lamp, he saw Gabby sitting on a low quilt-covered bed, her knees drawn up to her chin, and her borrowed shift gathered around her ankles. Her head was turned away from him.

She looked so small and helpless that he felt his throat tighten painfully. "Are you all right?" he asked, his voice low and thick.

When she didn't answer, he crossed the room and eased down beside her on the bed.

Lightly he touched her shoulder. "I'm sorry. I should have figured out some way to keep you safe."

Her face turned toward him, and he saw tear tracks on her cheeks. "What could you have done?"

He sucked in a knife-sharp breath. "I don't know. I

should have done something," he answered, the self-loathing coming through in his voice.

SHE SOUGHT HIS EYES, saw the pain and the guilt that were never entirely absent. And she knew that whatever she needed from him, it was no more than what he needed from her. "You mean like you should have done something to save Dave's life?"

"Yes!" he shouted, his voice reverberating in the small room.

"You were just a boy back then," she reminded him.

"And now I'm a man."

"Yes, a man. But not a man with superhuman powers. You made decisions based on your best judgment."

"Which apparently wasn't very good. Lord, Gabby, they were going to kill me and then do God knows what to you." He shuddered.

"They didn't do either. Because you got us out of there."

"Yeah, at least I managed that."

"That wasn't insignificant." When he didn't reply, she went on, "So are you open to the concept of repairing damage?"

"What do you mean?"

"I mean, I'm quaking inside after what happened to me. I keep thinking about that animal on top of me, tearing at my clothes." Her face contorted. "And I need you to help me get past it. I need you to hold me."

She saw his hands tighten and untighten. "If I put my arms around you, it's going to go farther than holding."

She permitted herself a tiny smile. "I guess I was counting on that. Mrs. Chaisson asked me a lot of questions about how I was feeling. She asked if I wanted to be alone here with you, or if I wanted her to stay and chaperon us. I told her I wanted us to be alone."

"Gabby."

"And when I said that, she left us a present."

When he arched an inquiring eyebrow, she reached under the pillow beside her and pulled out a small cardboard box.

As she watched him stare at the package of contraceptives, compressing his lips over his teeth, the air around her suddenly felt almost too thick to draw into her lungs.

But she managed to drag in a breath, managed to say, "Tyler, being touched by Benny was terrifying and disgusting. What I need is to feel your hands on all the places where he squeezed me and poked me, so when I remember this night, I'll think about being with you. I'll think about the way you touched me, not him."

She turned toward him, opening her arms, waiting, time frozen around her. For a terrible moment she was afraid he would turn away. Then he leaned toward her like a man moving through a dream, and she expelled the breath she was holding. When he sank into her embrace, she let out a quivering sigh.

She held on to him, rocking gently as she whispered, "Tyler, I need you. But this isn't just about what I need. It's what you need, too. Because if you let me get as close to you as two people can get to each other, maybe you'll understand that I never blamed you for what happened to Dave. I know you were his friend. I know you couldn't save him from himself."

"Is this how you usually tell guys you forgive them?"

She might have been insulted if she hadn't known he was making one last desperate attempt to save his honor. "No. I'm trying to make you understand there's nothing to forgive."

"Gabby—"

Before either one of them had more time to think, she cut off his protest by bringing her mouth to his.

She'd thought she was prepared for the instant flash of

fire that ignited between them, but at the touch of his lips she felt the heat curl her toes, curl her hair.

Earlier she'd been frightened by the intensity of his response to her, by the speed at which everything started happening. Now she was prepared to give him anything he asked, any way he wanted it. She had loved him and lost him a long time ago, but fate had given her a second chance to show him what she felt.

When he lifted his head, they were both breathing hard. He lurched away from her, pulled off his shirt and reached for the placket of her cotton shift.

As he undid the buttons, she stared at the broad expanse of his chest, at the dark hair that flared around each nipple. Reaching out, she gently touched the place where she could see his heart pounding.

"Let me give you what you need, Tyler," she whispered.

She saw his hands go still, heard an oath well up from deep in his throat.

When his hands dropped away from her, she raised questioning eyes. "Tyler?"

"Gabby, you don't want to be with a guy who hasn't touched a woman in two years. A guy who's been living in a cage like an animal."

The words tore at her. Lifting trembling hands, she undid the final two buttons of the shift, then pulled it over her head.

She heard his breath catch in his throat when he saw her, braless, naked except for the lacy panties she still wore.

In case he was planning to attempt an escape, she pulled him close, her gasp of pleasure mingling with his as her breasts flattened against the hard wall of his chest.

"Gabby, are you trying to drive me crazy?"

"I just want to love you."

His hands stroked up and down the silky skin of her back, along the ridges of her ribs, threaded through her hair.

Sensing his surrender, she melded her mouth with his, drinking in the potent taste of the man who had haunted her dreams for so long.

"Tyler, tell me what you want," she whispered.

"I want to make sure I'm taking you with me."

"You are."

"I will," he corrected.

He eased her down to the mattress, his lips leaving hers to chart a course along her jaw, her collarbone, the tops of her breasts. His fingertips caressed her nipples, causing them to tighten with pleasure. When his tongue swirled around one distended peak, she couldn't hold back a high strangled moan.

He lifted his head, his mouth coming back to hers in a teasing nibbling caress. "Yes, that's right. Tell me how much you like what I'm doing to you," he said, his lips playing with hers as he spoke.

She was drowning in bone-deep aching pleasure. Arching her back, she begged for more. And he was eager to oblige, caressing her breasts again, then stripping off her one remaining garment so he could touch her, stroke her, arouse her until she was the one in danger of spontaneous combustion.

When he finally skinned off his trousers and briefs and pulled her naked body to his, she melted against him, kissing him, sliding her hands over his hips, greedy for the feel of his skin.

"Gabby," he gasped, "I don't think I can wait any longer."

She caressed his face, his lips. "You don't have to."

He reached under the pillow for the box of contraceptives and readied himself. Then he levered his body over hers, his dark gaze holding her eyes as he entered her on a groan of pleasure that welled from deep in his throat.

"Tyler," she answered him, caught in the wonder of the moment. Finally, after all these years, he was hers.

When he began to move, it was like an explosion of heat radiating from her center to every one of her nerve endings. Matching the rise and fall of his hips, she clung to him as the pace quickened and the tension mounted.

"Gabby," he cried, a long shudder of satisfaction going through his body. As he plunged over the edge, she followed him into the rapture of free fall.

She came back to earth slowly. Turning her head, she kissed his damp cheek. He shifted to his side, and she followed him, snuggling close, feeling warm and contented.

"Thank you," she breathed. "Thank you for giving me yourself."

He was silent, holding her, stroking her, kissing her.

"What are you thinking?" she finally asked.

"That my life's a tangled mess. That I don't have anything to offer you."

"What do you want to offer me?"

He laughed softly. "The moon and the stars."

She nodded against his shoulder, wanting to press for something more tangible—like marriage, a home, children. But she'd known what she was getting into when she held out her arms to him. "Just promise me that you won't disappear from my life again."

Once more he was silent.

"Tyler?"

"I'm in the middle of an undercover operation. I can't promise anything."

She ducked her head so that he couldn't see the moisture filming her eyes.

"Gabby, I—"

She waited for him to finish the sentence. When he didn't, she swallowed. "I guess it wasn't all that good for you. I'm sorry, I tried to…to give you what you needed."

TYLER CURSED under his breath, then tipped her face up to his. "Are you crazy? That was more than I ever thought I could feel."

"Oh, yes. That's a good description."

"But—"

She pressed her fingers to his lips. "Don't tell me you don't deserve me. Don't tell me you let Dave down. I'm tired of hearing that stuff from you," she said, frustration hardening her voice.

"Why? It's the truth. And it's not just because of what happened all those years ago. Don't you understand? I was in prison! I was locked behind bars, treated like something less than human. And when you're in that environment day after day, it changes you." A shudder went through him as terrible memories assaulted him. Like the time two guys had cornered him in the shower and he'd only escaped being raped because he was a better fighter. Or the times he'd awakened in the middle of the night, his body covered with sweat and a scream locked in his throat.

"When you're in the joint, it doesn't matter why you're there," he said, his voice going raspy. "What's important is that you turn into something hard and bitter and cynical. And afraid." The last part was the hardest to admit, but he made himself say it because he wanted to make damn sure she understood what he had become.

His breath stilled as he waited for her reaction.

"I know it must have been a terrible experience, but I know it didn't damage the core of you—the rock-solid part that nobody can destroy. I know what kind of man made love to me. He was hard," she said, with a satisfied smile, then sobered again. "But he wasn't bitter and cynical. Or afraid of anything. He was a wonderful lover. Considerate, tender thrilling. The kind of man I always dreamed of being with."

She ignored his look of disbelief and went on, "So now that we agree about your character—"

"We don't."

"Well, at least tell me what I want to hear. Tell me you want to make me happy—not just for tonight," she whispered.

God, how he wanted to tell her all the things that were in his heart. All he said was, "I'm not free to do that."

"Then I'll wait till you are."

He stared down at her in exasperation. "Gabby, you are without a doubt the most bullheaded woman I've ever met."

"I'll take that as a compliment." This time when she wrapped her arms around him, he didn't protest.

He clasped her in his embrace, held her until she drifted off to sleep. Then he slipped out of bed and retrieved the papers. After pulling his pants on, he sat down at the table with the oil lamp and turned up the flame. Smoothing out the sheets, he began to read.

As far as he could see, it was a list of land transactions. He ran his finger down the lines. None of the notations meant anything to him—until a name leaped out at him.

Nick Ryan. His friend Nick. His blood brother. He looked again, his eyes narrowing. Nick was on this list. What the hell…?

A tight feeling gathered in his chest, making it difficult to breathe. What were the odds of this being a coincidence? he wondered. In his job he'd learned that coincidences were as rare as hundred-dollar bills falling from the sky.

Nick Ryan. Ryan Industries. Was there more about it on the disk? Was his friend somehow involved in this mess?

For several moments he couldn't draw in a full breath. Then he inhaled and pulled himself together.

His orders from the bureau had been to bring the computer disk back to headquarters. In the back of his mind he'd been thinking about just leaving the damn thing at the Honore place and telling Special Agent Swenson that completing the assignment was impossible.

Now he wasn't so sure.

He swept his fingers through his hair. Damn. He needed a telephone. He needed to talk to Nick. Then he cursed under his breath. Nick thought he was dead. That was going to make the conversation a little awkward.

Plans and contingency plans ran through his mind, but he could implement none of them at the moment. So he slipped back into bed and gathered Gabby close.

Slowly, inevitably, he saw the blackness outside the window brighten, and the sky above the trees took on a pink-orange hue. The night was ending, but he couldn't bear the thought of parting yet. Closing his eyes, he stroked her arms, moved inward to her breasts, hearing her breath quicken as her body responded to his touch.

"Tyler," she breathed.

Opening his eyes, he saw she was smiling at him. Lifting her head, she sought his lips with hers in a long intoxicating kiss that sent a lightning bolt of need zinging through him. But this time he kept his passion in check. This time he made slow delicious love to her, pushing them both to a high plateau where the air seared his lungs and every breath was a gasp of mingled pleasure and pain.

Even after he had entered her, he held himself back, marveling at the way arousal tightened her features, tightened her body around him, until he felt her convulse under him, heard her cry out in ecstasy. Only then did he allow himself the same satisfaction.

Afterward she locked her arms around him as if she knew he was planning to leave her.

"Are you going to take me back to the city?" she asked.

"I want you to get dressed, go next door and stay with Mrs. Chaisson until the men come home. If they'll let you stay here for a few days, that's even better."

"How will I find you?"

"I'll get back in touch with you."

She raised her head, her eyes burning into his. "Will you?"

"Yes," he answered, not knowing if it was possible—because he had no idea what was going to happen in the next few hours, let alone later.

Gabriella picked up her dress, holding it in front of her body as she disappeared into the bathroom. But she wasn't hiding the rear view. And he had a very satisfying look at her nicely rounded bottom before she shut the door.

He was pulling on his borrowed clothing when he heard the sound of footsteps on the porch. Cursing his lack of a weapon, he looked around for something to use. As he was picking up the kerosene lamp, he heard the old woman's voice in the other room.

"It's only me."

"Just a moment." He zipped up his pants and opened the door, then forced himself to stand still under Mrs. Chaisson's scrutiny.

"Gabriella is all right?" she asked.

"Yes."

"I think you didn't get much sleep," she observed, looking pleased.

"She slept for a while." When he'd been busy with the list.

"Good."

Gabriella poked her head through the doorway, saw the old woman and blushed prettily.

"You passed a good night, *chère?*"

She dipped her head. "Yes."

"I came to tell you that breakfast is ready. In the house next door." She preempted Tyler's argument when she said, "You can't leave with an empty stomach."

He thought about that and realized he was ravenous. "All right."

He washed quickly, and when he stepped outside, he was struck by the desolation of the setting. Several hundred feet behind the house he could see the brown water of the bayou and two weathered gray docks. In front was low marshy land. And beyond that stretched what looked like endless swamp.

Entering the house next door, he found Gabriella and Mrs. Chaisson standing in the kitchen area, deep in conversation, their voices low. They stopped talking abruptly when they saw him.

"Am I interrupting anything?" he asked.

"Woman talk," Mrs. Chaisson said.

He tipped his head to one side. "Like last night."

"Exactly," she agreed as she poured a mug of strong chickory coffee and set it on the old wooden table. "Sit down."

He took the coffee and pulled out a chair at the place she'd indicated.

Gabriella helped set out a breakfast feast, then sat next to him, her knee pressed to his. Under the table he caressed her thigh and allowed himself to imagine sitting with her like this every morning.

When he caught the old woman watching them with knowing eyes, he heaped food on his plate.

He was halfway through his second helping of French toast when a boy of about eleven or twelve with dark hair and brown eyes came into the room. He looked shyly at the visitors, but the old woman urged him forward.

"This is Jacques, my grandson," she said. "Him, he knows the swamp as well as any man. He can take you back to the house that you ran from last night, if that's where you still want to go."

Tyler jumped in quickly. "I don't want a kid involved in this!"

Ignoring him, Mrs. Chaisson said, "He will show you the way, then come back here as soon as you ask him to leave."

Jacques slid into a chair, then helped himself to a sticky bun.

The old woman reached into a drawer by the stove and pulled out a pistol. From a high shelf she produced a box of shells. "You might need these."

Tyler took the weapon, made sure the safety was on and checked it over. As he inserted bullets into the chambers and shoved the gun into the waistband of his slacks, he sensed the boy watching him.

"Out here we must be prepared to defend ourselves," his grandmother said. "Jacques knows the rules with guns."

Tyler nodded.

When Mrs. Chaisson and her grandson stepped onto the porch, Gabriella got up and gripped Tyler's arm. "Can't you call for backup or whatever you're supposed to do when there's trouble?"

"I'll decide when I get there," he said, more to reassure her than anything else.

She reached for him, pulled his body against hers, and for several heartbeats all he could think about was how good she felt in his arms and how much he wanted to stay with her. But when her hold tightened, he knew he was only delaying the inevitable.

"I have to go," he whispered.

She held him for a moment longer, then eased away. When he stepped outside and climbed down the ladder, the old woman was waiting.

"Thank you for everything," he said, feeling the inadequacy of the words.

"You are welcome."

He lowered his voice. "I don't have the right to ask, but

I hope you'll take care of Gabriella.'' At her nod he touched the boy's shoulder. "We'd better go.''

Because he couldn't deal with the expression on Gabriella's face, he didn't look back as he followed Jacques across black mud toward the gray-green swamp glistening in the sunlight.

Instead of taking him through thigh-deep water, the boy led him on a roundabout route that avoided the worst of the muck.

They had paused beside a vine-covered cypress when one of the vines detached itself from the rest and started slithering upward. The hairs on the back of Tyler's neck pricked as he remembered pressing his back against a tree trunk in the dark. Lord, how many of those vines last night had had scales and forked tongues?

Apparently the boy caught his reaction. "That's only a black snake there. It won't hurt you.''

"Right,'' he agreed, keeping his distance anyway.

Ten minutes later Jacques paused under a broad-leafed tree and pointed toward a house with weathered siding and a tin roof. "That it?''

Tyler squinted at sun glinting off the roof. "Yeah.'' He started forward across a patch of ground that looked relatively dry. Before he had gone more than a few feet, the boy grabbed his arm.

"Not that way. That's quicksand.''

He went stock-still, a sick feeling rising in his throat as he pictured himself running headlong through the night-dark swamp, pulling Gabby along.

Keeping his voice steady, he asked, "Okay, how do we get there?''

The boy indicated a route that wound through trees heavy with Spanish moss.

"Thanks. I'll go on from here.'' When Jacques looked

disappointed, he said, "Gabriella's worried about me. You need to tell her we got here safely."

Apparently the assignment satisfied the youngster. He took off in the direction from which they'd come.

Tyler started moving from tree to tree, closing in on the house. His best option was to copy the computer disk so nobody would know the original was missing. That was if Lex and Benny hadn't cut and run after last night's fiasco.

He crossed twenty feet of open ground in a final dash and pressed himself against a wall, gun drawn, waiting to see if his presence had been detected. When there seemed to be no reaction, he moved around the foundation and spotted the van parked in front.

Relieved that the thugs were still at the house, he found a spot where heavy vines climbed up the weathered siding. As insurance against snakes, he gave them a shake, wincing as the branches scraped the worn siding. When he detected no movement, he jammed the gun into the waistband of his slacks, grasped the lower branches and hoisted himself up, half expecting to feel fangs clamp onto his shoulder.

When he was high enough to peer through a window, he found the room beyond it empty, although he thought he heard voices inside. Moving to the right, he inched toward the next window. What he saw on the other side of the glass made him thrust his head back so quickly that his neck muscles twanged.

Chapter Six

Two men were standing in the room—Benny and the boss man, Harris Framingham, who wasn't even supposed to be in town. In his fifties, with salt-and-pepper hair, a crisp knit polo shirt and neatly pressed blue trousers, he looked out of place in the bayou hideout.

Tyler pressed his ear to the siding and listened. The thin walls carried the sound from inside, and he could hear Benny whining, "I told you, he beat up me and Lex. And he hightailed it into the swamp in the dark. I mean, what were we supposed to do? He and the girl are probably in some alligator's stomach by now."

"Well, that's not good enough. I want a body. Two bodies—now. Because we've got a better scenario—he and the girl were working together."

Tyler's hands clenched on the vines.

Framingham was talking again. "All you had to do was let him stay upstairs screwing the girl. Then we would have gotten our fat bonus from the guy who wants him dead. That guy was willing to pay plenty. Now we've got nothing."

Somebody wanted him dead? Tyler clung to the vines outside the window, trying to interpret what he was hearing. It sounded as if his cover had been blown before they'd pulled the robbery, and they'd been planning to make him the fall guy all along. The dead fall guy.

He'd thought Framingham was stealing corporate information for himself. Now it appeared he was working under contract for someone else.

Tyler's mind spun back to the moment Benny had walked out of the computer room carrying a manila envelope much too large for the floppy disk they'd come to steal. God, was that where the papers with the land information had come from? He'd sensed something wrong, something "off" in the look the big man had given him. But he'd had his hands full with Gabriella and hadn't pressed.

Tensely he listened for more details, but the conversation was apparently over, as far as the boss was concerned. It crossed his mind that this might be a good time to cut and run. But then, what about his blood brother Nick, whose name was on that list? And Nick wasn't the only reason for getting the disk. The disk was covered with Benny's fingerprints. Maybe Lex's and Framingham's, too. If he needed proof he wasn't the only one involved in the theft, he needed that disk.

Inching forward, he peered inside again and saw the room was empty. Quietly he pushed the window up and climbed through the opening. Drawing his borrowed weapon, he moved stealthily toward the door, listening for voices or any other sounds that would indicate whether the occupants of the house were still inside.

GABRIELLA STOOD on the porch, scanning the swamp, her fingers twisting the ends of the rope belt she'd used to gather in her borrowed shift. Tyler and the boy had been gone almost an hour, and it felt like a lifetime. Closing her eyes, she pressed her fist against the aching place in the center of her stomach, hoping to stop the pain. But there was no remedy for what she was feeling—the awful fear that she would never see Tyler again.

Lord, what if he had planned all along to leave her with

just the memory of one achingly beautiful night together? Or worse, what if something awful was going to happen when he got back to the hideout?

When she heard a noise in the distance, her eyes snapped open and zeroed in on a running figure. Jacques.

"What happened?" she asked when he reached her side, breathing hard.

"I took him to the house over at the edge of the swamp," he told her between breaths. "He climbed the vines and stayed there for a while. Then he climbed inside."

The boy's next words made her heart skip a beat, then start to pound double time. "After he went in the back of the house, I saw two men with guns go in the front."

Gabriella's fingers dug into Jacques's shoulder. "You have to take me there."

"Grandmaman won't like it. You're supposed to stay here."

"But I have to help Tyler. Do you have another gun?"

The boy shook his head, looked doubtful. "I'm not allowed to touch the guns unless my papa is here. Are the men back?"

Gabriella shook her head.

The boy's features were cast into gloom. Then his face brightened. "I don't have a gun, but I have something almost as good."

SLIPPING OFF HIS SHOES, Tyler made his way on stocking feet toward the front of the house, stopping every few seconds to listen.

When he heard footsteps in the hallway, he flattened himself against the wall. Through the crack in the door, he saw the muscular driver who'd been with Framingham at their meeting.

Tyler took a couple of slow steady breaths. He'd thought he knew the odds when he'd climbed inside. Now he realized the situation was more dangerous than he'd imagined. Getting the disk was one thing. Waltzing into a convention of wise guys was another.

On silent feet he reversed directions and had almost reached the window when he felt the unmistakable thrust of a gun muzzle in his back.

"Don't do anything stupid," a harsh voice commanded. "Nice and slow, set your gun down on that chest of drawers."

With a silent curse Tyler did as he was told.

"Now turn around—slowly."

Again Tyler obeyed and found himself facing a big bruiser of a man, one he didn't recognize.

"I think we got him," the guy called out, then gestured Tyler toward the front of the house. Moments later he was in the dining room, facing Framingham and the driver.

"Well, well, Tyler Belton," the boss man said, standing up and propping his hands on his hips.

"The name's Troy Burns."

"You can stop with the fake-identity crap. You've been pegged for a Feeb," he said, using the common term of disrespect for the FBI.

"That's bull."

"Hold him, Oliver," Framingham commanded.

The driver stepped around Tyler and grasped him by the arms while the bruiser stood with the gun still trained on him.

His expression completely bland, Framingham stepped forward and drove his fist into Tyler's stomach. It was a surprisingly solid blow, and Tyler doubled over, gasping for breath. When he finally straightened, Framingham's face wore a challenging look.

"Tyler Belton," he said. "Let's hear you answer to your name."

"Troy Burns," Tyler gasped.

His reward was a crack on the side of the face that made his eyes tear.

"Now we need the girl," Framingham said.

Tyler raised his chin. "She's back in the city. I put her on a boat last night."

"Oh, yeah?" Framingham gave Tyler another vicious punch in the gut. This time he was glad Oliver was holding him up, because he wouldn't have stayed on his feet unaided.

"You're going to end up singing your heart out to me," Framingham said, his voice mild, "so you might as well save yourself some grief."

Tyler took a cautious breath, the movement of his diaphragm sending fire through his midsection. "I'm not going to say a damn thing unless you tell me who you're really working for."

Framingham looked at him as though he couldn't believe what he'd just heard. "I don't have to tell you squat." He studied Tyler, his eyes running up and down the length of his body as though he was trying to decide where to injure him next, then he turned to the bruiser. "Okay, Tommy, I see our macho federal agent has taken off his shoes, which should make it simple for you to shoot off one of his toes. How about the little one on the left foot? It's okay if you miss and get two."

Tommy smiled, and Oliver let go of Tyler's arms, moving back so that his own feet were out of harm's way. Tyler tensed, prepared to spring forward the moment the gun lowered toward the floor.

Before Tommy could pull the trigger, a series of gunshots sounded from outside the house.

Everybody whirled toward the windows. All except Tyler, who brought his arm down in a chopping motion, slicing his fist into Tommy's hand. With a scream the bruiser dropped his pistol, which skittered across the floor and disappeared under the buffet.

After landing a satisfying kick to Framingham's rear, knocking him into Tommy and blocking Oliver's path, Tyler leaped toward the front door, doubled over by the pain in his gut but moving fast.

Just as he reached the door, Lex charged inside, his eyes wide.

Tyler's head was already lowered. All he had to do was butt the other man in the stomach. As Lex crumpled, Tyler hurtled out the door, clutching his middle to contain the pain.

His stomach muscles were on fire, but he kept running toward the safety of the swamp.

"Tyler! Over here, Tyler."

He raised his head, his eyes widening as he saw Gabriella frantically waving her arms.

"Get back," he gasped. "Before they start shooting."

Ignoring the warning, she waited until he reached her side, then pulled him behind a water oak.

"What the hell are you doing here?" he gasped.

"Saving you."

He realized suddenly that he was inhaling the smell of gunpowder. On the ground a half-dozen feet away were several green-and-red cylinders, blackened at one end. Seconds later his befuddled brain recognized them as firecrackers.

The thugs in the house had thought they were being fired at. But the sound had been firecrackers. And he knew where Gabriella had gotten them when he saw the boy sprinting from the direction of the house, heading into the murky light of the swamp.

Gabriella pulled Tyler after the boy. When he saw they were headed in the direction of the quicksand bog, he gasped, "Not that way."

"Yes. It's all right."

As she led him around the treacherous spot, he saw that

her belt was lying like a lure in the middle of the deceptively firm-looking muck.

They reached a fallen log on the other side and dropped behind the protective cover. When Tyler turned, he could see that the goon squad had already crossed the muddy stretch of ground in back of the house. A bullet whizzed over his head and he ducked.

"This way," Oliver shouted, pointing to the belt that floated on top of what looked like solid ground.

He and Tommy made a beeline for the trap, their forward momentum carrying them into the ooze. Framingham, Benny and Lex were close behind them. Benny couldn't stop in time and joined his friends. Framingham and Lex pulled up short, teetering at the edge of the deadly mire.

The three men who had gone in were desperately kicking and thrashing as their voices rose in terror.

As Framingham and Lex ran in the other direction, Tyler saw Gabriella coolly striking a match, and he realized there was another pile of firecrackers behind the log. She lit the fuse on one and then another, which she thrust into his hand. He gauged the distance carefully before lobbing the missile after the fleeing thugs. It burst in the air directly above them and seconds later smoke began to rise from their clothing. Then flames danced along the fabric. Shrieking in fear, both men fell to the ground, rolling in the damp earth, desperate to extinguish the fire.

Tyler turned to Jacques. "Go. Get your grandma to call the police and an ambulance."

The boy rushed off, moving at a crouch through the thick vegetation. When Tyler dodged from behind the log, Gabriella grabbed a handful of his shirt, trying to hold him back.

"No. Stay here."

"It's okay," he told her, yanking away and circling around the quicksand.

Both Framingham and Lex had dropped their pistols to beat frantically at the flames. Tyler scooped up the weapons, stuffed one in his belt and trained the other at the two men. Both had extinguished their burning clothing, but they were moaning and pleading for help.

Turning back, he saw the men in the quicksand were now mired up to their waists.

"Help. Damn you, help," Oliver shouted, waving his fist.

"What's it worth to you?" Tyler inquired. "Who sicced Framingham on me? Who's the mastermind behind this plot to discredit and kill me?"

"I don't know," Benny wailed.

"You gonna talk?" Tyler asked the boss.

"Somebody who hates your living guts!" Framingham answered. "He didn't give me his calling card!"

Gabriella had come up beside Tyler. Calmly she flicked her cold gaze over the flailing men, then addressed them in a conversational tone. "My grandmother told me that if I ever fell into quicksand, I had to keep myself from thrashing. If you hold still, you'll float—long enough for the police to get here and arrest you."

Their angry response was drowned out by the sound of male voices coming from the swamp.

TYLER KEPT THE GUN trained on Framingham and Lex, but turned far enough to see half-a-dozen men running toward them, Jacques in the lead.

Mrs. Chaisson's relatives, Tyler thought as they filled the clearing.

Jacques pointed to the thugs, then to Tyler. "They were using him for a punching bag in the house. Then me and Gabby got them outside with firecrackers."

Gabriella's eyes flew from the boy to Tyler. "They were beating you?"

"I'm okay."

Before she could argue the point, he addressed the dark-haired man at the front of the group who identified himself as Lucas Chaisson. "Somebody needs to call the police," he told Lucas. "And an ambulance."

The man pulled out a portable phone and punched 911.

Tyler turned toward the house, bent at the middle now from the pain in his stomach. Gabriella kept pace with him. "You need a doctor."

"Maybe later. First I have to get the disk. Then I have to get you out of here." He made it to the house, stopped in the room where he'd discarded his shoes and slipped them on. Then he checked on the disk. It was still in the floppy drive. Or maybe Framingham had brought a new computer, for Tyler remembered the old one flying across the room when he'd wrestled Benny off Gabriella.

"Could you make sure this is the data from the Blankenship office?" he asked Gabby.

She sat down at the machine, typed rapidly.

"Got it," she said after what seemed like an eternity.

He peered at the screen, saw a directory with files. "Open a couple just to make sure," he said.

She did as he asked, and he saw listings like the ones from the sheets he'd stolen, but there was no time to study them. "We have to get away before the cops arrive," he told her as he carefully removed the disk and wrapped it in a paper napkin.

"Why? I thought you were on their side."

"I thought so, too. But it looks like somebody was playing me for a chump, and I don't know who."

FORTY MINUTES LATER he and Gabriella were on a fishing boat heading toward Lake Pontchartrain. In the cabin she slumped against him, and he slipped his arm around her. They needed to talk, but not until both of them were in better shape.

When they docked at the marina, he stopped at a nearby souvenir shop and bought a clean T-shirt and a straw hat, which he pulled low over his eyes. Then, calling a cab, he gave the address of an elegant bed-and-breakfast in the French Quarter, figuring it was the last place anyone would look for them. After getting a room, he cleaned off under a hot shower.

When he came out, Gabriella was sprawled on the wide bed, eyes closed. She jumped when he stroked her arm.

"I'm sorry I startled you," he murmured, nuzzling the side of her face with his lips.

"I'm okay." She tried to look alert, but he could see she was barely functional. He ached to hold her in his arms; instead, he said, "I have to go out. I need my identification and some money."

"How long will you be gone?"

"A couple of hours. Will you be all right?"

"Yes."

"Get some sleep. And don't open the door to anyone but me," he cautioned as he jammed the hat back on his head.

His first stop was the bus-station locker where he'd stashed the proof of his real identity. Relief washed over him when he saw the driver's license, social security card and FBI identification. At least now he could prove who he was.

He tested the theory by stopping at his bank, since it was a pretty good bet nobody knew he was back in the city yet. The teller didn't question his identity when he asked to withdraw twenty thousand dollars from his account. He distributed the wad of cash in his pockets, then gave out a quick two hundred bucks on the street, paying some usually reliable sources for information about Framingham and the ex-con named Troy Burns. There had been plenty of guys in prison who would have turned him in for the price of a pack of cigarettes if they'd known he was actually an FBI agent.

But now that he was back on his old turf, he couldn't get a line on anyone specific. Ironically the only hard information he got was from a TV set playing in one of the bars off Bourbon Street. As he walked past the door, he saw the news was on. For the price of a beer he found out that Framingham and his buddies had been arrested for the Blankenship break-in.

Then Special Agent Swenson came on, saying a man named Troy Burns—alias Tyler Belton—was wanted for questioning in connection with the burglary.

When Tyler saw his own face flash on the screen, he threw some money on the counter and headed for the door, his shoulders hunched, grateful that the photo was a few years old.

Ten minutes later he was back at the bed-and-breakfast, where he found Gabriella pacing across the carpet, the TV playing quietly in the background. The look on her face made his heart squeeze.

"You said a couple of hours! Oh, Tyler, I was so worried. The newscasts say they're looking for you!"

He crossed to her and pulled her into his arms. "I'm sorry. I expected to get back here sooner."

She lifted her face toward him. "Will you tell me now what agency you work for?"

"The FBI."

He felt her relax several notches. "Can't you go to them?"

Wishing he didn't have to shatter her false sense of security, he answered, "Not when it looks like my boss is the one who sold me out. He's the guy you saw on TV putting out an APB for me."

"Why would he do that?"

"Somebody paid him a lot of money."

"Framingham?"

"No. Somebody else—the same person who hired Framingham.'' *Somebody who hates my living guts,* he thought. There had only been one person in his life who had sworn to get him at all costs. Boyce Sincard. And it couldn't be him. Then who?

A shiver crossed his skin, and he reached for Gabriella, stroking his hand up and down her arm, needing the contact. He found he couldn't simply sit there brooding. ''I need to look at the computer disk.''

Turning away, he booted up the machine and began methodically scanning the information, trying to figure out what Framingham would have been interested in.

What he found was similar to the information on the sheets, only more detailed. Especially on Nick's property. Staring at the screen, he swore.

''What?'' Gabriella asked.

''One of these properties is owned by my friend Nick Ryan.''

''Nick Ryan? You mean one of the guys you got tight with at Peltier Point?''

''You remember his name?''

''Yes. You talked about him a lot when you came back to the city. And Jules Duquette. You were all Dave's friends. It's a pretty odd coincidence, one of their names coming up now.''

''Is it a coincidence?'' He gestured toward the computer screen. ''What can you tell me about this stuff?''

''Not a lot. Blankenship keeps track of investments and potential investments for clients. Sometimes that includes real estate.''

''I've got to get in touch with Nick. Ask him if his property's for sale. Or if he knows anything about this.'' He turned his head toward her. ''But not from the room here. Are you going to be okay if I leave you again?''

''Yes.'' Her voice was shaky, but there was a determined look in her eye.

He left in the evening darkness and for the most part glided through the shadows. At a phone in front of a dry cleaners, he stood for several moments, wondering how his friend would react to a call from a dead man. Each ring of the phone increased the tightness in his chest. Then he heard Nick's voice and his heart leaped—until he realized it was an answering machine.

He swallowed hard, tried to organize his thoughts. He wasn't sure how to condense the past few days into one answering-machine message. But he did know how to make Nick believe it was really Tyler Belton speaking. "I hope you're sitting down. This is Tyler. And I'm not calling from the other side of the great beyond. I was on an undercover assignment, and the bureau wanted Jules to stop looking for me so they fed you that plane-crash story. If you want to be sure it's really me now, I'll remind you of something only you and I know. Remember that night at your stepdad's when I got sloshed on his liquor and threw up all over myself and you cleaned me up and swore you'd never tell anyone? You and I are the only ones who know about that." He sucked in a breath and let it out in a rush. "I'm in trouble again. Maybe you've heard about it on the evening news. It's a frame, but I can't come out of hiding, for obvious reasons. I was still working undercover, and somebody tipped off the gang I infiltrated. The weird thing is that your name surfaced in the middle of my investigation. On a list of properties for sale, which the bad guys and I stole from the Blankenship Corporation. Are you selling out? Or is something else going on? I'll try to reach you again later. Meanwhile, watch your back."

He hung up, trying to imagine Nick's reaction to all that. Shoulders hunched, hands thrust into his pockets, he started back to the bed-and-breakfast. But as he passed a sandwich shop, he realized that neither he nor Gabriella had eaten since breakfast. So he pulled his hat low over his face and bought coffee and *muffaletta* sandwiches.

When he walked in the door, Gabriella caught his mood at once.

"You didn't get Nick?"

"Just his answering machine. I'll try again later."

The look on her face told him she'd been dealing with her own issues. She licked her lips, then asked, "If the FBI and the police think you're one of the bad guys, and somebody else is after you, too, what are you going to do?"

"*We're* going into hiding—both of us."

She stared at him. "Are you saying you expect me just to disappear from my job? From my family? Without telling anyone where I am? Mom will be frantic!"

"Would you rather disappear for a while or turn up dead?"

"Put that way, it looks like I don't have a choice." He heard her swallow. "Can I at least write my mom and tell her I'm okay?"

"Yes, you can do that. I'll arrange to have the letter sent from another city."

Her hands clenched and unclenched. "Are we staying together?"

"Unless you want me to stash you with Mrs. Chaisson's relatives."

"Maybe you'd better tell me exactly what you have in mind," she said carefully.

"I'm going to be your bodyguard—protect you from whoever set me up and tried to get us killed."

"Because you feel a sense of obligation to me?" she asked in a steady voice. "Because of Dave?"

He stared at her, seeing the question in her eyes. He had felt drawn to this woman most of his life. She'd been his best friend's sister. Then Dave had died, and he'd felt he was doing her a favor by staying away. Now he understood what he had given up.

He took the biggest chance of his life and answered her question with all the honesty in his heart. "Because I love you."

"Tyler. Oh, Lord, Tyler, I never thought you'd say that. I love you so much, and I thought you didn't want to hear it."

She was in his arms then, kissing him, tears thickening her voice. "I was afraid you were too honorable to let yourself love me."

"Yeah, too honorable," he agreed. "And too worried about what that eighteen months in prison had done to me. Then I realized that loving you was the only thing that was going to save me."

"Thank God."

He held her against him, feeling suddenly better than he had in a long time, as if everything might come out okay, after all. Now that he'd told her how he felt, the place in his heart that had been empty for an eternity was suddenly filled.

She raised her face toward him, and the look of love he saw drove every coherent thought from his brain. Swiftly he lowered his mouth to hers for a kiss that he hoped said all the warm tender needful things that were clamoring inside him. All the things that a guy like him found hard to say.

When he finally broke the contact, his head was spinning. With unsteady hands, he fumbled at the sash of her robe, then parted the fabric so that he could skim his fingers over her satin skin, bend to swirl his tongue around the dark centers of her breasts and feel them tighten for him.

For years he had told himself she was forbidden territory. Then, when she should have run away as fast as she could, she'd held out her arms to him, asked him to make love to her, and he hadn't had the strength to turn away.

Now he knew that the strength came from accepting what she offered.

She helped him pull off his clothing. Then, naked, they tumbled onto the bed, touching, kissing, rocking together. He wanted to savor and seduce, but desire built to a quick hot intensity that left his head spinning.

Afterward he felt wonderfully peaceful. More complete than he ever remembered feeling in his life. Needing to tell her the rest of what was in his heart, he propped himself up on one arm and gazed down at her, brushing her damp hair back from her forehead.

"Gabby, I want to marry you. I want a life with you. A house, kids. The two of us sharing everything."

"Oh, yes."

"I want you to know all that. I also want you to know that I can't ask you yet, not until I get us out of the jam we're in."

"Suppose I don't care about that?"

He laughed, this time without mirth. "Remember that old problem of honor? Well, I can't make any lifetime commitments until I know I'm not tying you to a hunted man."

"But you'll be with me till then?"

"If you'll let me."

"I'll take what I can get…for right now. But I'm holding you to the marriage promise."

In answer his lips lowered to hers for a hungry kiss. Then, holding her gently in his arms, he said, "First, I need to figure out where to keep you safe. I was thinking Jules might be able to hide us. But anybody who knew my background could come looking there. Maybe I'll think of something over dinner."

"We're going out?" she asked, running a hand through her tousled hair.

"No. I brought in some real New Orleans gourmet food. I just forgot about it when you started kissing me."

They pulled on robes and sat at the table by the window. Gabriella looked as if she was thinking hard about something. About halfway through the meal, her eyes lit with excitement.

"I've been trying to figure out where we could stay, and I think I know."

"Where?" he asked, setting down his sandwich.

"One of my old girlfriends, Ann Marie, married a guy from Lafayette. They run a guest house up there. I was always too busy to visit, but now I guess we've got the time."

"You're sure she won't mind putting up both of us?"

"She said she loves having company. And I can earn my keep by helping her take care of the business. We can call her later."

They sat close together at the small table, eating, their gazes catching and holding. When he slipped off his shoe and stroked her foot with his toes, she responded with a sexy grin.

It was hard to believe they were on the run. Not when he felt so happy. Not when he was convinced everything was going to work out okay.

"Thank you," Gabriella breathed. "For letting yourself make the right choice about us."

"When we ate with Mrs. Chaisson, I imagined what it would be like sitting across from you every morning and every evening," he said, his voice thick with emotion.

She raised her gaze to his, and he had the feeling that her blue eyes could see past any pretense, into his very soul. "The night you brought me to Mrs. Chaisson's, she asked me how I felt about you. I told her I had loved you for a long time, but I'd given up on your returning my feelings. When she asked if I had the courage to reach out to you, I decided all I had to risk was a broken heart."

"Lord, Gabby, you were brave." Braver than a certain macho FBI agent he could name.

She shook her head. "Not brave. Desperate." Smiling, she went on. "And I got what I wanted, didn't I? You."

The declaration made his eyes mist as he slipped his arm around her and pulled her close. "How did I ever get so lucky?"

"I think we've made our own luck. You said you wanted to give me the moon and the stars. You already have. Next comes all eternity."

He clasped her to him, holding tight, thinking eternity wouldn't be long enough to show her how much he loved her.

NICK
METSY HINGLE

For Rebecca York, Joanna Wayne, Denise O'Sullivan, Karen Kosztolnyik and the Harlequin Intrigue fans for allowing me to join in this sultry tale of murder and love

Chapter One

The full moon should have tipped him off, Nick Ryan decided as he pulled his Jaguar into the parking lot of the Breauxville Country Club. Hadn't Mamie, his father's housekeeper in New Orleans, always claimed that a full moon brought out the crazies? Crazies like that idiot driver who'd jumped three lanes and crashed into an eighteen-wheeler in his attempt to outrun the state police. Luckily no one had been seriously injured, but the wreck had shut down the interstate for four hours—and had made him nearly three hours late for his stepbrother's wedding.

Finally spying an empty space at the far edge of the parking lot, he slid the Jag between two pickups and shut off the engine. Grabbing his black suit jacket from the passenger seat, he exited the sleek blue car. The oppressive Louisiana heat hit him square in the face. So did the stench of the nearby bayou. Flexing muscles stiff from sitting in the car for hours, Nick tensed at the sound of a twig snapping. He whipped around, scanned the cluster of trees that skirted the edge of the parking lot. "Who's there?" he called out.

No one answered. He gave himself a mental shake as he slipped on his jacket and started toward the club. Evidently the message he'd found on his answering machine from Tyler—telling him he wasn't dead, but working undercover—had spooked him more than he'd thought. No one was hiding out in the woods watching him, because everyone was at the wedding reception. Everyone, that is, except him. Shells crunched beneath the soles of his Gucci loafers as he strode toward the plantation-style house ablaze with lights and music. Judging by the crowded parking lot, the entire town of Breauxville had turned out for Paul's wedding to Caroline.

Caroline.

Although it had been thirteen years since that long-ago summer he and Caroline had been lovers, he could still recall every detail about her as though it were only yesterday. The thick chestnut hair that always smelled of strawberries. The soft smooth skin that felt like silk. The sweet womanly taste of her exploding beneath his mouth. Nick whooshed out a breath. She had been a potent combination of innocence and passion. That was the reason he'd never forgotten her.

And this trip down memory lane was the last thing he needed. Whether he approved of his stepbrother's decision to marry Caroline didn't matter. He owed it to Paul to accept it. After all, Paul had been the only person who had wanted him around when they were growing up.

His stepfather sure hadn't wanted the brat from his wife's first marriage. Not that he blamed the man. After all, Nick's presence each summer served as a reminder to Al Marchand that his wife had chosen a rich city boy over him before she'd come to her senses and returned to Breauxville. He'd known his visits were difficult for his mother. It had been there in her eyes—both the sadness and the relief—when it was time for him to return to his father. It had been the relief that had hurt the most, even though he'd understood it. With her small-town roots, his mother had been out of her depth in New Orleans society. She'd been miserable as the wife of a rich man who was too busy to spend time with his wife and son. Even as a five-year-old, Nick had understood her reasons for leaving his father. What he hadn't understood was why she had left him, too.

Then there had been Paul. Happy, lovable and two years younger than him, Paul had been the one bright spot in the whole mess. At first he had resented Al Marchand's only child, Nick admitted. Paul got to live with their mother all the time, while Nick only had her during the summer months. But it had been difficult to hold on to that resentment when Paul had been so genuinely happy to have him as a brother. Yes, he definitely owed Paul.

And how do you repay him? Not only do you miss the ceremony, but half the wedding reception, as well.

Cursing himself for not coming a day earlier as Caroline had suggested, Nick scowled as he recalled their conversation. They had both known that his excuse of a meeting had been just that—an excuse. He could have easily rescheduled the meeting and been back in New Orleans in plenty of time to make the trip for the wedding. But he hadn't rescheduled for the simple reason that he hadn't wanted to watch his brother marry Caroline.

A hot evening breeze ruffled the leaves of the oak trees. Shoving a hand through his hair, Nick continued toward the clubhouse at a slower pace. Damn, but this was the last place he wanted to be, he thought, as the familiar scents brought other memories tumbling back. Memories of summers spent here as a kid, wanting to be a part of his mother's new family, knowing he'd been tolerated, but never accepted. Memories of the summer thirteen years ago just before his eighteenth birthday when he and Caroline had made love the first time. Memories of the remainder of that summer spent locked up at Peltier Point, the military-style boot camp for troubled teens, the place where he had grown up overnight after Dave Lanier's murder. Memories of the night beneath another full moon when he, Tyler and Jules had met in the bayou and, using his pocket knife, swore an oath of friendship as blood brothers.

As he recalled that night, Nick's thoughts turned once

again to Tyler Belton. *Tyler was alive.* He still could hardly believe it. But there was no question that the voice on the phone had belonged to Tyler, because no one—not even Jules—had known about that incident when Tyler had gotten sick on the liquor they'd swiped from his stepfather.

Jules! Did he know yet? Had Tyler contacted him to tell him he was alive before that news story broke claiming that Tyler was an agent gone bad? Nick felt a prickle of guilt as he thought of his other friend, recalled phoning the NOPD and being told that Jules had left the force. When in hell had that happened? And where was Jules now?

Had he really allowed more than a year to pass without at least talking to Jules? Although the three of them had lived in different cities, traveled in different circles, they had always managed to stay in touch, always known they could rely on one another. Even before Tyler had disappeared eighteen months ago and they had launched the search for him, he had detected the bitterness festering in Jules. So why hadn't he followed up after they'd learned that Tyler had been killed in a plane crash while on assignment for the bureau in Alaska?

Because he'd been too busy zipping from one city, one country to another, chasing after new deals to make money, acquiring everything from race cars to hotels to computer-software companies, filling his life with things he didn't need. If he'd lived up to his vow of friendship, he wouldn't be wondering where in the devil Jules was now.

"Well, what do you know, fellas? Looks like one of the bayou bad boys is back."

Nick jerked his attention to the police officer leaning against a white column at the club's entrance. With a cigar clenched between his teeth and two scrawny cops flanking him, Tommy Joe Gaubert looked every inch the jerk he'd shown promise of becoming when they were kids. As the son of Chief of Police "Big Tom" Gaubert, Tommy Joe had had a mean streak a mile wide and had delighted in bullying Nick and his friends. "Hello, Tommy Joe," Nick said, keeping his voice deceptively relaxed. "Still working for your daddy, I see."

Anger flashed in the other man's eyes. "I work for the good citizens of Breauxville. But then, you wouldn't know much about real work now, would you, city boy? I mean seeing as how your old man left you all that money. Guess it was his way of making up for not wanting you around as a kid, huh?"

Refusing to take the bait, Nick simply smiled. "I see it still bugs the hell out of you that I have money and you don't."

Tommy Joe shrugged. An evil grin snaked across his lips. "Why should you having money bother me? I don't recall your old man's money or influence doing you much good. It certainly didn't keep you out of Peltier Point."

But only because of his own stupidity, Nick admitted silently. He'd allowed Tommy Joe to goad him into holding up that gas station. Later the knife he'd been carrying and his refusal to implicate Paul had made it impossible for Nick not to be convicted. "Maybe my father just didn't offer the right person enough money," Nick countered, and had the satisfaction of seeing Tommy Joe's face redden in anger. "As much as I'm enjoying reminiscing, you'll have to excuse me. I'm late for my brother's wedding."

"Speaking of Paulie," Tommy Joe drawled, "guess I'll have to pay him that ten bucks, after all, since I bet him you wouldn't have the guts to show up."

"You never were very bright, Tommy Joe. Making that bet just proves it."

Tommy Joe's expression hardened. He tossed his cigar to the ground, crushed it beneath his boot. "But you didn't come to the wedding," he reminded Nick, his voice mocking. "Not that I blame you. I mean, I imagine it's not easy to watch your stepbrother marry Caroline Donovan, seeing as how you were the one who bedded her first.''

Fury ripped through Nick. Ignoring the fact that Tommy Joe was a cop and had forty pounds, as well as three inches, on him, Nick grabbed the front of the other man's shirt and shoved him up against the column. ''Why you lousy son of a—''

''Nick!''

Nick whipped his gaze from Tommy Joe's face to the doorway. And there she was—Caroline—in her wedding gown. The sight of her hit him like a fist to the jaw, and the momentary lapse was all Tommy Joe needed. He broke free of Nick's grasp.

''Cuff him,'' Tommy Joe ordered, and the two officers moved in, yanked Nick's arms behind his back. They slapped on the handcuffs.

''Tommy Joe, what's going on here?'' Caroline demanded.

The burly cop smoothed his shirtfront. ''You saw for yourself. Ryan here attacked me. I'm afraid your new brother-in-law still lacks respect for authority. He seems to have forgotten that the law in this town isn't impressed by his name and money the way those folks in New Orleans are,'' Tommy Joe said, crowding him, so that Nick caught the scents of stale tobacco, bourbon and sweat on the bigger man. ''Maybe you can get away with assaulting a police officer in the big city, Ryan, but that's not how it works here in Breauxville.''

''Give me a break. I didn't assault you and you know it.''

''What I know,'' Tommy Joe said, poking a finger in Nick's chest, ''is that you're going to be spending the night in jail.''

Chapter Two

"Bobby," Tommy Joe addressed the lanky cop with the pockmarked face, "read him his rights, then take him down to the jail and lock him up."

"You have the right—"

"Wait!" Caroline cried. "Please don't do this. I'm sure Nick didn't mean anything. It was just a misunderstanding."

"She right, Ryan?" Tommy Joe asked. When he didn't respond, Tommy Joe said, "Go ahead and take him in, Bobby."

Caroline rested her hand on the cop's beefy arm. "Please, Tommy Joe. Don't ruin my wedding day."

Tommy Joe hesitated. "All right. I'll let him off this time, but I'm only doing it because of you and Paul."

"Thank you," she whispered.

It galled Nick for Caroline to have pleaded with that dim-wit on his behalf. And it shamed him to realize that he'd nearly created a scene at her wedding reception. She didn't deserve that and neither did his stepbrother.

"Lucky for you I'm the sentimental type," Tommy Joe said to him as he had the cuffs removed. "Otherwise you'd be spending the night in jail."

Adjusting his jacket, Nick promised himself he would deal with Tommy Joe and his snide remarks later.

"You planning to be in Breauxville long?" Tommy Joe asked.

"I haven't decided," Nick said, even though he expected to leave in the morning.

"Don't push your luck, hotshot," Tommy Joe warned, his eyes narrowing to angry slits. "You cross me and, instead of Breauxville jail, you might find yourself sharing a cell in the pen with your old pal Tyler Belton."

Nick stilled at the mention of Tyler's name. It had been all over the news in New Orleans—Tyler Belton, an FBI agent gone bad. Using the alias of Troy Burns, he was wanted for burglarizing a downtown New Orleans office. And two nights ago Tyler had called him and left that message on his machine. It had shaken him, hearing his friend's voice. He'd believed he was dead. He thought again about Tyler's warning—that Nick's name had turned up in records that Tyler had been sent to steal from the Blankenship Corporation for a crime boss. But why would a crime boss be interested in his, Nick's deal with Blankenship? And had the person who'd sent Tyler to steal those records known that Ryan Industries had acquired the Blankenship Corporation more than a year ago? The coincidence bothered Nick. But since the message had been left on his private line and Tyler didn't have his cell-phone number, there was no way for Tyler to reach him now. And as long as Tyler was in hiding, Nick had no way to contact his friend. Now Jules had disappeared, too.

Suddenly Nick wondered if Gaubert had had a hand in what had happened to Tyler. "What makes you bring up Tyler?" he asked.

Tommy Joe's lips pulled into a thin evil smile. "Thought you'd heard. The police are looking for him. Seems he robbed a place a few nights ago."

"He's wanted for questioning," Nick insisted.

"Right," Tommy Joe said, chuckling. "Things have sure

changed for you and your pals Belton and Duquette, haven't they? I remember how the three of you strutted around this town like you were freaking heroes after the DA bought your story about Boyce Sincard killing that Lanier kid. All anybody talked about for months was how brave all of you were. Of course, it was nothing but a load of BS. I knew that. None of you were at Peltier Point because you were choirboys.''

No, they hadn't been choirboys. They'd been three mixed-up kids one step away from going to prison. And if the time they'd spent in that hellhole hadn't served as a wake-up call to get their acts together, Dave's murder had. The only consolation was that Boyce Sincard had gone to prison for killing Dave. Recalling the madness in Sincard's eyes that night he'd sworn vengeance on the three of them for fingering him, Nick could only feel relief that the guy hadn't gotten the chance to make good on his threat. Perhaps it was fate, but somehow it seemed just that Sincard had died in a boating accident six months after he'd been released from prison.

"My old man always says once a thief, always a thief," Tommy Joe said, pulling Nick's thoughts back to the present. "Guess he was right. Because Belton turned out to be nothing but a two-bit thief, after all.''

"Tyler's no thief," Nick countered. Even without Tyler telling him the news reports were a lie, he would never have believed that Tyler Belton, the friend whose blood he'd mixed with his own and claimed as a brother, was a thief. Not the Tyler who had stood on one side of him, with Jules on the other, at the funerals of both his mother and then his father. Not the Tyler who had tracked him down and, taking turns with Jules, had spent an entire weekend trying to pound sense into his thick head until he'd finally realized that with his wealth came responsibility—to himself, to his friends, to the people he employed, to the community. And that trying to kill himself by racing cars and letting his father's company go to hell wasn't going to fill those empty corners in his soul.

Tommy Joe laughed. "Sure, he is. That's why when they find him, this time his sorry butt isn't going to be shipped off to some kiddy camp like Peltier Point. He's going to be locked up in a cage where crooks like him belong."

When he would have argued further, Caroline clutched his arm. "Come on, Nick. Let's go find Paul. He's going to be so glad that you're here."

BUT PAUL HADN'T SEEMED at all glad that Nick was there, Caroline admitted thirty minutes later. In all the years she had known him, she had never heard or seen Paul treat Nick with anything but affection. Yet, tonight he had been deliberately rude to Nick and referred to him more than once as his *step*brother, instead of as his brother. Never before had he done such a thing. Caroline winced as she watched Paul shrug off Nick's hand and disappear onto the gallery with two men he claimed were friends from New Orleans. Judging by Nick's expression, the pair obviously weren't friends of his, too. Caroline took a sip of water to chase down the pain pill for the migraine that had been plaguing her.

"Don't tell me you've got another one of those pesky headaches," Marilee Chauvin, the mayor's daughter, said in that musical drawl of hers. "And today of all days?"

"Trust me, Marilee. It's not something I planned."

"Of course, you didn't plan it," Marilee said as she twirled the straw in her frozen daiquiri. "Oh, well, what's a little headache when you're lucky enough to not only get a sweet husband like Paul, but a rich hunk like Nick Ryan for a brother-in-law."

"Believe it or not, landing myself a rich brother-in-law didn't factor into my decision to marry Paul," Caroline informed her. At least not in the way Marilee believed. When she had first agreed to Paul's scheme, she'd worried over the prospect of Nick entering her life again—even in such a remote capacity. Their paths had crossed only twice since they'd parted that long-ago summer, and it had been two times too many as far as she was concerned. Evidently her reservations had been well founded or seeing Nick again would not have resurrected this ache and shame inside her now.

"Oh, Caroline, I never meant that you didn't marry Paul for love."

Yet she hadn't married Paul because she loved him, but because it had been her last hope of hanging on to the only home she'd ever known. Another pang of guilt sliced through Caroline. A month ago she had convinced herself that she could live up to the marriage bargain she'd struck with Paul. She'd also convinced herself that she could handle seeing Nick today. After all, she'd come a long way from the naive sixteen-year-old who'd fallen in love with him. But suddenly she didn't feel nearly so sure of herself on either count. Not with Paul behaving like a stranger, instead of the childhood friend she'd agreed to marry. And as for Nick... She sighed. Perhaps she hadn't come nearly as far as she'd thought—not if every time he looked at her, her heart stammered and her pulse raced.

"And speaking of Paul, I was wondering..."

"What?" Caroline asked, wishing the pain in her head would subside.

"Well, Nancy Sue said that you and Nick Ryan used to be...involved. Of course, I told her she was mistaken. I mean, I'm your best friend, and you've never said a word to me about having any kind of romance with Nick Ryan."

Because for her it had been much more than a romance, Caroline thought. "Our folks were neighbors and Nick and I have known each other since we were kids," Caroline responded, proud of how calm she sounded. Yet she couldn't help but wonder how many others remembered that summer she and Nick had been nearly inseparable. How many of them were watching even now to see if there were any lingering sparks between them? It was one of the drawbacks of growing up in a small town like Breauxville—people knew all your secrets and didn't forget them. "Nick and I were…are friends."

"But Nancy Sue said—"

"I'm not interested in what a gossip like Nancy Sue said. You shouldn't be, either. Why, what would your daddy say if he knew you'd been gossiping with Nancy Sue?"

"I was just making conversation while we were at Opal's getting our hair done," Marilee insisted. "So all that stuff about how you two used to be lovers isn't true?"

Caroline's pulse jumped. Sweet heavens! Had the entire town known they had been lovers? Swallowing back the bubble of panic and shame, she kept her voice even as she said, "We were just kids. And we dated a few times. It wasn't anything serious." Or rather, it hadn't been serious for Nick. She, on the other hand, had given him her heart and her body, and though he'd never said so, she'd foolishly thought he'd loved her. Of course, he'd corrected that misconception the night he'd broken things off. For a long time after he'd left and gone back home to New Orleans, she'd told herself he hadn't meant it. That it was the trouble he'd gotten into, his getting sent to Peltier Point and then that nasty business where Nick, Tyler Belton and Jules Duquette had testified against Boyce Sincard. They had been the reason he'd pulled away from her. But as the months went by and her calls and letters went unanswered, she'd finally had to accept the truth—Nick Ryan didn't love her. He never had.

"Omigosh! Here he comes," Marilee said as she clutched Caroline's arm. "Mercy, he is s-o-o handsome."

Nick was handsome, Caroline conceded. With his six-foot frame, razor-sharp cheekbones and that poet's mouth pulled into a sexy scowl, he looked like he'd stepped out of a storybook. His dark blond hair was still a tad longer than conventional. His shoulders were slightly broader, and lines that hadn't been there thirteen years ago bracketed his eyes. But those eyes were the same piercing shade of blue that she had looked into for the first time as a shy young girl and fallen in love.

"You've just got to introduce me," Marilee insisted.

Caroline introduced Nick to Marilee and the flock of females eager to meet him or renew his acquaintance. When she'd had her fill of watching half the women flirt with him, while the other half cast speculating glances at the two of them, Caroline opted to escape. "I think it's time to cut the cake. I'd better go find Paul."

"Why don't I come with you?" Nick offered. "I never got a chance to properly congratulate him before his friends whisked him off. Ladies, if you'll excuse me," he said smoothly.

They started across the room. Caroline's skin burned where Nick's fingers rested at her back. She felt as though he'd branded her. In many ways she supposed he had. He had been her first and only lover. And today she had married his brother.

"What's wrong with Paul?" Nick asked. "Is he angry because I missed the ceremony at the church?"

Caroline paused, cut a glance at his face. "Why would you think he's angry?"

"Are you kidding? He's been acting strange since I got here."

She'd thought the same thing herself, but didn't say so.

"Come on, don't tell me you didn't notice the way he brushed me off when I congratulated him."

She had noticed and been confused by it. "There are a lot of people here, and he wants to be a good host," she defended Paul, her sense of loyalty making her reluctant to give credence to Nick's impression. "I'm sure he never intended to brush you off, Nick."

"And I suppose you're going to tell me I'm imagining that he's well on his way to getting drunk?" When she didn't reply, he said, "Come on, Caroline. When have you ever known Paul to have more than two drinks in an evening?"

Never, she admitted silently. "So he's had a few more drinks than usual. It's not every day that a man gets married," she reasoned. At least that was what she'd been telling herself the past few days to explain Paul's strange behavior. Now she wondered if maybe she'd been mistaken. Had she been so caught up in her own misgivings about the wedding that she had failed to recognize that there was something more serious behind Paul's odd mood? "Now if you'll excuse me, I need to go find Paul."

Nick caught her wrist, stopping her before she'd taken a step. "What's wrong?"

She looked away from that probing blue gaze. "Nothing," she insisted.

"Then why is your pulse racing?" he asked, smoothing his thumb over the inside of her wrist.

Averting her gaze, she attempted to pull away, but his fingers tightened.

"Something's off here, Caroline. With you and with Paul. I can feel it. When Paul first told me you were getting married, I didn't buy the idea of you two suddenly falling in love after all these years. But then, I figured, I haven't been around here for a long time. Maybe things really had changed between the two of you. So I was willing to accept the fact that maybe it could be true, that the two of you were in love."

"My, how magnanimous of you," she said sarcastically, and attempted to pull free.

Nick's grip on her wrist remained firm. "Believe me, I

was trying to be," he said, his eyes as hard as his voice. "But after seeing you two together, I think my initial instincts were right. You aren't in love with Paul any more than he's in love with you. So why don't you just cut the act and tell me what's going on here?"

"That's what I'd like to know," Paul said loudly from the doorway of the gallery as he started toward them. "I don't know who in hell you think you are, but I want you to get your hands off my wife."

"There you are," Caroline said, even though she could feel the heat shooting up her cheeks as people stopped to stare at them. Quickly she moved to Paul's side and gave him a brilliant smile. "We were just about to come look for you."

"She's right, little brother," Nick replied. "I wanted to talk to you. What do you say we take a walk outside?"

"How about we not? I'm not interested in anything you have to say. And you can quit with the 'little brother' crap. We're not brothers. We never were."

Pain flared in Nick's eyes for an instant, but disappeared so quickly Caroline wondered if she'd imagined it. "Paul, you don't mean that," she said.

"I do mean it," he shot back. "He isn't my brother. I never wanted him hanging around when I was a kid. None of us did—not even his own momma. And I sure as hell don't want him hanging around here, flaunting the fact that he used to be your lover."

Caroline gasped. She felt the blood drain from her face. All chatter, even the music, ceased as everyone's attention was riveted on the three of them.

"If I were you, pal, I'd lay off the champagne," Nick said, his tone deadly soft.

"But you're not me. So you can take your advice and shove it."

"Paul! Nick's your brother. He's—"

He whipped around, glared at her. "You're *my* wife. Or is that the problem? I saw how cozy the two of you were when I walked in. Maybe you're having second thoughts? Hoping that if you go to bed with him now, maybe he won't walk out on you the way he did the last time?"

Something dark and dangerous flashed in Nick's eyes, and Caroline could see the effort it took Nick not to grab Paul. His expression lethal, his eyes shards of blue ice, he moved a step closer to his brother. His voice was deceptively soft as he said, "I don't know if you're drunk or crazy. And to tell you the truth, I don't much give a damn. Say whatever you want about me, but show Caroline some respect."

"Get out of my face." Paul's speech was slurred, his face flushed. "I need some air." He stormed out of the clubhouse.

Long past embarrassed, Caroline ignored the murmurs and ran after Paul. She didn't realize that Nick had followed her until she heard him ask one of the policemen, "Where's Paul Marchand?"

The taller of the scrawny pair jerked his head toward the red Porsche at the far curb with white streamers and the words Just Married painted on the windows. "Said he was leaving."

Nick swore. "Couldn't you see the man was drunk? He doesn't belong behind the wheel of a car." He cursed, then shoved past the policemen. He continued right past her.

"Nick, wait," Caroline called after him. "I think it would be better if you stayed here and let me go talk to Paul."

He hesitated. For a moment she thought he was going to refuse. Then he sighed. "All right. Go ahead. But I'm not leaving before I talk to Paul."

Caroline nodded. Lifting the skirt of her gown, she moved quickly to the end of the walkway and started toward the parking lot after Paul. She'd gone no more than a dozen steps when suddenly the red Porsche exploded.

Chapter Three

"Get down!" Nick shouted.

Caroline swung around, her eyes wild, panicked. "Paul," she choked out. "I think...I think he was in the car." Then she turned and started running toward the burning Porsche.

Swearing, Nick charged after her. He snagged her waist and yanked her back across the pathway, then dove for the grass. With her anchored to him, he rolled once, twice, putting distance between them and the fire until she lay face-down, his body covering hers like a shield. They'd barely hit the ground before another blast sent more metal and glass flying. Flames ripped through the sky, and fiery orange tongues licked at the heavens. Nick turned his face away from the horrifying scene.

Even with the noise of the explosion still ringing in his ears, Nick could hear the chaos erupt around them—the shouts, the cries of shock, the slap of running feet, the repeated commands to stay back. Somewhere in the distance he heard the shrill of a siren. But he didn't move. For several long seconds he barely breathed as the scent of burning rubber and scorched metal filled his nostrils.

He squeezed his eyes shut, but the sight of the car exploding replayed painfully behind his shuttered lids. Rejecting what he'd just witnessed, Nick buried his face in Caroline's hair. He breathed in the scents of strawberries and flowers. Blocking out the fiery images of death, he tightened his hold on Caroline. And suddenly he went stone still. He nearly swallowed his tongue as he opened his eyes and realized where he had his hands—one palm clutched her breast and the other her hip.

He scrambled to his feet. "Are you all right?" Nick asked, his voice sharper than he intended.

"Yes." She accepted the hand he offered, but the moment she was on her feet again, he released her. He took a step back, needing, wanting distance. As he did so, he noted her trampled wedding veil on the pathway, her gown torn and stained with grass, her hair tumbled around her shoulders and face. Suddenly the image of Caroline all mussed reminded him of another summer night when they'd gone for a picnic on the bayou and made love for the first time. It had also been the first time she'd said she loved him, swore she would always love only him.

"I need everyone to get back," a police officer shouted as a fire truck roared into the parking lot with its sirens screaming and yellow-slickered men armed with hoses.

"Oh, my God! Paul!" Caroline started to push her way through the crowd.

"Caroline, it's too late."

She stared at him, her green eyes filled with horror. "No. It can't be."

He caught her when she tried to turn away again. "He's dead. Paul's dead."

She struggled for freedom. "No! You're wrong! You can't be sure!"

But he was sure. He'd seen his share of car accidents on the racing circuit, enough to know that no one could have survived that explosion. His brother was dead. Grief and guilt hit him like fists as he thought of Paul, replayed the explosion in his head. Why Paul? *He* was the one who should be dead. Not Paul. *He* was the one who'd always thumbed his nose at fate, at death. Not Paul. Paul was the good son, the one who mattered. Paul was the one who'd be missed.

When Caroline started to weep, Nick took her in his arms. As he held her, he stared at the inferno where the Porsche had been. And he thought of his brother, of the anger and hatred he'd read in his eyes when he'd stormed out of the room. For a moment, just a blip of a second when Paul had looked back at him from the doorway, there'd been something else in his brother's eyes, too. Regret? Had Paul regretted the harsh words that had passed between them? Or was it just wishful thinking on his part, a way to ease his guilt? Because he did feel guilty, Nick conceded. Paul's accusations hadn't been totally without merit. He *had* wanted Caroline. And heaven help him, he had been fiercely jealous of his brother.

"Caroline! Nick!" Marilee Chauvin pushed her way through the crowd lining the walkway in front of the country club. "Honey, I'm so sorry," she said her voice as thick as maple syrup. She hugged Caroline, patted her back and made soothing noises. "Oh, honey, bless your heart. This has got to be so awful for you. I mean, becoming a bride and a widow on the very same day. Why, if you had been in that car with Paul—"

"Excuse us," Nick snapped, wanting to strangle the insensitive female when Caroline's already pale skin turned gray. "We need to go find the police."

THE POLICE FOUND HER, instead. Late the next morning she opened her door to Chief of Police Big Tom Gaubert and Nick. Feeling numb and exhausted from a night spent seeing the car explode every time she'd closed her eyes, Caroline stared across her kitchen table at the chief. She'd known him most of her life. He'd been the assistant chief of police of Breauxville when Will and Jenny Donovan had adopted her. A shy and skinny eight-year-old when they'd introduced her to Big Tom for the first time, Caroline had been in awe of him because of his size, as well as his position. Never once in the twenty-one years since that time had she given him less than her full attention. Until now. Of course, never before had she been in such a position—with Paul, her friend and new husband dead, and Nick Ryan back in her life.

"Caroline girl, you listening to me?"

She shut off her wandering thoughts. "Sorry, Chief. What did you say?"

"I asked if Paul had any enemies that you know of."

"No," she said, and stared at the rings on her left hand. There was so much about Paul she didn't know, she realized. Things a real fiancée would have made it her business to know. Like how he'd been able to buy the expensive engagement ring. Where he'd gotten the money to buy the flashy sports car and the new boat he'd purchased. And where he'd really gone when he'd disappeared several nights each week. "Everyone liked Paul. I can't think of anyone who would want to hurt him."

"That's what I thought, too," the chief said. "But Ryan here seems to think differently. He insists Paul was murdered."

"Murdered?" Caroline repeated, stunned by the idea.

"I don't think my brother was murdered, Chief. I *know* it. That wasn't a short in the electrical system that caused that car to explode last night. It was a bomb—one somebody set to go off when Paul started the engine." Nick shoved away from the counter. His hands clenched into fists at his sides. "My brother's dead. Why aren't you questioning the people who were at the wedding reception—the guests, the country-club staff, the people who decorated Paul's car? Whoever rigged that bomb did it while Paul was inside at his reception."

"You listen to me, boy," Big Tom said, his voice hard,

a menacing scowl on his face. "I don't need you to tell me how to do my job. I've been keeping law in this town since before you were born, and I know what needs to be done."

"Then why aren't you doing it?" Nick challenged, and Caroline winced at the fury behind the accusation.

"As it happens, I did talk to quite a number of people who were at the club last night. And based on what I've heard so far, if I were to buy into your theory of foul play, the person who'd top my list of suspects would be you."

"Me?"

"That's right," Big Tom said, his lips flattening into a grim line. "The one thing that stood out in people's minds was that you arrived late and got into an argument with your brother over your relationship with Caroline."

"We don't have a relationship," Caroline said quickly.

"I'm sorry, Caroline, but I have statements from at least half-a-dozen people who claimed Nick threatened Paul last night."

"It was a misunderstanding," Caroline told him.

"Maybe. But I have to look at all the facts. As Nick's pointed out, he's spent a lot of time on racetracks and he knows his way around a car engine."

"You accusing me of killing my brother, Chief?" Nick asked, his voice deadly soft.

"I'm not accusing anyone of anything—yet. Like I said, we'll know more when the report comes in." Big Tom's cell phone rang and he snatched it from his belt. "Chief Gaubert." A thunderous expression settled over his wind-burned face. "I'm on my way out there now. Call the coroner's office and then call Tommy Joe. Tell them both to meet me there. And, Millie, I want this kept quiet." He slapped the cell phone closed.

"What's wrong?" Caroline asked, concerned at the request for the coroner.

"It looks like Reynard Duquette managed to get himself murdered last night."

Nick frowned. "Jules Duquette's cousin?"

"That's right."

Caroline knew that Nick had spent time at Peltier Point with Jules and Tyler Belton and that the three of them had been close friends. "How did he die?" she asked.

"I'm not at liberty to discuss it. But what I can tell you is that this town isn't a hotbed of crime. Generally I don't have to deal with much besides a fender bender or some little squabble between neighbors or a kid swiping a pack of smokes."

"You have a point, Chief?" Nick asked.

"Yeah. I find it odd that the last murder in this town was thirteen years ago—when the Lanier kid got himself killed up at Peltier Point—while you were there."

"You'll remember that Boyce Sincard was found guilty of murdering Dave."

"I also remember that you, the Belton boy and Jules Duquette were the ones who had Sincard put away for murder. Things have been peaceful here for the most part since that time. Then you show up here yesterday and suddenly I've got myself with one confirmed murder and another possible homicide on my hands."

Nick's eyes hardened. "Like I said, what's your point, Chief?"

"My point, son, is that I don't believe in coincidences. Don't make plans to leave town anytime soon. And, Ryan," he said as he paused at the door, "you might want to give your lawyer a call."

Chapter Four

The silence that filled the room after Big Tom's departure was as oppressive as the summer heat. So were the thoughts running through Nick's head. He kept feeling as though he were in the midst of a nightmare. First Paul dying right before his eyes, now Jules's cousin murdered. Only it wasn't a nightmare. It was reality. His stepbrother was dead and the chief of police considered him a suspect.

"Do you want some more coffee?"

Nick shifted his attention to Caroline. For the first time since he'd arrived, he allowed himself to really look at her. Her face didn't have much more color than the white blouse she wore. From the shadows under her eyes, he suspected she hadn't gotten any more sleep than he had last night. Judging by the way she kept rubbing her temples, she had another headache. His gaze slid to her mouth, and desire pulled at him. Furious with himself and with her because he still wanted her, Nick ground his teeth. "Do you believe the chief? You think I had something to do with Paul's death?"

"Of course not," she said.

"There's no 'of course not' about it. You heard what he said, what others are saying." He straddled the chair. Because he wanted to touch her, he wrapped his hands around the mug she'd set in front of him. The last thing he needed was more caffeine in his system, but he drank the brew, anyway, to fill the hollowness inside him.

"My momma always said that gossip was the product of small-minded people with too much time on their hands. She said I shouldn't pay any attention to gossip or to the people spreading it. Maybe you should follow that same advice."

Mention of her parents reminded Nick that it had been less than a year since she'd lost both of hers. "I was sorry to hear about your parents."

"Thank you." Abandoning her coffee, she pushed away from the table and walked over to the window. "Sometimes I look out this window and still expect to see Momma working in her garden or hear Daddy coming through the door yelling for his two best girls. I miss them so much," she said, her voice cracking. "If it hadn't been for Paul, I'm not sure how I would have gotten through this past year. And now that's he's dead, I...I'm wondering how I'm going to manage without him."

Nick went to her, turned her to face him. The tears brimming in those big green eyes ripped at him. He eased his arms around her and pressed her head to his shoulder. "You'll manage," he assured her. "The Caroline Donovan I remember was always a fighter. I don't imagine she's changed that much."

She lifted her head, stared at him. "Why wouldn't I have changed? You did."

Nick knew she was referring to how he'd ended things between them. As far as she knew, one day he'd loved her and the next he had stopped. What he hadn't told her was that he'd loved her enough to let her go. She'd needed what he could never give her—roots, family, the things that money couldn't buy. He'd come to terms long ago with the fact that he was the unwanted result of a moment of passion between his parents. Their marriage had been a mistake from the start, and they'd spent a lifetime regretting it. They'd been stuck with him. He hadn't fit in with his father's all-business high-society world or with his mother's new family and simple lifestyle. At best he'd been tolerated. But after that stint at Peltier Point, his stepfather's tolerance had run out. When Al Marchand had ordered him to stay away from Paul, Nick had known he had never really been a part of their family, after all. His father's answer had been to ship him off to an Eastern school.

That was when he'd realized there could never be a future for him with Caroline. He could never give her the sense of family, of belonging, that she needed and deserved. The scars from her years at the orphanage ran too deep. She'd loved Breauxville, her home and her family and had told him more than once that she never wanted to live anywhere else. So he'd let her go. After thirteen years he thought what he'd felt for her was dead—only to discover that she still stirred his heart and his blood. She made him want things—things he could never have.

"Everyone changes, Nick. It's called growing up."

"Maybe you're right," he conceded. "Obviously from Paul's reaction last night, I was wrong about your relationship. I'm sorry for not believing you."

Caroline took a step back, avoided his gaze. "You weren't wrong," she told him, worrying her bottom lip with her teeth. "Paul and I...we were friends and we loved each other. But not like— Our marriage was never supposed to be a real one."

Nick's eyes narrowed. "Maybe you better define what you mean by 'real.'"

"We weren't lovers," she said, her voice breathless, her cheeks pink. "We got married so I could get the refinancing I needed to keep this place and so that Paul could fulfill his crazy dream to reunite the two pieces of land—the way it was in his grandfather's time."

Nick swore. "He had that crazy dream even when he was a kid. But I don't understand why *you* went along with it."

"Because I didn't want to lose my home," she snapped, then clutched her head.

"Hey, take it easy," Nick said, trying to calm her and himself. "Why don't you sit down and I'll go get your migraine pills?"

Once she'd taken the medication and calmed down, he asked, "Do you feel up to telling me what happened? Why you needed to refinance this place?"

She nodded. "Last year, after my parents died, I was in a state of shock. When I finally started to put my life back together, I began getting past-due notices from the bank. That's when I learned that Daddy had taken out a second mortgage on the house and land, and that he'd also borrowed against his life-insurance policy."

Surprised by the news, Nick asked, "Why?"

"My guess is, he was worried about the future. He'd made comments a number of times about all the money people were making in the stock market. He used to joke that if he won the lottery, he'd take the cash and invest it, too."

"So he mortgaged the house and land to get the cash."

Caroline nodded. "I think he intended to make a fast profit and put the money back. Only…"

"Only he lost it," Nick finished.

"I made up the missed payments out of my savings, and I could have handled the monthly note. But there's a balloon payment due on the loan at the end of next month. I knew there was no way I could meet it. So I went to the bank and tried to renegotiate the loan terms. They turned me down. And I couldn't get another loan because my income as a teacher is too low. Without a new loan, they were going to foreclose."

"Why didn't Paul just lend you the money?"

"He didn't have it—at least not the cash. That's when he

came up with the idea of us getting married. Paul said that under Louisiana's community-property laws, my husband's assets would be taken into consideration and I could get the loan.''

"For God's sake, we're talking about wood and dirt here,'' Nick snapped, incensed by her foolish decision. "Why didn't you just sell this place?'' The moment the words were out, he knew he'd made a mistake.

Eyes blazing, she said, "I would *never* sell this place. It's my home. But that's something you wouldn't understand, would you? You've never known what it's like not to have a home, to belong.''

He understood far better than she realized. He recalled the years of shuffling between his parents' homes. He thought about the houses he owned in New Orleans, New York, L.A. Though he occasionally stayed in them, he had never considered anyplace home. "Didn't it ever occur to you that you could ask me for help?''

"No.''

"Well, you could have,'' he said, stung. "I would have given you the money. All you had to do was ask.''

"You're the last person I would ever ask for help, Nick.''

"So you sold yourself to my brother in a loveless marriage, instead,'' he accused. Even though he saw the slap coming, Nick didn't try to avoid it. And as she stood there looking horrified that she'd hit him, the anger gripped him by the throat and refused to let go. Before he could stop himself, he lashed out, "But then, I guess with Paul dead, the price doesn't seem nearly so high, after all, does it?''

"What's that supposed to mean?''

"That with Paul dead, your troubles are over.''

She eyed him warily. "What are you suggesting, Nick?''

"Just stating the facts. As Paul's widow, you'll inherit his assets. I don't imagine you'll have any trouble securing that loan now.''

Nick

Caroline flinched, and Nick immediately regretted his sharp tongue. "Despite what you think, Paul was my friend and I loved him. And no matter how much I would hate to lose my home, I'd walk away from it in a heartbeat if it would bring Paul back." She tipped up her chin. "Now if you don't mind, I'd like you to leave. I need to make funeral arrangements for my husband."

Ashamed, he started to apologize. "Caroline, I—"

"Just go." She yanked open the door. "I'll leave word at your hotel about the funeral service."

CAROLINE HELD HERSELF together through the funeral service and the reading of Paul's will, determined not to allow Nick to see the tiniest chink in her composure. But once she was alone in the privacy of her home, the tears fell.

Sobbing, she cried for Paul—for the tragic way he'd died, for the life he'd had snatched away too soon, for the dreams he'd never see fulfilled. And she cried for herself because she missed him and because the guilt she felt about his death was eating her up inside. Crying harder, she admitted that while she had told Nick the truth—that she and Paul had been only friends—in her heart she'd suspected that Paul's feelings for her ran deeper. She'd married him knowing that she could never return those feelings because she was still in love with his brother. The admission brought another rush of tears and intensified the migraine she'd been suffering all day.

When the tears finally stopped, Caroline sat up and sucked in a breath as another blinding pain shot through her head. She glanced at the clock, but it took too much effort to make out the time. Late, she decided, judging by the darkness outside her window. Moving carefully, she headed for the bathroom and searched the medicine cabinet for the pain pills she'd been taking most of her life. As she reached for the bottle, she noticed the sleeping pills Doc Pritchard had prescribed for her following her parents' deaths. Unable to remember the last decent night's sleep she'd had, Caroline stared at the bottle a moment. It would be nice, she thought, to be able to just fall asleep and not dream, to pretend that the past few awful days had never occurred.

The Caroline Donovan I remember was a fighter.

Nick's words came back to her, and she tried to block him from her thoughts. She didn't want to contend with her mixed feelings about him. Except for the funeral and the reading of Paul's will that afternoon, she'd managed to steer clear of him for the past three days. There had been a moment during the reading of Paul's will when their eyes had met and she'd actually felt sorry for him. While Nick hadn't needed any monetary bequests from Paul, she was certain that Paul leaving everything to her and making no mention of Nick had hurt him. Since Paul had drawn up the will only two weeks ago, she'd have thought he'd have at least left Nick a note.

But then, she'd been too shocked upon learning the state of Paul's finances to worry about Nick. Discovering that Paul was deep in debt and that his house and land were heavily mortgaged had come as a blow.

Yet Nick had been right about one thing. She *was* a fighter. She'd survived being abandoned as a child, having Nick break her heart and losing her adopted parents in a freak accident. She would survive losing Paul and her home, too, if that time came. And she'd survive without resorting to sleeping pills or antidepressants. But right now, she decided as her stomach began to pitch—a side effect of the excruciating pain in her head—she would not survive the night unless she took the pain medication for her head. Bypassing the bottle of sleeping pills, she reached for the migraine pills, instead. After shaking out two capsules, she returned to her bedroom, feeling a bit unsteady. She paused at the doorway and tensed as she thought she saw something move in the shadows outside her window.

She crossed to the window and stared out into the darkness. Great, she thought as she moved to the nightstand and reached for the glass of tea she'd poured herself earlier. All Nick's talk about Paul being murdered had her jumping at shadows now. She washed down the pain pills and set the glass down. More tired than she'd ever remembered feeling in her life and promising herself she'd change clothes later when the headache was under control, she stretched out across the bed. Clutching the pillow in her arms, she began mapping out a plan to pay off Paul's creditors while she waited for the pills to take effect. The one thing she would not do, Caroline vowed as she drifted off to sleep, was ask Nick Ryan for help.

HE NEEDED Caroline's help, Nick conceded as he sat in his car outside her house. He'd made no headway with the police chief. Big Tom obviously didn't want to be bothered with his suspicions about Paul's death when Reynard Duquette's murder had the townsfolk up in arms. And when his slow-moving experts got around to confirming it was a bomb that had caused the car to explode and not a faulty fuel line, Big Tom would come looking for him. He didn't blame the chief. It was no secret that he knew his way around a car engine. He imagined it wouldn't take Big Tom long to discover that among his investments was a munitions plant—one he had visited only last week. After that, it wouldn't be long before the chief charged him with Paul's murder. Was he being paranoid? Or was someone trying to set him up? If so, who? Who hated him so much that he'd go to such lengths to hurt him?

Suddenly the hair on the back of Nick's neck lifted, and he recalled the image of a young man's face, twisted with rage, his eyes wild and dark, as he swore he'd get even with the three of them—him, Tyler and Jules. "Yeah, right," Nick muttered and shook off the crazy notion. Whoever killed Paul, it wasn't Boyce Sincard—not unless the man had managed to come back from the grave.

He gripped the steering wheel, thought of the way Paul had died. Once more pain tightened his chest. He'd failed him. Had Nick been a real brother to him, Paul would never have gotten himself into such a fix. It may be too late for regrets about his relationship with Paul, but it wasn't too late to bring Paul's killer to justice and find out who was trying to frame him. But to do that, he needed Caroline's help.

Before he could ask for her help, however, he owed her an apology. Exiting the Jag, he started up the drive. Located on the outskirts of town, the house looked small and lonely sitting amidst the oaks. The place was in darkness, which meant he should probably have waited until morning. But he'd waited too long already. He should have apologized days ago. He still couldn't believe the things he'd said—all but accused her of having a hand in Paul's death so she could get her hands on his money. His being blind with jealousy at the time didn't excuse him.

Feeling lower than the belly of a snake, Nick climbed the stairs to the porch. He rang the doorbell and told himself he wouldn't blame her if she slammed the door in his face. He deserved her scorn and had even braced himself for it at the reading of the will. Instead, in that brief glance they'd exchanged, he'd seen only sympathy.

But she hadn't been feigning shock over the state of Paul's finances. He could hardly believe it himself. Not only had Paul gone through his inheritance, but he'd been up to his eyeballs in debt. And, according to the detective Nick had hired, Paul had also been in deep to a loan shark with mob connections.

Nick rang the doorbell again. When no movement or

lights came from within, he frowned. Caroline was home. He'd seen her truck in the driveway, and he didn't recall her being someone who went to bed when the sun set. Of course, these past few days had been rough on her.

He would come back in the morning, he decided, and descended the stairs. Not sure why, Nick decided to circle the house. He could see a dim light burning in Caroline's bedroom window. Pressing his face to the glass, he looked inside. And then he saw her—lying on the bed. One arm dangling over the side like a rag doll's with her palm out and her fingers pointing to the empty medicine vial on the floor.

Chapter Five

Nick kicked in the front door and raced into Caroline's bedroom. "No!" he shouted at the sight of her lifeless body on the bed. With his heart in his throat, he ripped open the collar of her blouse. He pressed his fingers to her throat and nearly choked with relief at the faint pulse.

Recalling the first-aid training he'd learned during his stint in the navy, he checked her air passages, made sure they were unblocked. After rolling her into the recovery position, he snatched up the phone and punched in 911. "This is Nick Ryan," he spit out when the dispatcher answered. "I'm at 555 Old Bayou Road, the Donovan place, and I need an ambulance. I've just found Caroline Donovan unconscious."

"Hang on," Nick told Caroline after he hung up the phone. Sitting on the bed beside her, he brushed the hair from her face. "I promise you're going to be just fine."

"YOU'RE GOING TO BE just fine," Doc Pruitt told Caroline several hours later as she lay in the hospital bed. "You'll probably have a bellyache and your head isn't going to feel too good. But otherwise, you'll be as good as new. Just make sure the next time you take medication that you turn on the lights and get the right bottle."

"But I didn't—"

Nick listened as Caroline bit off another denial that she'd taken the sleeping pills, instead of her migraine pills, by mistake. He suspected the doctor had concocted the story to avoid classifying Caroline's overdose as a suicide attempt. From the concern in the good doctor's eyes, he obviously believed she had tried to end her life.

"Doc, I'm feeling okay now. Can't I just go home?" Caroline asked, anxiety in her voice.

Doc rubbed the gray whiskers on his chin. "Well, now, it's pretty late and you'd be all alone out at your place—"

"What if I were to stay with her?"

The older man looked at Nick. "Well, I guess it would be all right. I'll go take care of the paperwork."

"Thanks," Caroline said, and was climbing out of the bed before the door closed.

"Hey, take it easy," Nick cautioned, catching her when her legs started to buckle. "You're sure you don't want to stay until morning?"

"Hospitals give me the creeps," she replied, and quickly stepped away from him. "They remind me of when…when I was little and my first mother died."

The words tugged at his heart as he recalled Caroline confiding in him that when she was four years old, her birth mother had committed suicide. "I'm sorry." And he *was* sorry that she had suffered so much in her life. It made him all the more ashamed to realize that he had added to her suffering with his ugly insinuations.

"It was a long time ago," she said, and lifted her gaze to his. "I want to thank you for saving my life. Doc said if you hadn't come by the house when you did…"

Nick went to her, cupped her cheek. "Try not to think about it." He'd thought about what might have happened enough times while they'd pumped her stomach. And each time he had, he'd felt ill. "The important thing is, you're all right."

"Thanks to you." Reaching up, she caught his hand and squeezed it. "Thank you, Nick. I don't know how I'll ever be able to repay you."

"You can start by accepting my apology. The other day, those things I said—"

"Don't." She pressed a finger to his lips. "It doesn't matter."

But it did matter. The gentle look in her eyes, her touch, sent heat streaking through his veins and had every cell in his body on full alert. She was so close. He could see the flecks of gold in her green eyes, feel the warmth of her body, hear her sharp intake of breath as he lowered his head to kiss her.

Despite the hunger clawing at him, he kissed her softly, gently. She had been through enough today. The last thing he wanted to do was frighten her with the depth of his desire. But when she parted her lips, touched her tongue to his, need exploded inside him. He lifted his head, looked into eyes that had gone all smoky and dark.

"Nick?"

Desire fired through him at the sound of his name on her lips. Still, he tried to hold back. But when she moved closer, pressing her body against his, he lost the battle. Groaning, he anchored his fists in her hair and took her mouth again. This time he kissed her hard and deep, feasting on her sweetness like a starving man. Caroline met each thrust of his tongue, fed the fire raging inside him.

Long past sanity, he ran his hands down her shoulders, filled his palms with her breasts. Driven by greed, he shaped her, sloping his hands along her waist, cupping her bottom. He pulled her into his heat. He felt on the verge of stripping off her hospital gown and carrying her over to the bed when a knock at the door sent him crashing back to reality.

Nick yanked his mouth free and dragged in a breath. A

second rap sounded, and he positioned himself in front of Caroline just before Tommy Joe Gaubert strolled in.

Tommy Joe cocked his brow. "Didn't expect to see you here, Ryan."

"Then we're even, because I didn't expect to see you here, either. What do you want?"

Narrowing his eyes, Tommy Joe looked past him to Caroline. "I'm here on official business. I received a report that your sister-in-law tried to commit suicide tonight."

"That's not true," Caroline countered, pushing Nick to the side so that she faced Tommy Joe. With her chin tipped defiantly, she met the cop's gaze. "I don't know who told you that, but I did not try to kill myself."

"I'm sorry, Caroline. But when that report came in from the ambulance dispatch that you'd taken an overdose of sleeping pills...well, given Paul's death and your family history, naturally I thought—"

"You thought wrong," Nick informed him. He draped his arm around Caroline's stiff shoulders. He gave her a squeeze, hoping she'd take his signal to go along with his explanation. "It was an accident. Caroline had a bad headache and didn't turn on the lights when she went to get her medication. Instead of the migraine pills, she grabbed the sleeping pills by mistake."

"That right, Caroline?" Tommy Joe asked.

"Yes," she replied, her tone curt. Nick could feel the anger humming through her. "If that's all, Tommy Joe, I'd like to get dressed so I can go home."

"Sure thing. Glad you're okay," Tommy Joe offered.

"I'll wait for you outside," Nick said. The moment the door closed behind him and Tommy Joe, Nick was in the cop's face. "You always did go for the cheap shot. But hitting Caroline with that bit about her family history was low even for you, Gaubert."

"I was just doing my job."

Nick shoved his fists into his pockets to keep from using them on the cop's face. "Well, now that you've checked it out, make sure the report you write up for your daddy gets it straight. It was an *accident.*"

Anger flashed in Tommy Joe's eyes. His nostrils flared. "If I were you, I'd be worried about my own skin. The report came back on Paul's car. It was a bomb that caused the explosion that killed him. Last I heard, Big Tom was going over to your hotel so he could bring you in for questioning."

"He must have missed me," Nick said, but could feel that noose around his neck tightening. His history with cars, the fight with Paul over Caroline, his access to explosives. It all made him a perfect suspect in Paul's murder. He was being set up. He could feel it in his gut. But by whom? The door to Caroline's room opened. "I'm taking Caroline home now. Tell your daddy I'll come by his office in the morning."

And maybe by then he'd have a lead on who'd gone after Paul to get at him. He thought about Tyler's warning about the Blankenship operation and wished he'd been able to speak to his friend. Since he had no way to contact Tyler and he still didn't know how to reach Jules, he was on his own—at least for now. He just hoped he'd be able to come up with some answers about who was behind this before he found himself in jail facing a charge of murder.

CAROLINE CUT A GLANCE at Nick, who sat behind the wheel of the Jag. He'd barely said ten words since they'd left the hospital, and the brooding silence had her already taut nerves stretching even tighter. Unable to bear the quiet a moment longer, she asked, "Did you mean what you said to Tommy Joe back at the hospital? Do you believe me? That I didn't try to kill myself?"

"I believe you. Suicide is a coward's answer. And you're not a coward."

Momentarily relieved by his reply, she wondered if his faith in her would remain so firm if she told him the truth. She struggled with how to phrase her misgivings, but finally just blurted out, "What would you say if I told you that I didn't mix up the prescription bottles and take the sleeping pills by mistake the way Doc claimed?"

He shifted his gaze from the dark wet road to her. "Tell me what really happened and then I'll tell you what I think."

"That's the problem. I don't know what happened." Caroline's breath came out in a *whoosh*. "I know it sounds crazy, but I know I didn't take those sleeping pills—either deliberately or by mistake. I was in pain because of the migraine, but I wasn't confused. And I *do* remember what I did. I'm very careful when it comes to taking medication because of…the way my mother died. Anyway, the mirror in my bathroom is well lit, so I could see what I was doing. I didn't get those vials mixed up, Nick. I took the migraine pills. I know I did."

"Then how do you explain the other drug in your system and the empty prescription bottle on the floor next to your bed?"

"I can't," she said in frustration.

Nick pointed the car toward the unlit stretch of road that would take them to the narrow bridge that crossed the swamp on the border of her property and Paul's. "If you didn't take those pills by mistake, it means that someone wanted it to look like you committed suicide."

A chill ran down her spine. "You mean, you think someone tried to kill me?"

"Yes."

"But who? Why?"

"I don't know. I've been asking myself the same questions. Unfortunately all I've come up with so far are more questions." He sighed. "I might as well tell you what I've uncovered so far. Maybe together we can come up with some answers."

But instead of answers, Caroline had only more questions as she listened to Nick explain how Paul had been gambling at the casinos for more than a year, and as his problem worsened and the money ran out, he'd turned to a loan shark to cover his debts.

"It was a dumb thing for him to do. There was no way he could make the ridiculous interest payments they were charging him and pay back the money he'd borrowed. When he died, Paul owed them close to half a million dollars."

"Half a million dollars," Caroline repeated. She felt hysteria bubble inside her. Until now her greatest concern had been paying off Paul's credit-card balances and other debts. "I didn't even know Paul gambled."

"That makes two of us."

But she should have known, Caroline reasoned. Paul had been her oldest friend and she'd even married him. Yet she'd had no inkling that he'd been in trouble. She stared out the window as Nick eased the car around the steep mud-slicked curve and took the shortcut to her place. For some reason the old two-lane bridge that crossed the swamp seemed darker than usual tonight, she thought. And the tree limbs jutting from the swamp below seemed like tentacles reaching for her, to drag her down into the inky black waters. Uneasy at the images, she repressed a shudder.

"I don't want you worrying about the money," Nick said. "I intend to handle it. I've tracked down the name of Paul's money contact—a guy named Landry. But my guess is he's just a front man for somebody else." He slanted her a glance. "Have you gotten any calls from this Landry fellow or anyone claiming that Paul owed him a lot of money?"

"No," she said, and swallowed hard as she realized she hadn't even considered this loan shark might come after her for the money. "Do you think this guy Landry is responsible for Paul's death?"

"What would he gain by killing Paul? He'd still be out the half-million."

"Then who?"

"Someone who wants to make it look like I killed my brother."

Stunned, Caroline stared at Nick in disbelief. "You? But everyone knows how much you loved Paul. What possible motive could you have for killing him?"

"You," Nick said the word softly.

So softly that Caroline was sure she'd misunderstood him. "Me?"

"Yes, Caroline, *you.* I was eaten up inside with jealousy from the moment he called and told me the two of you were getting married. I was so angry with him for taking you I wanted to kill him."

"I..." She swallowed, fingered the chain around her neck. "I didn't know."

His expression grim, Nick shifted his attention back to the road. "When a woman gives a man her innocence, tells him she'll never love anyone but him, he's not likely to forget it. I didn't forget. That summer after I left you, I couldn't get you out of my head. I missed you so damn much, I thought I'd go crazy. I got in my car at least half-a-dozen times and started to come back here and beg you to give me another chance."

Caroline pressed a fist to her heart to ease the ache. "Why didn't you?" she asked, remembering how many times she'd hoped he would come back to her, that he would tell her those awful things he'd said weren't true.

He glanced at her again, and Caroline's stomach fluttered at the emotion shimmering in his eyes. "Because I knew I could never give you what you wanted, what you deserved.

As much as I wanted you, as much as I still want you, I can't give you those things, Caroline. Not then. Not now.''

And just as it had thirteen years ago, pain ripped through her. The same pride that had kept her from begging him not to end things then gave her strength now. Battling back the tears burning her eyes, she hiked up her chin. ''I don't recall asking you for anything, Nick. Not then. Not now. As a matter of fact, as soon as you drop me off at my house, you can go back to doing what you do best—running away from life and the things you claim you want.''

''Got me all pegged, do you?''

''I just know that—''

Caroline saw the truck running without lights straight at them and screamed, ''Look out!''

Nick swore as he jerked the wheel of the car out of the truck's path. The Jag fishtailed on the damp road before it struck one of the bridge railings. The air backed up into Caroline's lungs as a section of the wooden barrier toppled into the water below.

She could barely breathe as the car continued to slide, its metal striking the wooden posts and felling them like dominoes into the water below before the car finally slammed against a post and stopped. The tires on her side of the car spun, hit air. And as she caught sight of the dark watery grave awaiting below, she began to pray.

Chapter Six

"Quick! Unfasten your seat belt and give me your hand," Nick commanded. Grabbing her arm, he hauled her across his lap and shoved open the driver's door. "Hurry! Get out!"

"But—"

"Do it!" The car rocked as she fell to her knees on the dark wet road. "Are you all right?"

"Y-yes." She scrambled to her feet, but her eyes widened when the car swayed. "What are you doing?" she demanded when he started to pull the door closed. "Nick!"

"Stand back," he yelled. "I'm going to try to get it off the railing."

"Nick, no!"

"I know what I'm doing," he snapped, and prayed that he did. "Start walking along the shoulder. I'll meet you." He yanked the door closed, cutting off her protests. Taking care to keep his weight on the left, Nick cut the wheel hard and hit the gas. The tires spun. The car wavered. Swearing, he shifted gears and punched the gas again. Suddenly the Jag leaped forward. For a moment Nick thought he'd bought it. Then the car jerked again, metal crunched and was followed by the slap and skid of rubber as the Jag hit the roadway. With his heart still racing, he backed off the gas and eased the car to a halt where Caroline waited. After a moment he opened the door and climbed out.

The rain had started again, but she didn't seem to notice as she came at him, emerald eyes flashing. "You fool!" she accused as she clung to him and sobbed.

"It's okay," he soothed. He stroked her back, kissed her hair.

"No, it is not okay. You could have been killed. If the car had fallen—"

"Hey, I'm all right," he murmured, struck by guilt when she shuddered in his arms. "I'm sorry I frightened you, but everything's all right now. We're both okay."

"Oh, Nick, for a minute, I thought…I was so afraid…"

The sight of tears streaking down her cheeks hit him like a fist. "Baby, please don't." He brushed the tears from her cheek with his thumb, felt her cool smooth skin.

"I thought the car was going to go over and that you—" Her voice hitched.

Unable to bear seeing her hurt, he silenced her the only way he knew how—with his mouth. He'd meant only to calm her with the kiss. But when Caroline curled her arms around his neck and opened her mouth to him, Nick did what he'd sworn he wouldn't do—he gave in to the need that had been burning inside him from the moment he'd seen her again. Lost in the feel and the taste of Caroline, he wasn't sure just how far he would have taken things were it not for the flash of headlights and the sound of a noisy muffler coming their way. Jerking his head up, he positioned Caroline behind him as the driver of a battered pickup pulled to a stop beside them. "You folks all right?"

Nick studied the weathered old man. "Yeah. We had a little car trouble, but it's under control now. Thanks for stopping."

The old guy eyed him closely. "No problem. Your car the one that took out that bridge rail a few yards back?"

Nick hesitated, wondered how much he should tell him. "I lost control of the car."

"What about that little gal you got tucked behind you? She okay, too?"

"I'm fine, Mr. Lemieux," Caroline said, and stepped from behind Nick.

"That you, Caroline?"

"Yes, sir," she replied. "This is Nick Ryan, Paul's brother. He was driving me home when…when we got into a little accident."

"Marchand's brother, hmm? He liked to drive fast, too. And from the looks of that rail, you two came a might close to following him to the Almighty. You ought to remember that the next time you go tearing down the road in your fancy car, son."

"I will," Nick assured him. "Thanks again for stopping." He ushered Caroline into the Jag.

"Why did you let Mr. Lemieux think you were hotrodding? What happened wasn't your fault. It was the driver of that truck running without lights."

"Because I think whoever was behind the wheel of that truck wants one or both of us dead."

DESPITE NICK'S SUSPICIONS, Caroline hadn't allowed herself to believe Paul's death had been anything but an accident. So when Chief Gaubert advised her the next day that a bomb had killed Paul, she was shaken. She was also shaken by the police chief's questioning of Nick as a suspect. "I'm sorry, Nick. I still can't believe Chief Gaubert thinks you could have had anything to do with Paul's death."

Nick shrugged. "The man's just doing his job."

"Well, I'm glad you and your lawyer convinced him he was wrong."

Nick shifted his gaze from whatever it was that had captured his attention outside her living-room window. "Don't kid yourself, Caroline. Big Tom released me because he didn't have enough evidence to hold me. But you can bet as soon as he finds out that I own a munitions plant, he'll be back with a warrant for my arrest.''

''But you didn't have anything to do with Paul's death.''

''Thanks.'' Nick gave her a weak smile. ''But someone's gone to a lot of trouble to make it look like I did. And until I find out who that someone is, I'd feel a lot better if you'd agree to go away for a while—someplace where I know you'll be safe.''

''Forget it. I'm not leaving.''

He strode across the room, hunkered down in front of her and stared into her eyes. Caroline's heart kicked at the intensity of his gaze. ''I'm serious. I've got a bad feeling about this. Whoever killed Paul may have planned for you to die in the explosion with him.'' When she started to protest, he held up a hand. ''Think about it. If everything had gone as planned, you and Paul would have left the reception together.''

And they'd both be dead now. Her blood ran cold as the realization hit her.

''Last night someone staged things so that it looked like you'd tried to commit suicide, and a few hours later someone tried to run us off the bridge.''

''But who would want to kill me? And why would anyone try to frame you?''

''I don't know.'' Nick stood, paced the room. ''There's any number of business competitors who may hold a grudge, but none of them would go this far. Actually, the only person who comes to mind that would is Boyce Sincard. The night before he was arrested, he followed Tyler, Jules and me into the bayou and swore he'd get even with each of us someday for squealing on him to the DA and causing him to go to prison.''

Caroline fingered the cross at her throat. ''But I thought

he was dead, that he drowned in some kind of boating accident not long after he got out of prison.''

"He did," Nick replied, and jammed his hand through his hair. "I thought his father might be behind what's been going on, but I found out this morning that Old Man Sincard is in a nursing home."

"Yes," Caroline confirmed. "He practically became a recluse after his son went to prison. Then when Boyce drowned, I heard he suffered a stroke. He was moved to a nursing home in the next parish more than a year ago."

"Which brings me back to square one. I've got a detective in New Orleans checking on a couple of other leads, including a tip I got from Tyler about one of my business interests. In the meantime I've made arrangements for you—"

"No. I have no intention of letting you or anyone else run me out of my home." She stood and walked over to the telephone. "I'm going to call Chief Gaubert and tell him what's going on. He can protect—"

Nick captured her wrist. "What are you going to tell him? That a truck tried to run us off the road last night?"

"Yes."

"And what do you think he's going to say when you tell him you can't describe the truck or the driver and that you didn't get a license-plate number?"

Caroline frowned. "There's still the matter of someone switching my pills."

"Where's your proof?"

"I don't need proof. It's what happened."

"Is it? How can you be sure? You've been under a lot of stress—struggling to hang on to your home, losing your new husband so violently and then finding out he was in serious financial trouble."

Furious with Nick, she fired back, "Aren't you forgetting

the bit about my birth mother and the fact that she committed suicide?''

"I'm sorry," he said, and stroked her cheek. "Big Tom's a cop, Caroline. He's going to see this with a cop's eyes and he's going to want proof."

She knew he was right, knew it and hated the fact that he was. The police chief would not believe her. Nor would probably anyone else.

"Trust me, Caroline. I'll get to the bottom of this, I swear I will. But I need to know that you're somewhere safe."

And what about him? Who would protect Nick? If what he said was true, he was in as much danger as she was—maybe more. She couldn't abandon him now.

"Trust me," he said, his voice softening.

She'd always been susceptible to Nick. Now with him so close, so gentle, his eyes filled with such concern, it would be easy for her to do as he asked. But she wouldn't. Not this time. This time whatever happened would be as much her decision as his. "All right, I'll go. But only if you come with me."

He scowled. "I can't go. Not until I find out who killed Paul."

"Then I'm not going, either."

Nick swore and marched back to the window. He flicked aside the curtain and peered out into the gathering darkness. After a long silence he turned to face her once more, a frown etched across his face. "All right. Go pack a bag—enough for a few days. We're getting out of here."

"We?"

"Yes, 'we,'" he said, and started toward her bedroom. "If you won't leave town, then I have no choice but to take you with me." He opened her closet, pulled out an overnight bag.

"Hold on a minute. Where are we going?"

"Someplace safe, away from here."

"But—"

"Do you want to stay here and end up dead? Someone's already gotten in here once and tried to kill you," he ranted as he yanked open the chest of drawers that contained her lingerie.

She pulled the lacy things from his fists. "Why are you so angry?"

"Because I don't want to waste any more time arguing with you. Something tells me that the guy who followed me from the police station to the grocery store and then back here wasn't out for a leisurely drive."

"What guy?" Caroline asked, adrenaline pumping through her system.

"The one parked behind the cluster of oaks on the main road to your house."

When Caroline fled to the living room and started toward the window, Nick pulled her back against him. "Wait," he ordered. "I don't want him to know he's been spotted."

Her heart pounded. She swallowed hard, aware of the strength and warmth of his body, pressed against hers, the heat of his breath against her ear as he spoke. She wasn't used to such close contact with a man, she told herself. That was why her pulse was racing, her breathing uneven.

Liar! a voice inside her head accused. Her limited experience with men had nothing to do with her reaction to Nick. It never had. A simple look, an innocent brush of fingers, was all that had been needed to make her heart ache, her body throb with longing for him. Her heart ached, her body throbbed now. She still loved him, she realized, and her knees went weak at the admission.

"Look out at the oaks and you'll see the gleam of his truck's bumper."

Caroline's stomach dipped as she saw it. "Do you think it's the same truck that tried to run us off the bridge last night?"

"Probably."

"Then we should call Chief Gaubert. Now we'll have proof—"

"All we've got are my suspicions."

"But—"

Nick caught her by the shoulders and moved her away from the window. He pressed her against the wall. "I need you to trust me on this, Caroline. Thirteen years ago I didn't follow my gut, and a friend ended up dead. Right now my gut tells me that we need to get you out of here."

Caroline swallowed. "You think he'll try to kill me again and frame you?"

"I don't know, but I don't intend to wait around to find out. Paul told me a couple of months ago that he bought a new powerboat. Does he keep it at the old dock?"

"Yes, but—"

"Good. Then we'll use it. Now, are you going to go pack that bag, or do I do it for you?"

Chapter Seven

"Nick, this is crazy," Caroline declared as he maneuvered the small speedboat through the dense growth and bends of the dark bayou. "At least turn on the lights."

"Can't risk it. We may have lost the tail, but he'll figure out soon enough that we're on the water. When he does, he'll come after us. There's no point in making ourselves an easy target."

"Are you sure you remember where this place is?"

"I remember," he told her. He wasn't likely to forget the rustic hideaway he'd purchased the year after he'd been released from Peltier Point. After being banned by his stepfather from Paul and his mother's home and shipped out East to college by his father, he'd felt more alone than ever. His only family of sorts had been Tyler and Jules. Then he'd remembered all that land surrounding the bayou where the three of them had taken their oath after Dave's murder. He'd never thought of himself as sentimental, but he'd wanted a place that would serve as a reminder of what they'd been through together, of the oath that had bound them as brothers in blood. So he'd used part of his inheritance from his grandfather and bought the excuse for a house and the land surrounding it. Although he hadn't been to the place in years, he'd known it was there in case he ever needed it. And he and Caroline needed it now.

"Look out for the cypress knees!"

"I see them," he told her, and steered the boat around the trees jutting from the water. "Try to relax. I know what I'm doing," he assured her, and prayed that he did. With only the moonlight to guide him, he kept his eyes fixed on the darkness in front of him and on the pairs of red eyes that watched them from the murky waters. He had to give Caroline credit. Most of the women he knew would be freaking out at the idea of traveling through the alligator-infested waters in the dark. But then, Caroline wasn't most women. Maybe that was the reason he'd never been able to forget her. No, he amended, knowing he'd only been kidding himself. He hadn't forgotten her because he had never stopped wanting her.

"Listen," she hissed. "I think I hear another motor."

Cutting back on the throttle and filtering out the sounds of the nightlife around them, Nick caught the faint putter of an engine some distance away and swore. "Judging from the sound, I'd say we've still got a pretty good start on him."

"What are we going to do now?"

"We're not too far from the cabin I told you about. It should be about another hundred yards or so up ahead. There's an inlet not far from it that's barely visible. We'll hide the boat there and make the rest of the trip by foot."

Just as he remembered, the twisted clump of cypresses that formed an odd-looking triangle came into view and marked the entrance to the inlet. With a skill he'd gained from years spent racing boats, Nick eased the boat in past the trees and guided it toward shore. He turned to Caroline. "You up for a little hike?"

She nodded and took his hand.

Once she was on the shore beside him, he grabbed a satchel of supplies and started toward the overgrown path. Thunder sounded in the distance. Dark clouds crowded the moon, cutting off much of the light. "From the looks of things, it's been a long time since anyone's been down this way. It'd probably be a good idea if you stick close and let me take the lead."

"All right. But we'd better hurry," she said after another burst of thunder. "It sounds like that storm's going to hit any minute."

THE STORM HIT just before they reached the cabin. And by the time Caroline raced up the stairs to the small house behind Nick, she was soaked to the skin. They both were, she realized, as Nick turned to her with rain dripping down his face. "You okay?"

"Yes. Just wet."

"There's a bathroom inside where you can dry off and change." He hesitated in front of the door. "I wasn't kidding about the place being rustic," he warned.

Caroline followed him inside. Nick hadn't exaggerated. From what she could see beneath the layer of dust, there was lots of wood—both the walls and the floor—and the furnishings could only be described as basic.

He dumped the overnight bag on the floor and moved across the room to open a window. "There's a small generator out back, but I can't risk turning it on right now. Any light would act as a beacon for whoever's tailing us. So we'll have to make do with whatever light the moon provides."

"I understand." The faded curtain rippled in the breeze, and Caroline was suddenly grateful for the clean rain scent that chased away some of the stale-smelling air. Aided by what little moonlight spilled through the window, she took stock of the cabin. It was tiny. Other than the room they were standing in, she saw only one other door and suspected it led to the bathroom. The only furnishings were a woodstove, a small table and chairs, a small chest with a kerosene lamp, and a bed. One bed, she noted, with a frown.

"I'm going to take a look around outside. The bathroom's through that door if you want to change into something dry," he told her. "There's no window in there, so you can use the flashlight. Clean linens and towels are in the cabinet."

Once Nick headed back out into the storm, Caroline scooped up her bag and the flashlight he'd left her and hurried into the bathroom. After changing into dry clothes, she felt almost normal again—until she exited the bathroom and found Nick waiting. Her heart stopped, then started again at the sight of him. His clothes were plastered to his body, shaping the broad chest, the ripple of muscles along his arms and thighs. Raindrops glistened on his sun-darkened skin, in his hair, on the tips of his eyelashes. With the whiskers shadowing his chin he looked sexy and dangerous.

"Either we lost him or he's holed up somewhere until the storm passes," Nick said, his husky voice adding to the spell she'd fallen under. "Either way, we should be safe here until morning."

Her heart still pounding, Caroline didn't even try to speak. She simply nodded her head. And while Nick took his turn in the bathroom, she went about making up the bed. From the looks of it, she guessed the bed was technically a double. But while it might prove plenty big for one person, for two people it would be...cozy.

When the bathroom door opened again, Caroline looked up. There was just enough moonlight for her to get a tempting glimpse of his bare chest and the way the low-fitting jeans hugged his hips. Her throat suddenly dry, she swallowed hard as he approached her, unable to look away.

"You go ahead and take the bed. I'll sleep on the floor," Nick offered, his voice gruff. He reached for the blanket and pillow in her hands and looked away—but not before she recognized the hungry gleam in his eyes.

Caroline held on to the blanket and pillow, and he lifted

his gaze to hers. For a long moment she simply stood there. When his eyes moved over her face, down her throat to her breasts, her heart beat faster. Desire curled in her belly. She thought about all that she and Nick had been through during the past few days—Paul's death and funeral, the attempts on her life. What if the killer found them tomorrow morning? What if this was her last night alive? She knew that if it was, she didn't want to spend it in bed alone. "I don't want you to sleep on the floor," she finally told him. "I want you to sleep in the bed—with me."

Nick tensed. In the faint light she could see the sharp angles of his face, the flare of his nostrils, the narrowing of his eyes. "If I get in that bed with you, it won't be to sleep."

"I know," she whispered. After toeing off her shoes, she pulled off her T-shirt and jeans, tossed them to the floor. He didn't move a muscle. But his eyes, those piercing blue eyes, tracked her every movement. Still, he said nothing. He simply stood there, watching her, waiting. With trembling fingers, she reached for the snap on his jeans.

Nick caught her hand. "Be sure this is what you want, Caroline. I want you more than I want my next breath. But when this mess is behind us, nothing will have changed. I still can't offer you any future."

She met his gaze. "I'm not asking you for anything beyond tonight. No commitments, no promises. Just tonight. Tonight I need to feel alive. I need to remember what it feels like to be wanted. Make love to me, Nick."

Nick groaned and pulled her into his arms. His mouth devoured hers with hot hungry kisses while his hands shaped her, cupped her, pulled her into his heat. He pushed her back against the bed, came down between her thighs. And then his hands—those oh-so-clever hands—were everywhere. So was his mouth. Tongue and teeth teased her nipples, tasted her flesh, while his fingers—those strong, knowing fingers—

continued to play over her body like a master musician with a violin.

He touched her, stroked her, made his way down to the sensitive spot at her center. He slid his fingers inside her and she arched her hips. "Don't fight it, angel," he urged as he brought her up, took her to the brink, then sent her over the edge.

She was still panting from the shattering release when he moved lower, replaced his hands with his mouth. "Nick, I can't—"

"Yes, you can. Let me love you," he murmured, and flicked his tongue over her tender flesh until she was soaring once again.

"Nick, please. I need you."

"Not nearly as much as I need you," he murmured, and slid his knee between her thighs. He entered her in one swift thrust. Caroline's breath caught as he filled her. Thunder roared outside as he began to move inside her. Rain beat down on the roof, lightning exploded outside the window. But the storm raging outside paled against the storm of emotion she read in Nick's eyes, against the storm of love in her heart for this man. "Show me, Nick. Show me how much you need me."

And he did, sending them both tumbling over the edge headfirst into the storm.

Chapter Eight

Making love with Caroline had been a mistake, Nick thought as he lay awake in the darkness much later. But try as he might, he couldn't regret what had happened between them. Was Caroline right? Had he been running all these years from life, from her, the one person he needed and wanted most?

He had told himself that he'd done the right thing by walking away from her all those years ago because he'd feared he would be unable to give her what she needed. But it hadn't been Caroline he'd been protecting, he saw with sudden clarity. It had been himself. He'd walked away from her before she could leave him, just as his mother, his father and everyone else he'd cared about had done. What a fool he'd been! So many wasted years, years they could have had together.

And now? Now it was too late to change the past. But not the future. He wanted a future with Caroline, he realized, and tightened his arms around her. But first, he had to get her away from here, take her someplace where she would be safe until he found the scum who had tried to frame him for Paul's murder and had tried to kill her. And then he would try to convince her to give him, to give them, another chance.

Once again Nick went over the series of events in his

mind, beginning with Paul's odd behavior at the wedding reception. Thinking back to that night, he recalled his brother's face. While Paul's slurred speech had made him conclude that his brother was drunk, he didn't remember smelling liquor on Paul's breath. And his eyes hadn't had that glazed look of someone who'd been drinking heavily. Nick frowned. If anything, Paul's eyes had been clear that night when he'd hurled those accusations at him. Clear and…panicked. Not angry, Nick realized, his muscles tensing.

Had all those ugly things Paul had said to him been an act? An act for whose benefit? Who had Paul been trying to protect? The answer hit him, stole his breath. Caroline…and possibly him. Nick's chest tightened. Of course. Why hadn't he seen it before now? Paul must have known someone was trying to kill him. So he'd staged the angry scene and stormed off to make sure they were out of danger.

But why, Paul? Why didn't you tell me? Why didn't you let me help you?

Squeezing his eyes shut, Nick mourned his brother anew. If only he had kept the lines of communication open, been able to see past his own jealousy over Caroline. Nick went over everything again in his head—the car explosion, Caroline's nearly fatal overdose, the truck trying to run them off the bridge. Who was calling the plays from behind the scenes? Who knew enough about him to stage the incidents so that the evidence pointed to him? Because everything *did* point to him—his history of racing and skill as a driver, his ownership of the munitions plant, his romantic involvement with Caroline. He thought again about Tyler's call telling him he'd been set up. Was it possible whoever was trying to frame him for Paul's death was also behind Tyler's problems? And what about Jules? Where was Jules?

"Do you always wake up with a frown on your face after you've spent the night making love with a woman?"

Nick opened his eyes. His chest tightened at the sleepy well-loved look on Caroline's face. "I don't know. I've never spent the entire night with a woman before."

She pulled free of his embrace and tucked the sheet around her breasts before sitting up. Her expression somber, she said, "If you're saying that for my benefit, I can assure you it isn't necessary. I knew what I was doing, and I don't have any regrets."

Nick captured her face between his palms, kissed her soundly. When she was breathless and her eyes dreamy, he said, "I'm not lying. There have been other women, but I've never spent the night with any of them. Only you, Caroline. Only you."

"Is that why you were frowning? Because you broke one of your rules?"

"Actually I was frowning because I was thinking about Paul," he said, and explained the conclusions he'd reached about his brother's actions before his death. He further explained that if anyone questioned her supposed suicide, the police chief could easily have verified that Nick had been to her house and could have switched the pills. And had the car been run off the bridge, there was always the argument that his training as a driver would have enabled him to escape even if she had not.

"I'm not questioning what you're saying," Caroline told him. "But who would want to frame you? It doesn't make any sense."

She was right. It didn't make any sense. He was missing something, something obvious but important. What? The detective he'd hired had told him to follow the money trail. The money trail. Tyler's message about Blankenship. Then it hit him. Sitting up, he asked, "Who stands to gain if something happens to you?"

"No one I can think of."

"Who's the beneficiary of your will?"

Caroline frowned. "Actually I never got around to making out one. I suppose since Paul and I married, if he were still alive, he would inherit. With him gone, I'm not sure. But I really don't have much in the way of assets other than my house and the land—and even that's not worth much, according to the geologist's report."

"You had a geological survey done on your property?"

"Paul and I both did about eight months ago when we were approached about selling it. Some development wanted to turn it into a company resort for people who wanted a taste of the bayou country."

"What happened?"

"They made us an offer, but Paul thought it was too low. He said his grandfather had always claimed there was oil on the Marchand land that just hadn't been found yet. So Paul had surveys done on both properties."

"And?"

"And there was no oil."

"So why didn't the two of you sell?" Nick asked.

"Paul would have, but the company insisted they needed both pieces of property."

"And you wouldn't sell."

Caroline nodded. "I know it sounds crazy, but I couldn't."

"I understand," he told her, and drew her into his arms. He did understand—just as he'd understood all those years ago.

"Maybe none of this would have happened if I had sold. Because it was only a couple of months later when the bank called in the loan and I found out about the balloon note. Then when I was at my wit's end, Paul came up with the idea for us to marry and join our assets." She paused. "The crazy thing is that, given Paul's financial condition, the bank would never have given me the refinancing."

And maybe his brother had counted on that, Nick thought.

Even as a kid, Paul had stubbornly refused to accept defeat when he'd made up his mind about something. Nick felt a swift kick to his gut as he recalled a young Paul defying his own father and sneaking food to Nick when he'd been sent to bed without supper.

"I don't know why I insisted on hanging on to the place. It's not like it was some sort of legacy. I mean, I don't have any family."

"Wait," Nick said as some of the puzzle pieces began to click into place. "Caroline, think carefully. Do you have any living relatives at all?"

"No. The Donovans were both only children, and they adopted me because they were unable to have any children of their own. Why?"

"You have no heirs," he told her. "Neither does Paul."

"What about you?"

"Legally there's no blood tie between us." Nick blew out a breath and continued, "Louisiana's still governed under the Napoleonic Code, meaning we have forced heirship. In most cases when there's no surviving heir or beneficiary, the city claims the land and sells it for the taxes due."

Caroline paled. "Which is what would have happened if both Paul and I had died."

"Yes. Do you remember the name of the firm that wanted to buy the property?"

"Blankenship Corporation."

Nick froze. "You're sure?"

"Yes. Why? Do you know who owns the company?"

"Yes," Nick replied. Once again he felt that web closing in around him. He had never authorized or even discussed any bayou-themed resort. Until he spoke to Jeff Robelot, the man he'd appointed to run Blankenship after its acquisition, he didn't want to scare Caroline. And she would be scared if she thought that he might be the one responsible for his brother's death and the attempts on her life. "I'll make a few phone calls and see what I can find out."

"Now?" she asked when he started to get up. "It's still dark."

She was right. But he was eager to speak to Robelot and get some answers.

"Can the calls wait until morning?" she asked, and ran her fingers down his chest.

Nick sucked in a breath as she smoothed her palm over his stomach and moved lower. Despite his worries and the fact that they had made love twice already, he was hot and hard in an instant. "Why? Did you have something special in mind?"

She smiled a womanly smile that he suspected Eve had used on Adam. "As a matter of fact, I did," she whispered just before she dropped the sheet covering her breasts. She pushed him back down to the bed and positioned herself over him. And as she filled herself with him and began to move, every thought, every concern went right out of Nick's head, save one—the need to love and be loved by Caroline.

"I DON'T CARE what it takes. I want to know who Robelot is working for and how he managed to get past the personnel checkpoints and infiltrate Ryan Industries!"

Caroline's eyes snapped open at the angry sound of Nick's voice. Sitting up in bed, it took her a moment to adjust her eyes to the darkness, and when the door to the bathroom opened, she realized he'd been talking on his cell phone. "Who was that you were talking to?"

He paused. "The private investigator I told you about. He's checking on a few things."

"You're dressed," she said, stating the obvious. Her own nakedness beneath the sheet left her feeling vulnerable. "Is it morning already?"

"Almost. The sun will be up soon. We'll need to get moving."

His distant manner sobered her far more quickly than his words. The tender lover of only hours ago seemed almost a dream. Chastising herself for thinking last night might have meant more to Nick than sex, she tugged the sheet more tightly around her. "Do you think whoever was following us yesterday will be able to find us here?"

His expression grim, Nick said, "I don't want to take any chances. I'm going to check on the boat. You get dressed, and when I get back, we'll take the boat to the nearest town. If memory serves me correctly, they have a small airport there where I can charter a plane."

"A plane?"

"I'm not going to argue with you about this. Whoever killed Paul and tried to set me up knows a lot about me. So they'll know that the best way to get at me is through you. I want you to leave Louisiana until I find out who's behind this."

Caroline's stomach dipped at the prospect of leaving Breauxville and Nick. "What if I called Chief Gaubert, explained everything to him? He could arrange protection for me. It's what I should have done, instead of dragging you into this mess."

Nick's mouth thinned. "You didn't drag me into anything. And I've already called Big Tom and told him what's going on. But there's no way I intend to rely on him to keep you safe."

"I appreciate your offer, but I'm not your responsibility, Nick. I can take of myself."

"Dammit, but if you aren't the most stubborn woman…" He caught her by the shoulders, gave her a tiny shake. "Get it through that thick head of yours—I am not going to risk losing you again."

Stunned, Caroline blinked. The vise around her heart loosened. While it wasn't a declaration of love, it was close enough, she decided.

"Do you trust me?" he demanded, his blue eyes stormy with temper.

"Yes," she murmured.

"Good," he said, and then kissed her hard before storming out the door. Too dazed to move, Caroline sat there for several heartbeats. Then a smile broke out on her face, and scooping up her clothes, she dashed into the bathroom.

WHEN SHE EXITED the bathroom fifteen minutes later, Caroline was still smiling—until she saw the man waiting for her. A man with a gun in his hand.

"Well, well, look what we have here. Where's your friend, little lady?"

The hairs on the back of Caroline's neck stood on end as she viewed the dark-haired giant with the cold black eyes and lascivious grin. "He's not here, and if I were you, I'd leave before he gets back. He's bringing the police."

"Is that so? Then I guess you and I will just have to wait for them to get here. In the meantime why don't you come have a seat over here, darling?"

Caroline made a dash for the door. For a big man, grizzly face moved fast. He closed a beefy fist around her arm. "That wasn't smart," he said, and dragged her over to the chair. When she struggled, he smacked her across the face. Caroline's head rang under the blow. Her cheek throbbed so fiercely she barely registered the stinging pain in her arms as he bound her hands behind her back with rope.

"You'll never get away with this," she told him. "My friend knows who you're working for and he's told the police chief."

"Is that so?" he replied as he gave the rope another vicious yank and sent pain shooting up her arms.

"Yes. The police are on their way here now. Nick will be back with them any moment."

His task finished, the man retrieved the gun from his waistband and trained it on her. "What did you say your friend's name was?"

When she hesitated, he lifted his hand and she said, "Nick. Nick Ryan. He's a very important businessman from New Orleans. He'll never let you get away with this."

"Well, I'll be damned," grizzly face said, and started to laugh.

There was something in his tone, accompanied by the feral gleam in his eyes, that sent ice trickling down her spine. "I'm serious. Nick will hunt you down. He'll never let you get away with killing me."

"Darling, who do you think hired me to kill you in the first place?"

Chapter Nine

The blood in Nick's veins turned to ice when he heard the voices inside the cabin. Flattening his body against the outer wall, he moved slowly to the window. He bit back an oath at the sight of the goon holding a gun on Caroline.

"You're lying!"

The gunman laughed, and as the man shifted, Nick was able to get a clear view of Caroline's face. Fury gripped him by the throat and refused to let go when he saw the angry bruise forming on her right cheek. Clenching his hands into fists at his sides, it took everything in Nick not to burst into the room and ram a knife through the other man's heart.

"Believe what you want, darling. It's no skin off my nose. But you're the one who wanted to know who I was working for, and I told you. Nick Ryan hired me to kill you and his brother."

Nick stilled. His heart slammed against his ribs. Surely Caroline wouldn't believe him. Then he thought about the conversation he'd had with his detective just before that crazy boater had come out of nowhere and nearly plowed him down. No doubt, the boater was meant to take care of him. But it was the info from the private detective that gave him pause now. Thanks to the tip from Tyler and what information he'd gotten from Caroline, the investigator had been able to quickly make a connection between Jeff Robelot and the Framingham organization that Tyler had infiltrated. Harris Framingham had long been suspected of having mob ties. It hadn't been difficult to tie Landry to Framingham's money-lending scam. Nick's stomach sank. And if his suspicions proved correct, Robelot was a plant by Framingham to infiltrate Blankenship. With Robelot working at Blankenship, he would have access to a great deal of personal and financial data on Nick. And with that information at his disposal, it wouldn't be too difficult for Robelot to provide the person after him with the means to set him up for Paul's death and the attempts on Caroline's life. Of course, his motive would be their land. And whoever had set up the scheme had left a smoking gun right in his hand.

"I've got to give it to this guy Ryan," the goon said. "When I heard he was the one who saved you after I switched those pills, I was pretty confused. Then when he left me instructions to put a scare into you that night on the bridge, I figured he'd lost his nerve. Either that, or he'd changed his mind because you and him were sleeping together. But when I got his message telling me where to find you, I realized the man was smarter than I'd given him credit for. I mean, who's going to suspect him of having you and his brother offed when he's the one who saved your life twice already?"

Caroline's face lost what little color it had.

"Although, if I was him, I'm not so sure I'd want to get rid of a pretty little thing like you," the gunman said. Moving closer, he ran the tip of his gun along the edge of Caroline's jaw.

Nick tensed, prepared to launch himself through the window at the man, when Caroline jerked her head to the side. "If you were hired to kill me, why don't you just shoot me and get it over with?"

"'Cause I'm supposed to make it look like an accident,

sweet thing. And I will. You and I are going to take us a ride in that fancy boat you came out here in. But we're going to have to wait until it gets dark.''

"No one will believe my death was an accident. I'm not lying. The chief of police knows someone's been trying to kill me.''

"All the chief knows is that you're a young widow who hasn't been herself since her husband died. Why, you even tried to overdose on sleeping pills, remember? And everyone knows how easy it is to get lost in the bayou at night.''

Nick stepped in front of the window and motioned for Caroline to keep quiet as he made his way to the door. As he did so, he prayed she didn't believe the things the gunman had accused him of and that she'd trust him just a little bit longer.

"In the meantime we've got us quite a few hours to kill while we wait for it to get dark. What do you say I untie you and the two of us get better acquainted?''

"I'd sooner sleep with a snake,'' Caroline hissed.

"What's the matter? Think you're too good for me?'' When she didn't answer, he said, "You were shacking up with that Ryan guy before your old man was even cold in his grave. Don't tell me it's because you were in love with him.''

"I hate Nick Ryan,'' she spit out. "I made a mistake trusting him, and if he were here now, I'd cut his heart out and feed it to the gators.''

Her words ripped at Nick, left him feeling raw. From the scorn in her voice and the expression on her face, he suspected she meant every word. But he could hardly blame her. He'd never even told her he loved her.

And he did love her, Nick realized, staggered by the discovery. Only, Caroline didn't know it. As far as she knew, last night had been nothing more than sex to him, and he was going to waltz right out of her life again just like the last time.

"I mean it," she told the gunman. "I'd kill him if he were here. I hate him."

The other man laughed. "You know, I think you just might."

"Please, mister—"

He hesitated a moment. "I guess since you won't be around to tell anyone... The name's Walt."

"Please, Walt, all I want is a chance to get even with that louse Nick Ryan. I don't think you really want to kill me. Don't do his dirty work for him. Cut me loose so I can go after him myself. I swear, if you do, I won't breathe a word about you to the police."

"Darling, you ain't going to breathe a word to anyone because you'll be dead."

"How much is he paying you?" she asked. "I'll double it if you let me go?"

He paused. "I don't know... You really hate the guy that much?"

"Yes," she said firmly. "I hate him."

CAROLINE NEARLY CHOKED on the lie. Her heart had been racing at breakneck speed from the moment she'd seen Nick at the window. Dear God, she prayed, let me be a good enough actress so that the man believes me. "What have you got to lose?" she asked as she continued to work at freeing her hands from the ropes.

"I don't know," Walt said. "It don't seem right."

Great, an honorable hit man, she thought. "Come on, Walt. I hate the SOB." She shifted her gaze to the window. For a split second her eyes locked with Nick's and she tried to tell him it wasn't true. That she loved him, trusted him.

Something in her face must have alerted Walt, because he

shouted, "Why, you bitch! You lying bitch!" Then he whipped around and aimed the gun in Nick's direction.

"No," Caroline cried, and despite the screaming pain in her arms, she launched her body and the chair at Walt's legs. The big man's knees buckled at the impact. The gun fired high. And then he swung back around and aimed the gun at her.

In agony from the pain in her arms, Caroline was unable to move quickly. She heard wood breaking, shouts and a gunshot. She held her breath, waited for the pain, waited for death. But all she felt was a sting at her temple. Before she could rejoice that Walt's shot had missed her, she saw Nick.

"Nick," she called out, and started to get up to tell him she was all right. But her legs refused to obey her.

"Caroline!" Her name was an animal cry from Nick's lips. He raced over to her, his face twisted with rage. Something warm and wet dripped in her eye, and Caroline thought she saw him hurl something sharp and shiny at Walt. Walt screamed, dropped the gun and grabbed his shoulder before slumping to the ground.

Feeling weak and light-headed, Caroline closed her eyes.

And then Nick was there, unfastening the ropes and cradling her in his arms. He brushed her hair from her eyes, kissed her face. "Caroline! Baby, can you hear me?"

She tried to tell him he didn't need to shout. She could hear him just fine. But her mouth didn't seem to be working.

"Hang on, baby," he urged, and never letting her go, he managed to dial the cell phone one-handed. After demanding to know where the chief was, he ordered somebody to get their sorry rears out here fast and to bring a doctor.

"I'm so sorry for everything I put you through, for being such a damn idiot all these years." Continuing to hold her, he pressed kisses to her head. "Please, don't leave me. I need you. And I love you so much. I swear, I'll never leave you again."

Even though she could feel herself fading fast, Caroline forced her eyes open a moment so she could see his face. Reaching up, she touched Nick's cheek. "I love you, too. And I intend to hold you to that promise," she told him just before she gave up the battle and allowed the darkness to swallow her.

NICK DIED A THOUSAND DEATHS as he waited outside the cabin with the police while Doc Pruitt tended to Caroline. He had refused to leave her when the police had tried to question him, but he had given in when the doctor had ordered him out. He vaguely recalled Big Tom, Tommy Joe and the two other officers arriving and pulling him off that goon Walt before he beat him to within an inch of his life for hurting Caroline.

"You realize I'm going to have to check out this story of yours," Big Tom told him.

"Go ahead," Nick said. "According to my detective, Robelot's already spilling his guts to the New Orleans police about Framingham planting him in my company. He's admitted that the geological reports on the land were faked and that the motive behind Paul's death and the attempts on Caroline was the land. According to Robelot, Reynard Duquette did another survey on the same properties, and it revealed there's oil on them."

"Which would give this Robelot character a reason to have Duquette killed," Gaubert added, and looked at the handcuffed bloody-faced Walt.

"I told you. I don't know nobody named Robelot, and I ain't killed nobody named Duquette. Ryan's the one who ordered the hits on his brother and the Donovan girl."

"Listen you son of a—"

"Back off, Ryan," Gaubert ordered, then motioned for Tommy Joe to take the prisoner down to the police boat. "I said I'd check out his story about getting his instructions over the phone and the money sent to a post-office box. What doesn't make sense is why he wouldn't cop to Duquette's murder, too.''

''That's your problem,'' Nick said, eager to get back to Caroline. ''But you can talk to the New Orleans police and to Pete Mackenzie, the detective working for me. They're trying to trace the source of the cash and the letters to the person inside Framingham's organization who set up the whole scheme.''

''Like you said, it's my problem. So I suggest you keep your nose out of it.''

Nick had no intention of keeping his nose out until he learned who had ordered his brother killed, had tried to kill Caroline and tried to frame him. Although discovering Robelot's and Landry's link to the Framingham organization filled in most of the blanks, he couldn't shake the feeling that he was missing a piece of the puzzle. Framingham had denied any knowledge of the land scheme. The same gut instinct that had made him wary of Boyce Sincard all those years ago was telling him that Framingham was telling the truth. Which meant that someone else had orchestrated the elaborate plot and had set Nick up for murder—someone with a motive that went beyond money and acquiring the land. If it had been only monetary gain, why not just kill him and be done with it? Why go to such lengths to have him convicted of murder and sent to prison when it would have been simpler and less complicated to have him dead? Why kill his brother and try to kill Caroline, but not make a serious attempt to kill him?

The door to the cabin opened and Nick rushed over to Doc Pruitt. ''How is she?''

''Fine. Why don't you come see for yourself? She's asking for you.''

Nick followed the doctor back into the cabin. He'd seen snow with more color than Caroline had in her cheeks. The sight of the bandage on her temple made his stomach weak. "Are you sure she's all right? I can have a chopper brought in to take her to the hospital."

"Take it easy, son," Doc said, resting a hand on his shoulder. "The bullet just grazed her temple. Other than a headache and a little scratch, she should be as good as new in a day or two. I'm beginning to think the girl's got more lives than a cat."

"Would you two quit talking about me like I'm not here?" Caroline demanded.

"She's all yours, son. The last thing I need is being around a prickly female. I'm going to go back with Big Tom and his men. I've given her something for the pain, and here's a prescription to get filled later." Standing, he picked up his bag and walked to the door, then paused. "You planning to stick around this time, boy?"

Nick smiled. "Yes, sir. I plan to stick around."

"Then bring her by my office tomorrow so I can check that head wound."

Nick nodded, and when the door closed behind the other man, he sat down on the bed beside her. "How are you feeling?"

"I'm fine."

"Caroline, about what he said—"

"I don't want to talk about what happened. Not right now. What I need to know is if you meant what you told Doc. Are you planning to stick around?"

"I meant it," he said. "I'll be here for as long as you want me."

"Because you're feeling guilty about what almost happened to me?"

"No," he said, smiling. He brushed a strand of hair from her eyes. "Because for the first time I have a reason to stay. I love you, Caroline."

"Enough to stay in Breauxville?"

"Enough to stay in Breauxville," he assured her.

"And what if I told you I've been thinking about selling my place and moving?"

Nick paused. "But why? You love that place. It's your home."

She caught his face in her hands and drew his mouth to hers. "No, it's not. My home is where you are. New Orleans. Breauxville. Tahiti. Where I live doesn't matter—as long as I'm with you. You're my home, Nick."

"And you're mine," he told her, and took her into his arms and kissed her.

LATER THAT NIGHT when Caroline awoke and went in search of Nick, she found him on the phone. "Waking up and finding myself alone because you're on the phone is becoming a habit," she said, sliding her arms around his waist. She pressed her face to his back and sensed the tension in him. "What's wrong?"

He hung up the phone and turned her into his arms. "Just a feeling I have that there's something I'm missing. Damn! I wish Tyler would call again or I knew how to reach Jules."

"It's over, Nick," she said.

"Not yet. But it will be." He looked at Caroline, a vision with the moonlight flowing around her. His heart swelled with love. "I love you and I want to marry you."

"Is that a proposal?" she asked, smiling.

"Yes. But…"

"But?"

"But I don't want a lot of press. While I'd like to shout to the entire world that you're my wife, until I'm sure this is all behind us, I want to be certain you're out of danger."

"So what are you suggesting?" Caroline asked.

"How would you feel about a quiet wedding and honeymoon away from here?"

She smiled. "Oh, I think I could be persuaded," she whispered.

Nick reached for the sash on her robe and set out to do just that.

JULES
JOANNA WAYNE

A special thanks to Linda Hayes
for having the vision that inspired this book,
to Denise O'Sullivan for having faith
that we could make it work,
and to Debra Matteucci for working so diligently
to keep us on track.

Chapter One

Jules Duquette guided the small pirogue deeper and deeper into the Atchafalaya swamp. A moonlit night, yet the stench of murder stalked the muggy wetlands. Death, dank and suffocating. That was all this area meant to him anymore.

First his grandmother, then his grandfather, both buried in a plot of swampland behind the old trapper's shack they'd called home. Now his only cousin, Reynard, lay with them. The Duquettes were a dying breed.

Reynard. The decent Duquette. They'd been as close as brothers, growing up, though different in a lot more ways than they'd been alike. Reynard had been the student, the peacemaker, the ambitious one.

Jules had been the rebellious one, had stayed angry for years about the car crash that had claimed the lives of both sets of parents when he was only eight and Reynard six. He and his cousin had spent the day with their grandparents while their parents had gone to the big Mardi Gras celebration in New Orleans. None of them had returned. Both boys and their grandparents had been devastated, but they'd all dealt with their grief in their own way.

Reynard had eventually gotten himself a college degree, learned to eat with the right fork and wear a tie without choking. Jules had bummed around a few years after graduating from high school, worked construction jobs when he could find them. Then, finally, after his buddies Nick and Tyler had refused to let up on him, he'd applied for and gotten accepted into the New Orleans Police Academy.

He'd loved it from the get-go, moved up quickly through the ranks, thought he'd finally found his niche. But in the end, wearing a NOPD badge hadn't been what he'd hoped. If anything, being a detective in New Orleans had made him more of an outcast, set him more firmly against the establishment.

You gotta learn to look the other way sometimes, Duquette. That had been the NOPD chief's advice. Translated, it meant you didn't rat on a fellow cop, no matter what he was doing. And blackmail and murder weren't crimes unless the chief said they were.

But Jules wasn't going to dish out injustice just because some louse with a badge and a title told him to. Not after the treatment he'd gotten the summer after his freshman year in high school. Sent to a detention camp for no reason, except that T. L. Breaux had decided he needed to be taught a lesson.

He'd learned a lesson, all right, just not the one T.L. had in mind. He'd found out that he couldn't trust rich or powerful men any farther than he could spit. It was a fact of life he hadn't forgotten. But he probably shouldn't be too hard on Breaux. The two best friends he'd ever had he'd made at that hellhole they called Peltier Point.

Friends. Blood brothers. Only, even they were gone now. One dead. The other who knows where, leading his own life.

Shifting and stretching the muscles in his neck, Jules peered through a veil of cypress and Spanish moss. He could see the Breaux house in the distance, the steep roof and chimney silhouetted in the moonlight. It dwarfed the landscape, flaunted its superiority over the surrounding swamp and the murky bayou that meandered just below its back border. He slowed his boat, then killed the motor altogether.

Taking the oars, he dipped them beneath the green slime that smeared the surface, then stroked smooth and sure, easing the boat slowly and silently past the imposing plantation house. This was the last place he'd planned to end up his first hour back in town, yet here he was.

He sat for a minute, letting old memories slink through his mind. Something splashed in the water, and he turned to see what had joined him. A second later he spotted the snout of a young gator, floating just above the surface like a gnarly log. The company didn't bother him. Gators were far less treacherous than a lot of cops he'd met in the Big Easy.

But his gaze caught and held on a smattering of color in the moonlight, a piece of clothing peeking from the jungle of cypress knees that dotted the bank. He rowed closer. The fabric took form. It was attached to a body, at least what was left of one.

He'd apparently disturbed the gator's dinner. But Jules had lived in the swamp too long to believe that the small gator had killed a grown man. The hungry reptile had just taken advantage of someone else's handiwork.

Another murder? Could peaceful little Breauxville finally be setting free the evil it had always masked in lies and deceit, or had the real world just dipped its deadly fingers into the bayou country?

Either way, Jules wouldn't be leaving until he'd found the man responsible for taking the life of his cousin. Then he'd be out of here. This time for good.

HOT, SULTRY, HUMID, like steam escaping a kettle. Adrienne Breaux turned restlessly, the cotton sheets tangling in her long legs. She'd only lived away for five years, and yet she'd almost forgotten how the August humidity took you like a deceitful lover. Intoxicating at first, then sucking the life from you until you collapsed into a perspiring, pulsating shadow of the person you'd been.

Only there was no reason for it to be this way inside Mims's house. Adrienne's father had insisted her grandmother have the rambling plantation home air-conditioned a decade ago, at the same time he'd pressured her into letting him oversee a major remodeling project. Discard the old. Trash the reminders of the past. Bury the memories.

Only, her dad was dead now, and the most valuable relic of the Breaux heritage was still breathing. Alive, though not the Mims Adrienne remembered. Age had stolen the twinkle from her eyes, the strength from her bones, the dance from her step. Worse it had attacked her mental processes, dulled her quick Cajun wit and punched crippling holes in her memory and ability to reason, and sometimes even to recognize people she'd known all her life. But it hadn't stolen Mims's sweetness.

Adrienne slung her legs over the side of the four-poster bed and stretched. Her white cotton gown pulled tight across her breasts and then fell in loose folds to skim the tops of her knees as she planted her bare feet on the hardwood planks of the floor. The house creaked and moaned as she padded across the room and down the wide center hallway to the air-conditioner controls.

As she expected, her grandmother had gotten up during the night and nudged the thermostat up to a sweltering ninety-five degrees. Most likely not because she'd gotten cold, but from the patterns of frugality she'd learned in her youth. The past was clear in her mind. It was the present that was blurred and splotchy.

The heart medicine she was supposed to take, the food she'd left cooking on the gas range. Those were the type of things that floated from her mind with increasing frequency.

Which was why Adrienne was back under her grandmother's roof, the reason she'd tendered her resignation at the law firm of Holt, Brown, Grennold and Wright and moved back into a world she'd thought had been put behind her forever. The reason she'd asked Maggie Prejean to start coming over every day to stay with Mims, instead of just dropping by a couple of days a week to help with the cleaning.

Adrienne adjusted the temperature setting, then continued down the hall. Her grandmother's bedroom door was open. Adrienne peeked inside. Mims's thin gray hair fell across her pillow in wiry waves and caressed her sallow cheeks. Moving as quietly as she could so as not to wake the dear, Adrienne tiptoed across the room and tucked the sheet around her frail body. The air conditioner was already spraying a cool breath across the high-ceilinged room.

Her grandmother was sleeping soundly, but Adrienne was wide awake now. *Never sleep unless your body craves it. Time is far too important a commodity to waste.* The edict was one preached by her favorite law-school professor. She'd adopted it, more out of necessity than pleasure. But it had served her well, not only at the university but as a fledgling with the powerful Boston law firm who'd recruited her from the ranks of summa cum laude graduates at Tulane University in New Orleans.

Shadows danced on the walls, and her bare feet slapped the polished wood as she descended the winding staircase. The house was quiet but not lonely. Too many ghosts walked the rooms and stared at her from the painted eyes of the Breauxs whose portraits lined the wall. The good, the bad, the ugly and the forgettables, like herself, had all lived under this roof at one time or another.

Forgettable. The word fit, but she'd never consciously used it to describe herself before. She wondered when her mind had pigeonholed her that way. Perhaps when her dad had forgotten her graduation or maybe when he'd failed to congratulate her when she'd won her first big case. Or had it been much earlier in her life?

Maybe eleven years ago. A hot August night, not much different from this one, except she'd been young, celebrating her eighteenth birthday. That night she'd been excited, giddy at the attention Jules Duquette was paying her. Crashing her party, then teasing, touching, whispering in her ear that she was no longer jailbait. Jules, the mysterious boy from the swamp who drove the girls mad with his dark brooding virility.

Her mouth went dry, her flesh suddenly clammy, as if that night so long ago still had the power to stir her blood. But it didn't. Jules didn't. It was just the heat and being back here at Mims's that made the memories so potent. That and the fact that she'd spent the day reviewing the few facts available concerning his cousin's murder.

The walls of the old house seemed to close in around her, and she walked to the back door, turned the key in the lock and pushed it open. The moon was almost full, bright enough that the back lawn and even the towering cypress trees in the swampy hollow beyond it were bathed in a silvery glow.

Slipping her feet into the pair of mud-encrusted tennis shoes she wore for her morning walks, she stepped across the porch, down the steps and onto a lush carpet of grass. She sucked in a breath of fresh air, hoping to clear her mind of the thoughts of Jules that had haunted her in the house. Instead, they resurfaced, stronger than ever.

She crossed the yard beneath the canopy of huge oaks that her great-grandfather had planted years before. Enticed by the scents and sounds of the night, Adrienne walked to the back of the yard and pushed through the iron gate. Past the fence, the manicured lawn gave way to the untamed. But the swamp didn't frighten her, at least not this part of it.

It had been her playground while she was growing up,

her personal hideaway. She knew where the high ground was, where the irises grew thickest, where the ground sunk low and was covered with a thin layer of sucking mud and slimy water once the spring floods receded.

She knew the bogs where the alligators nested and the nutrias fed. And there were the spiders, huge hairy creatures as big as your hand. Scary enough in the light of day, and she didn't even want to imagine the feel of one crawling up her neck at night. Nor did she have a craving to come face-to-fang with a water moccasin.

A breeze stirred, plastering her thin white gown to her thighs. She lifted her long dark hair from her neck to feel the whisper of coolness on her skin. But even the wind wasn't cool tonight.

She turned to go back to the house. A sound stopped her. A rustle. In the city she would have sworn it was a footstep, but Mims's house was isolated. The nearest neighbor was miles away.

She turned again, toward a sucking sound to her left, like mud oozing around a man's footfall. A rush of adrenaline set her nerves on edge, but she forced her mind to deal in reason. It was likely a skunk or an armadillo foraging for its dinner.

Still, she was more than ready to go back inside. She took one step and the prickly fronds of a giant palmetto parted and a man stepped into the clearing. Tall, broad-shouldered, shadowed by the scalelike leaves of a cypress. Her heart slammed against the walls of her chest.

"What are you doing here?" The words scratched across the dryness of her throat. She tried to swallow, but couldn't. "What do you want?"

"You'll do."

Chapter Two

He watched her, aware that she didn't recognize him. Strange. He would have known her anywhere. He stepped from the shadows. "It's been a long time, princess."

"Jules Duquette?"

"Yeah, *chère*. It's me."

"You frightened me."

She was still frightened. He could hear it in her voice. "I didn't mean to."

"What are you doing out here?"

"I'm not stalking you, if that's what you think."

"No, I didn't think that. I didn't even know you were back in town. The last I heard you'd quit your job with the NOPD and just disappeared."

"I tried."

"Where did you go?"

"Mexico. An easy place for a man to get lost."

"But why? Did you work there?"

"I made enough money to keep my throat wet and my belly full."

"And now you're back in Breauxville. Does that mean you heard about Reynard?"

"I heard." The grief cut into his composure, robbed him of the edge he needed to deal with the princess. "Murdered and left to die in the swamp. Reynard didn't deserve that."

"No one does. I tried to find you. I knew you'd want to know."

She stepped closer, and Jules struggled with the old longing. At nineteen he'd given into it. At thirty he knew better.

"Was it Nick Ryan who told you?" she asked. "I know the two of you are friends."

"No. Dennis LeBlanc has a cousin living down there. He got word to me." Jules scanned the area, made sure they were still alone, while emotions he couldn't quite identify warred inside him. Anger, regret? Guilt? Finally he turned back to face Adrienne. "I haven't heard from Nick in months."

"Then you don't know about his stepbrother?"

"Paul Marchand. What about him?"

"His car blew up last week, on his wedding night. He was marrying Caroline Donovan."

"Was she in the car with him?"

"No. Paul had been drinking. There'd been an argument, and he went out to the car and started it. At least that's what I heard. I wasn't at the wedding. Mims wasn't feeling well that night."

"Marrying Caroline Donovan. I never expected that." Never expected it because he always thought that if any of the blood brothers ever got the girl of their dreams, it would be Nick. Not that Nick ever admitted he was still in love with Caroline. But Jules had always known he was.

"The explosion wasn't an accident, Jules."

The news stunned him. "You're saying it was murder."

"They've arrested a man named Robelot. Apparently Paul owed him a lot of money. I don't know all the facts, but Caroline left town with Nick right after the arrest."

Reynard and Paul. Both dead. Just like Tyler. Here one day. Gone the next. Jules ached for his friend Nick, wished like hell he could see him, that it was like the old days when they'd been there for each other no matter what. He wondered if Nick had even tried to get in touch with him. Probably not, since he hadn't bothered to respond to Jules's SOS a few months earlier.

Adrienne touched his arm. "Why don't you come by my office tomorrow, and I'll tell you what little I know."

"Your office? Don't tell me the big-city attorney has set up shop in Breauxville."

"I'm home to take care of Mims. You probably heard that my dad died."

"No. I hadn't heard." Now that he had, he felt no remorse. The world would be a better place without T. L. Breaux. But that didn't lessen the pain Adrienne must feel at his passing.

She stared up at him, and her dark eyes caught a glint of moonlight. His muscles clenched. It had been three years since he'd even seen her, eleven more since he'd made love to her, and yet he ached to touch her.

The need galled him. He might have grown up in every other way, but he'd never had sense enough to quit wanting what he could never have.

"I'm sorry about your dad, *chère*. Sorry you had to face it."

"Thanks. I still have trouble believing he's dead. Sometimes Mims doesn't. But then, she doesn't even always remember that my mom is dead, and that happened years ago."

"Maybe they're not to her. My grandfather used to say that everything eventually winds up as a memory. When life gets tough, you just pull out the best ones and make them your reality."

"I like that philosophy."

The moment grew awkward. "A man and a woman alone in the moonlight with nothing to talk about but old folks and the dead. What's wrong with us, princess?"

"Eleven years. Different lives." She wrapped her arms

around herself, covering her breasts. "You never answered my first question, Jules. What are you doing out here this time of the night?"

"Renewing my friendship with the bayou. What about you?"

"I couldn't sleep." She turned and glanced back at the house. "It's late and I need to go inside. I'd like to talk to you, though. Will you come by my office tomorrow?"

"Probably not." For reasons he didn't care to go into. Not with the woman who was already eating away at his resolve, making him think about things he should have forgotten years ago. He stepped to her side. "But I'll walk you to your door tonight."

"That's not necessary. I'm a big girl now. I do just fine on my own."

"Is that so? You don't look so big. A man could grab you, throw you over his shoulder and carry you away to ravish you in some deserted shack along the bayou."

She exhaled slowly, her breath warm on his skin. "That might not be so bad. If it were the right man."

"No? You surprise me."

Worse, he surprised himself, because, heaven help him, he'd like nothing better than to be that man. Only, he wouldn't want to kidnap her. He'd want her to go willingly, to be trembling with anticipation the way he was right now. He'd want her so hungry for him that she'd scream out in pleasure and beg for more.

His stomach churned as he tried to ignore the emotions she stirred in him. "Let me walk you to the house," he said, his voice gruff with the longing he couldn't tamp down. She started to protest again. He stopped her. "I didn't just happen to be out here tonight, princess. I was in my boat when I spotted a body, at least what was left of it, tangled in the knots of cypress just a few yards down the bayou from the back of your place."

"Oh, no! Not again. Did you recognize the victim?"

"Yeah. He's changed, grown older since I've been away, but I knew him. It's James Trosclair."

"But he's fished the bayous around here and hunted the swamps all his life. He knows them as well as any man."

"The land didn't kill him. A bullet did."

"Are you sure?"

"I may not have been the most valued detective on the NOPD payroll, but I recognize a bullet wound when I see one."

"We have to call the police."

"Like I said, princess, I'll walk you to your door."

ADRIENNE HAD WALKED this same path only minutes ago. Alone, but still haunted by the memory of a young man who'd made love to her on a hot August night all those years ago. Now the man was beside her, and every nerve in her body was charged with awareness.

He wasn't here to renew old relationships. It was a dead body that had brought him sloshing through the swamp, but he must have seen her standing there or he'd never have walked so far from his boat. He'd have gone back to town to use the phone or to LeBlanc's bar down the bayou.

She shuddered, not sure if it was the nearness of Jules or the idea that a killer stalked the area that sent shivers slithering up her spine. She did know that Jules had changed.

The rough edge was still there. So were the brooding eyes and the coal-black hair. But he was no longer the boy who'd haunted her dreams. He was a man. More handsome, more dangerous, exuding a sheer animal magnetism that frightened as much as excited her.

They reached the back door and she stopped, remembering that James Trosclair had a son in his early twenties who was said to be autistic. She seldom saw James without

Pierre, but she'd never heard the young man say as much as hello. "What about Pierre? Someone has to tell him."

"I'll take care of it in the morning."

"What will he do now that he's all alone?"

"He'll make out. He's resourceful and a lot smarter than most folks give him credit for. Besides, the neighbors will watch out for him, take him in if need be. That's the way it is with the bayou people."

"Still, this will be hard on him. It all seems so sad. I can't imagine why anyone would kill either Reynard or James."

"I'll let you know when I find out who did it." He leaned closer. "And I *will* find out, with or without the help of Breauxville's infamous police chief."

"I don't know why Chief Gaubert wouldn't help."

"Neither do I, but that doesn't mean I expect him to be cooperative. There's not a lot of love floating between the two of us."

Her fingers circled the doorknob. "You can use the phone in the kitchen to report the murder, but try to keep it low. I don't want to wake Mims if we can help it. I never know how she'll react to disruptions in her routine."

"I'll leave the phone call up to you. I have other business to take care of."

"But you found the body. You have to be the one to make the call."

"There are no have-to's in my life anymore, princess. Not unless *I* decide them."

"But the police will want to talk to you."

"Then let them come calling on me. Like I said, I have business to take care of."

"At this time of night?"

"One world stops turning when the sun goes down. Another one starts." He pressed both hands against the door, trapping her between his body and the barrier of wood. "You take care of yourself, princess. Watch your back, since

T.L.'s not here to do it for you." He touched a finger to her forehead, then let it slide down her nose and settle on her lips.

She reeled from the touch, her stomach fluttering somewhere around her heart. She should push him away, exert her independence, prove to him he didn't wield any power over her anymore.

But she couldn't prove something that wasn't true. He bent his head toward hers. She knew he was going to kiss her, knew that when he did, she'd lose all perspective about the two of them again. And still she couldn't make herself move away.

A second later his mouth was on hers. Rough at first, he took more than he gave, but then the jagged edges of him seemed to melt away. The kiss deepened. Her body arched toward him and she wrapped her hands around his neck, tangling her fingers in his thick dark locks.

Desire welled inside her, heated, overwhelming. She kissed him hard, hungrily, as if she couldn't get enough of him. When he pulled away, she leaned against the door, too weak to move.

He dropped his hands to his side. "I didn't plan that."

That was all. No apology. No thank-you. No "I've missed you."

He backed away. "Lock your doors tonight, princess, and sleep with one of T.L.'s guns within reach."

"There's no reason to think the killer will show up here."

"That's probably what Trosclair thought, right up until the bullet penetrated his skull."

She shivered. "Come by the office tomorrow, Jules."

"Don't count on it." He turned and walked away.

"I'll be there if you change your mind," she called to him. "I have some information about Reynard's death you might find interesting."

He kept walking, just as he'd done eleven years ago. But

this time she knew he'd be back. She had something he wanted.

JULES CLIMBED the steps to Breauxville's police station. The building was old with cracking brick walls that had been painted white and then faded over the years to a grimy yellow. The last time he'd been here, he'd been a swaggering teenage boy, handcuffed and scared half to death, but determined not to show it.

He pushed through the door. The place looked different than he remembered, smaller, more disorganized, far less intimidating. There was a desk with a sign behind it that read Information, but the desk was unoccupied at the moment. It hadn't been that way long. There was a nearly full coffee cup with lipstick smudges sitting next to half an oyster po-boy.

"You looking for someone?"

He turned to find a uniformed cop staring at him from a cluttered cubbyhole off to the left. "I'm looking for Big Tom. Is he around?"

"Who wants to know?"

"Jules Duquette."

That got the man's attention. He stood and walked out to the reception area. "Chief Gaubert went out for a minute, but he'll be right back. You can step into his office and wait. He's been looking for you."

So Big Tom Gaubert wanted to see him. Evidently Adrienne had told him about the body Jules had found in the bayou last night.

The past came back to haunt him as the cop led him to Gaubert's office. A summer long ago. He, Nick and Tyler. So close over the years, but now, when he needed them most, they were nowhere around. Not that he blamed Tyler. A man didn't choose when his number came up.

He didn't really blame Nick, either, though there was no

denying his disappointment when his old friend hadn't returned the calls he'd made to him before he left the force
and moved to Mexico. He'd needed a friend then. Needed
someone who'd believe him and not the trumped-up charges
that the department had come up with. Charges he didn't
have the clout to beat.

Truth was, even though they'd shared a hundred good and
bad times, he and Nick were totally different. Nick with his
money and power, racing through the fast lane at breakneck
speed. Jules, the man who liked cold beer and fried oysters
and never going anywhere he couldn't go in a pair of jeans.
Still, they'd been friends, and much as he hated to admit it,
he still missed both of them more than he'd ever imagined
he would.

"Don't look like you'll have to wait long," the cop said,
sticking his head inside the room and interrupting Jules's
thoughts. "The chief's heading up the steps now."

JULES SAT ACROSS from Big Tom. A smoldering cigar dan-
gled from the police chief's mouth. The first button of his
cotton shirt was open, but still looked as if it was binding
the man's second chin.

Big Tom stamped his cigar into the ashtray at his elbow.
"It's about time you made it into the office, boy. A man
finds a body, he's supposed to report it to the authorities,
not go harassing the people who happen to live near the
scene of the crime."

"You might want to rephrase that comment, Big Tom.
One, I'm not a boy. Two, I didn't harass Adrienne Breaux.
I merely informed her in case she wanted to take extra pre-
caution with a murderer on the lose. Three, that wasn't the
scene of the crime. That was the location where the body
was discovered."

The chief glared at him, clearly annoyed that his intimidation routine didn't work on Jules. "That's right. I forgot you were a cop yourself for a while."

"A homicide detective with the NOPD, to be exact."

"But you're not with them anymore. I guess they didn't like your smart-ass ways in the Big Easy any more than we liked them around here."

"We could exchange insults all day, Big Tom, but I'd as soon get to the point. What have you done about Reynard's murder?"

"So that's what brings you back to town. You didn't bother to make it to the funeral, but now you come running in making accusations about the murder investigation."

"Accusations? You got the wrong man. I just asked a question. I want an answer."

Big Tom's face turned blood-red, and the meaty flesh swelled even more around his shirt collar. He took a deep breath, then worried the end of his cigar, obviously stalling.

"Seems like an easy enough question to me," Jules prodded.

The chief shrugged and leaned back in his chair. "Your cousin's body was found floating in the bayou, a quarter-mile from your grandpa's old place. No prints. No weapon. No motive. We've questioned everyone who lives out that way. No one saw or heard anything. If you have any additional information, I'll be willing to listen, but don't come in here acting like I'm not doing my job when you don't know a damn thing about what's going on in Breauxville."

"Then why don't you tell me what's going on?"

"I suppose you've talked to your buddy Nick Ryan."

"Not lately."

"Guess Nick and you aren't so close anymore. What's the matter? You not good enough for him now?"

"Why don't you just spit out the facts, Gaubert? And if I need any advice about making or keeping friends, I'll give you a call. Right now if you don't know anything about

Reynard's murder, how about filling me in on Paul Marchand's?''

Jules sat rigidly in the straight-backed chair while Gaubert spilled out a bizarre tale of Nick's stepbrother being murdered by someone out to get his hands on Paul's and Caroline's property, a few acres of marsh and swamp and a couple of old houses. Not much to kill for.

''So what makes you so sure Reynard's murder isn't linked to Paul's?'' Jules asked, determined to regain the focus of his visit to Gaubert.

''I've investigated both of them fully. There's no connection.''

''Then you won't mind if I snoop around a little myself.''

''You'll be wasting your time. Paul's murder case is solved. I'll solve Reynard's, too, in time. And James Trosclair's, as well. But right now I have a few questions to ask you.''

Jules stood up.

The chief banged his fists on his desk. ''Hold on a second. You heard what I said. We're not through talking here.''

''I am. I found out what I wanted to know—that you don't have a single lead in Reynard's murder.''

''No, but I do in James Trosclair's. You found the body last night. The person who finds the body is always a suspect. You were in homicide. You know that.''

''No weapon. No motive. Now witnesses. No case. Just like you said.'' Jules walked toward the door. ''Apprehend Reynard's killer and you've probably got the man who killed Trosclair, too. Unless Breauxville has turned into a regular war zone. And in that case, the citizens might be looking for a new police chief.''

Evidently Big Tom had no answer for that. He didn't protest when Jules left the office and headed down to pay a call on Adrienne Breaux. Jules's heart wasn't ready to face her again, and his body surely wasn't, but she might be the only one in this town with the answers he was looking for.

He'd never been the kind of family member Reynard could look up to, but he could do this one thing for him and for their grandparents. Then he could walk away from this town for good.

Walk away with only one regret. That he'd never get to make love with Adrienne Breaux again. That he'd never know for certain if they'd been as dynamite together as he remembered or if it was only that it had been his first time— and with the town's society princess—that made it live forever in his mind.

All he knew was that last night when he'd kissed her, it had taken all the strength he could muster to walk away. Now he was about to put himself to the test again.

Chapter Three

Adrienne hung up the phone, feeling better now that she'd talked to the housekeeper and heard that Mims was having a good day. That taken care of, Adrienne picked up her pen and went back to the notes she'd been scribbling.

Murders and Jules Duquette were adding heat to a summer that was already scorching. The events of last night replayed in her mind, the way they'd done a hundred times today. The crush she'd had on Jules in high school should have dissipated over the long years since she'd seen him last. The primal urges he'd ignited in her the night of her eighteenth birthday party should have been satisfied by someone else or at least dimmed by maturity.

Last night had proved all those should-haves wrong. Hours after his careless kiss, she'd lain between the sheets, her body burning with an all-consuming need.

But it was mere memories that haunted her, fantasies that had no place in the real world. Determined to put Jules out of her mind, she spread the information on Puckerton Oil and Gas and their dealings in the area around Breauxville across her desk.

Her inquisitive mind and her legal training took over, and even Jules drifted from her mind. When her secretary stuck her head in to say she was leaving for the day, Adrienne made the appropriate comments and then went right back to her notes.

"NICE PLACE YOU'VE GOT here, Counselor."

Startled, Adrienne jerked her gaze up and focused on the man lounging in her doorway. "Jules. I didn't hear you come in."

"Then lucky it was me and not the *loup-garou* come walking in on you, *chère*."

In her mind the legendary swamp werewolf would be less dangerous. Certainly less intriguing. Jules's dark hair fell over his forehead, and the top button on his white shirt was open, revealing a sprinkling of dark hair on a tanned chest. "I thought you'd decided to decline my invitation to stop by," she said, stuffing the papers back in the open manila file and closing it.

"Your offer was too tempting to resist." His tone suggested an intimacy that shouldn't exist between them. He scanned the room before he walked over to her desk. Picking up the silver frame that sat on her desk, he studied the photograph. It was one of her and Mims.

"Nice picture," he said, setting the frame down next to her pencil holder. He perched on the corner of her desk where the frame had previously sat. "You have your grandmother's eyes."

"Thank you."

"You're welcome. Now, that should do it for small talk. What was it you wanted to tell me that you couldn't last night? Do you know something about Reynard's death?" His tone grew edgy, guarded.

"Nothing concrete, but he called me the day before he died."

Jules's gaze bore into hers. "What did he want?"

"He said he'd come across a geological report that appeared to be altered."

"Did he say where he'd found the report?"

"No. I assumed it was at the courthouse, a part of the records for some land deal he was examining."

"Why would he call you about that?"

"I asked him the same question. All he said was that there was more, some suspicion about a man he was doing business with. We agreed on a time for him to come in the next afternoon. He never kept the appointment. A day later I heard that his body had been found floating in the bayou and that he'd taken a bullet in the back of the head."

Jules slid from the desk and paced the room. "This doesn't add up. Why would he want to talk to you about suspicious people or geological records?"

"All I know is that he seemed anxious."

Jules exhaled slowly, the muscles in his face and neck tensing. He strode over to stand behind her. Too close. She hated that his nearness affected her so. Hated the suffocating power of the virility that clung to him like a second skin.

He put his hands on the back of her chair. "What else did he say?"

"That's all, except for the usual formalities. He asked about my family."

"I've talked to his boss," Jules said. "They said Puckerton Oil had been looking at several areas in south Louisiana for possible exploratory drilling sites. They wanted an outside report. The company Reynard worked for supplied it for them, but Reynard had turned in his report on that a month ago. After he did, they concluded that there wasn't enough oil in this area to make drilling worthwhile."

"I know. I called them, too. They claim Reynard was down here on his own time when he was killed."

"So I heard. You called, but no one else from Breauxville did, not even the chief of police. Guess Big Tom had more on his mind than worrying about a—" Jules stopped in mid-sentence. He leaned over her shoulder and picked up the file she'd been working on. "Puckerton Oil and Gas. How interesting. A client of yours?" There was no mistaking the accusation in his voice.

"That's none of your business."

"No, but it would explain your sudden interest in my cousin's murder."

"I asked you to come here so that I could tell you about Reynard's call. I've told you. You can leave anytime now or else—"

"Or else what? You'll call Big Tom and sic him on me? He was your father's yard dog. I'm sure he'd provide the same service for you."

She stood and walked away from him. Her insides shook, and she was trying hard not to let the shudders become evident to Jules. Passion and fury. Strange bedfellows, but they always managed to pair up when she was with him. She turned and met his gaze. "You can leave or else I will."

"That won't be necessary." He put up his hands as if in surrender. "I was out of line, princess. You call the shots in this room."

"I call the shots in my life, Jules."

"I'm sure you do. Tell you what, *chère*. I won't bother you again. If you think of something else you need to tell me, you know where to find me."

"Does that mean you're staying in town?"

"Until my business is finished." He turned toward the door, but she couldn't let him go without telling him what else she'd discovered, though she definitely had no proof of wrongdoing on anyone's part. "There is one other thing," she said, keeping her voice steady.

"I'm listening."

"I hate to tell you this. If you go off half-cocked and start accusing people, you'll wind up in jail."

"That's a lot better sentence than Reynard got."

His argument won. "It's doubtful this has anything to do

with Reynard's death, but when I was looking over the land holdings in the area, I noticed that Big Tom had purchased a lot of acreage in the area a few months ago. The exchanges were made about the same time Puckerton was considering drilling in this area."

"Nice find, Counselor."

"More interesting is the fact that most of the land was acquired for far less than the appraised value."

Jules let out a low whistle. "A good reason to have someone alter reports, make it appear that our little neck of the swamp is rich in oil. Looks like Big Tom and I might need to talk again."

"Watch your step, Jules."

He met her gaze, holding her as surely as if he'd wrapped her in his arms. "Are you worried about me, princess?"

Yes, but she'd never let him know it. "I'm worried about the innocent people who might get in your way."

"I promise not to drop any bodies in the bayou."

"That should make me rest a whole lot better tonight."

"Good. I wouldn't want you to lose any sleep on my account." He leaned in so close she felt his breath on her flesh. "Not unless I'm there to make your sleeplessness worthwhile."

She waited, trembling, knowing he was going to kiss her again. She closed her eyes. When she opened them, he was gone.

ADRIENNE TRIMMED the stems from a bouquet of flowers she'd picked in the garden. Red roses, some baby's breath, a half-dozen zinnias in various shades of pinks and yellows. A thorn pricked her finger. She turned on the faucet and held her finger under the cool stream until the bleeding stopped.

Mims walked to the counter and took over, placing each flower individually into the crystal vase. For a second the problems of the day faded into the background. Mims had always loved the garden, had taught Adrienne the joy of digging in fresh dirt, planting the tiny seeds and then watching them come to life each spring.

Adrienne didn't remember her mom, though Mims had shown her countless pictures of her. She'd died of complications from a simple surgical procedure before Adrienne's second birthday. *Your mother was beautiful, always laughing. She was my ray of sunshine,* Mims always said. And Adrienne knew that Mims had never fully gotten over the loss of her daughter.

Early on Adrienne had realized that her dad shared an uneasy truce with his mother-in-law. Her dad provided the income. Mims provided the child care and the prestigious plantation home. They both provided love, but in very different ways. Mims was soft, assuring. Her dad's way had been harsh, demanding.

Mims stepped back to admire her handiwork, a perfectly arranged bouquet. "That nice man came to see you today."

"What man?"

"Oh, dear." Mims rubbed her left temple. "I know him. So do you. I just can't think of his name right now."

"Maggie never mentioned that anyone was here."

"*Mais non.* Maggie doesn't know everything that goes on around here."

Apprehension churned in Adrienne's stomach. Breauxville was normally a peaceful town. No reason for fear to choke off her breath at the mention of an uninvited man showing up at the house. Three murders had changed that.

"Think, Mims. What was the man's name?"

Mims's forehead drew into deep ruts, the wrinkles around her eyes multiplying. "Sorry, I don't remember so well."

"Did he say what he wanted?"

"*Mais oui.* He wanted to see you. He was in your room."

A man in her room. The story was too bizarre. Mims was probably confused. Of course, that was it.

"Set the flowers on the table, Mims, and I'll be back in a minute to make our dinner."

"You don't need to make dinner. I can cook. I'll make the gumbo your mother loves. That girl loves the shrimp, she does. You call her."

Adrienne hugged her grandmother and kissed her thin cheek. "I'll do that, Mims. You just sit down and wait until I get back."

It was all a mistake, an event from Mim's past that had become confused with the future, the way her memories of her beloved daughter did. Only, Adrienne wouldn't be able to get it off her mind until she at least walked into her room and checked to see that everything was in order.

She raced up the stairs. The door to her room was open. She stepped inside, breathing hard from the flight to the second floor. The room was just as she'd left it. The drawers closed. Her slippers peeking from under the edge of the quilt. The silver comb and brush set that had belonged to her mother sitting on the antique dresser.

And a white envelope propped against the lamp. She walked across the room and picked up the envelope. The outside was blank. Anger replaced the fear as she tore it open. How dare someone invade her private space? And where had Maggie been when all this was going on?

Reaching inside, she slipped out the folded note and opened it, turning it so that it captured the last glow of sunlight filtering through the lace curtains. The note was printed in red crayon, the letters thick and uneven:

Keep your nose out of Reynard's death or your body will be the next one found in the bayou.

Her hands grew clammy. She dropped the note to the dresser. The killer had issued his warning, and he'd been bold enough to walk into her home to do it. A killer in the house with Mims.

The familiarity of her surroundings offered little comfort as she walked down the steps and back into the kitchen. Crazy, but she longed to call Jules, to ask him to come over. The most dangerous troublesome man she knew, and yet he was the one she wanted beside her tonight.

JULES SAT IN A CORNER of LeBlanc's Bayou Hideaway. Some things never changed. The old Cajun diner and bar was one of them. The wooden floor was marred and coated with a thick layer of dried juices from thousands of pounds of crawfish and crabs. And the place reeked of beer and whiskey.

But Jules had always liked LeBlanc, had even worked for him a while when he was in high school. He should have kept working for him, instead of taking the job for T. L. Breaux down at the docks where the shrimp boats came in.

He finished his gumbo, tilting the bowl and drinking from it like a cup to get the last of the spicy liquid. If he'd missed anything about Breauxville, it was the food.

That and Adrienne. The forbidden fruit. Too rich for his blood. Not that she didn't want him. She did. He felt it when he was near her, felt the desire sizzle like a crackling fire between them. She'd like him for a night, maybe longer. But he'd never fit into her world. If he tried, it would destroy him, make him a shadow, a pretender. And soon she'd hate him the way he'd hate himself.

He forced her from his mind and scanned the smoky room with the mind and eye of a cop. Big Tom and his pompous son, Tommy Joe, were sitting in the opposite corner, feasting on fried seafood and guzzling draft beer. Some of the guys he'd gone to school with were cozied up to the bar, flirting with a waitress, who hung more out of her tube top than in.

Most of the other folks he could place even if he couldn't put a name to them.

All except the three guys who'd been sitting against the far wall when he'd first come in. They'd left by the back way a minute after he'd arrived, but he'd seen enough to think that the one with the jagged scar at this throat looked vaguely familiar.

Still, Reynard had talked to Adrienne of a suspicious stranger, and Jules would ask a few questions, make it his business to find out more about the rough-looking men who'd exited the bar so quickly.

He paid his bill and was about to go back to the kitchen to look for LeBlanc when Tommy Joe Gaubert sidled up next to him. "I hear you're back in town a day and already messing around where you got no business."

Jules stared straight ahead. "Are you keeping tabs on me, Tommy Joe? You must lead a boring life if that's your entertainment. You ought to find yourself a woman. I can lend you a few bucks if you want to buy one for tonight."

"Don't start that tough-guy routine with me, Jules. I wasn't impressed when we were in school, and I'm not impressed now."

"Then get out of my face."

"I'll get out of your face when I'm good and ready. And you don't give the orders around here. I do."

"You got an order, Tommy Joe? Let's hear it."

"Stay away from Adrienne Breaux. She don't need swamp trash like you around."

"Are you speaking for Adrienne now, or is that just another friendly service the Breauxville police provide?"

"Stay away from her. Fact is, you can just carry yourself right on out of town anytime now."

"I'd like nothing better. As soon as I find out who killed Reynard."

"That's a job for the police, and in case you forgot, you aren't a cop any longer."

Jules stood. He was taller that Tommy Joe, muscle where the arrogant cop was flab. He leveled a stare and moved into Tommy Joe's space. "Reynard's dead. The police have had almost a week to find a killer. You haven't made an arrest. So you can harangue and bluster all you want, but I won't be leaving Breauxville until I find some answers."

He pushed past Tommy Joe, strode across the barroom and walked out the door. The last thing he'd wanted when he came back to town was trouble, but he wouldn't run from it. He never had and he wouldn't start now. Besides, he still needed to talk to LeBlanc.

He turned back toward the bar, then stopped, suddenly aware of movement behind him. He whirled around, but not soon enough. Two brawny men in ski masks grabbed him and dragged him to the side of the building. He yanked, almost freeing himself before the fist of a third man pounded him in the gut. Three against one, a coward's way, but the fists kept plowing into him. He tried to fight back, but he couldn't get in a punch with two men holding him down.

"Hey, what's going on out there?"

A voice cracked through his splitting head. The men dropped him to the ground, all three of them kicking and grinding their heavy boots into his stomach one last time before they took off running into the boggy marsh behind LeBlanc's.

Someone flashed a light in his face, temporarily blinding him. He sat up and spat a mouthful of blood to the ground while a crowd gathered to watch the show.

"Looks like I'm home," he said to one in particular.

MIMS WAS ASLEEP upstairs. The house was quiet, dark except for the glow of the lamp in the parlor. The house that Adrienne had lived in most of her life, and for the first time she felt uneasy. There were no neighbors for miles around, nothing but one narrow road and miles of swamp between her and them.

Only, there was another way to reach the house. The way Jules had arrived last night. The bayou where the second murdered body in a matter of days had floated to the surface. Anyone could come up the bayou and step into her backyard. Into her house. Into her bedroom.

Car lights flashed across her front window. Panic swelled inside her, skidding like sharp glass along her already rattled nerves. She froze as male voices broke the stillness of the night. She had company.

Chapter Four

Adrienne recognized the vehicles in her driveway. The dented red Jeep belonged to Dennis LeBlanc. The black mud-splattered Honda was Jules's.

She watched as LeBlanc stepped from the red Jeep and then walked to the passenger side and swung open the door. A man staggered out.

Oh, no. It was Jules, and he was hurt. Not bothering to slip into her shoes, she raced out the door, across the *galerie* and down the steps.

"Hello, princess. Got an extra bed?"

She threw an arm around his shoulder. "What happened?"

"A little rumble, but don't worry. You should have seen the other three guys. They don't have a scratch on them."

"Help me get him inside, Dennis."

The man nodded. She pulled her blouse loose from her skirt and touched the hem of it to the bloody cut over his eye. "Does it hurt?"

"Only when I breathe."

THE KITCHEN WAS WARM, close. Adrienne dabbed antiseptic onto the jagged cut that ran down Jules's back, intensely aware that they'd crossed another line. He was inside her house, naked to the waist, so sore he could barely move, and still every touch of her hand on his flesh made her tremble with desire.

He reached up and caught her left hand with his. The antiseptic slipped from her right, falling to the floor, thudding against the tile.

"Are you sorry LeBlanc brought me here?"

"No. I doubt you could have made the trip home in your boat tonight." His grandparents' cabin was off the highway and so deep in the swamp that the last part of the way could only be reached by a network of shallow bayous. "Besides, you needed someone to tend your wounds."

"Mais oui." He tugged her around to face him, his gaze searing into hers, the bourbon LeBlanc had given him to curb the pain slurring his voice. "No one ever took care of me the way you did. You know what I'm talking about."

Her hands grew shaky and she struggled to breathe. She knew all too well what he was talking about, was still tormented by memories of what it was like making love with him.

"We were *chaud* together, princess. Very hot."

"Don't go there, Jules."

"I don't know how we're gonna avoid it." He reached up and trailed a finger down her cheek. "You want me. I want you."

"There's more to consider than just desire." Only, her hands were clammy, her body on fire. And all she could think about was the way he looked right now, his muscled chest bare, his jeans unbuttoned at the waist, his eyes dark and smoldering.

"Are you afraid it won't be as good as before?" he taunted. "Or afraid it will be better?"

She swallowed hard. "I'm not afraid of anything."

He reached up and cupped her face in his hands. "I think you are. You're afraid of the way I'll make you feel."

"Maybe you should be the one who's afraid. I'm a woman now, Jules. Fully grown. If we made love, it might not be that easy for you to just walk away again."

His hands roved her back, then slid lower, pulling her close. "I am afraid, princess. I'm scared to death. But tonight I'd pass a good time with you and take my chances."

"Tonight you'd probably pass out." She tried to move away from him, but he didn't release his hold on her. She touched her mouth to his battered lips. He winced in pain but didn't pull away.

She went weak with wanting, a need that overshadowed everything. Basic, primal, driven. The kiss deepened.

The past, the present, the future were nonexistent. Jules was here and now. He delved into places inside her soul and mind that didn't seem to exist until he touched her.

"Adrienne."

The word was sharp, high-pitched. Adrienne jerked away from Jules and looked up to find Mims in the doorway to the kitchen. Confusion deepened the lines in her thin face.

"I didn't know you had a gentleman caller," Mims said. "I would have kept myself upstairs and out of the way."

The fire that had raged in Adrienne a minute ago cooled to a blush that reddened her flesh. She smoothed her hair and tried to pull a shred of dignity from the situation. "I'm sorry, Mims. This is my friend Jules. He was attacked in town. I was putting ointment on his wounds."

"No wonder he come here and not to the hospital. I think the nurses, they not so personal with their ointment applications."

Mims's voice softened and Adrienne spotted the familiar twinkle in her grandmother's eyes, a sign that she was in one of her more lucid moments. Adrienne breathed a little easier.

"Your granddaughter took me in when I needed help.

She's a good person, like you," Jules said, flashing his devastating smile.

"*Merci.* My Adrienne is a very good person. *Jolie,* too, eh?"

"Very pretty. And very good at applying ointment." Jules laughed, and Adrienne realized it was the first time she'd heard him do it. She always thought of him as dark, brooding, sexy. But he laughed with the same passion as he did everything. She wondered what other sides of him lay beneath the ironclad surface.

Mims walked over and circled Jules, eyeing his wounds. "Somebody worked you over real good. You deserve it?"

"Maybe. Maybe not. The men didn't bother telling me what they didn't like about me."

"Breauxville is not the friendly little town it once was," Adrienne offered.

"Breauxville has always had its share of hate and evil," Mims said. "The men, they're just more open now. The women today let them do these things and still sleep in a warm bed at night."

"You never told me your *grandmaman* was so wise," Jules said.

That was because Adrienne forgot it herself most of the time. "Why don't I warm you some milk, Mims? It will help you sleep."

"No, I leave the kitchen to you two. If I don't sleep tonight, I sleep tomorrow. It doesn't matter when you get to be my age. The days and nights, they run together. The same with the past and the present. They slip in and out." She touched a thin hand to Adrienne's cheek. "But always there's my Adrienne."

Adrienne kissed her grandmother on the cheek and gingerly squeezed her hand. No matter what happened in her life or her career, she'd never be sorry she'd come back home to take care of Mims.

Her grandmother started back to the steps, then turned to Jules. A few seconds ago her eyes had been sharp and clear. Now they seemed glazed, the way they did when she was confused or bothered by something. "I'm glad you came back," she said. "Like I say to you today, my Adrienne, she works all the time the sun shines. You only find her here at night."

Anger swelled inside Adrienne as she watched Mims climb the stairs to her bedroom. She turned to Jules. "So you're the one who came out here today and left me the note. I should have known. You'd be glad to have sex with me for old time's sake, but don't mess around in your business. Still, leaving that threatening note was low, even for you."

"You're talking in circles, *chère*. I was here last night and I'm back again tonight, but I was not here today."

"You heard Mims."

Jules grabbed her upper arms, his fingers digging into her flesh. "I'm not defending myself against something that never happened. Now tell me what note you're talking about."

"The note that said for me to back off from questioning people about Reynard's murder."

"Get the note. I want to see it."

The intensity in his eyes, the urgency to his voice, almost convinced her that Mims had been mistaken. "It was a warning to keep out of Reynard's murder investigation," she said. "If you didn't leave it, then you can forget about it. I can handle it."

He dropped his grasp on her arms and let his fingers slide down to take her hands in his. "Three people are dead. I don't plan to stand by and watch you be the fourth. Show me exactly where you found the note."

JULES REREAD the printed warning as he listened to Adrienne's account of finding the message in her bedroom. The facts were sobering, clearing his mind and sharpening his focus.

"Who stays with your grandmother during the day?" he asked.

"Maggie Prejean. She's worked for Mims for years."

"Did you call her and ask her about this?"

"I talked to her. She didn't see anyone enter the house."

"So the man didn't knock or ring the bell. He just slipped inside and went directly to your bedroom."

She dropped to the side of the bed. "Which means this is someone I know, someone who's been in the house before."

"That, or Maggie Prejean is lying."

"That can't be, Jules. I've known Maggie all my life."

"You've known almost everyone in Breauxville all your life. That doesn't prove a thing." He placed the note back on the dresser, careful not to smudge the fingerprints, in case there were any. "I spent the afternoon talking to some of the old families along the bayou," he said, wondering how much of what he learned he should tell Adrienne.

"What did you find out?"

"That Big Tom did a little more than just offer to buy their land."

"What do you mean?"

"He told them the government was going to come in and appropriate their land, make it into a national park and rich man's resort."

"I still don't see why they sold to him."

"He convinced them that little guys couldn't fight the bureaucracy, but if one man owned a huge section of the wetlands, he could keep unwanted development out of there. He told them that if the government took over, they would be forced to move into town. If they sold to him, he'd let them live on the land until they died."

"The government's dedicated to preserving the wetlands. I can't believe they bought that story."

"Why not? He's Big Tom Gaubert. The law. Besides, you know the people who live in the swamps and along the bayous. They're fiercely independent, don't know any way to live other than the way they've been doing it for generations. Half the families barely speak English."

"So now Big Tom has the land, but Puckerton pulled out, in spite of fake reports claiming there are large deposits of oil in the area."

"Big companies aren't fooled that easily."

"Big Tom must be upset."

"Right." Jules nodded grimly. "Now he's making return visits to the ones who sold to him."

"That takes gall."

"This time he wants them to buy their land back, for a few dollars more, of course. A little lagniappe for his court costs and trouble. If they don't, he may be forced to offer it to some big developer. Which he would in a second if he could."

"Are the people buying their land back from him?"

"The ones who can. Most of them can't. They spent the piddling check he paid them on a new trolling motor, decent nets, and supplies to repair their homes. Bottom line, the money's gone."

"I have an office in town. No one's been there to see me with that type of complaint."

"No, and they won't be coming now. They don't trust the government, and they definitely don't trust lawyers."

"You found out all this in a day?"

"I'm one of them, Adrienne. And don't think they haven't noticed that two of their own have been murdered. They're scared."

ADRIENNE WRAPPED her arms around her middle, suddenly inundated with a chill. She crossed to the window to stare out at the swampy land that stretched behind her property, though there was little she could see by only the light of the moon. "But…Big Tom! He and my dad were friends."

"Your dad got him elected and made sure he stayed in office. Money's the same as power in Breauxville. Always has been."

"Still, the Gauberts have been to our house for parties and cookouts. I just can't see Big Tom as a killer."

"I never said he was. I'm just telling you what I heard."

"I'm going to talk to him tomorrow."

"Oh, no, you're not." Jules walked over to stand behind her. He placed a hand on her shoulder and tugged her around to face him. His eyes were dark, angry. "Stay out of this, Adrienne. Just like the note said. This isn't your fight."

"What makes it yours?" she asked, determined not to be intimidated.

"Reynard's death. And an old bone that's never been picked clean."

She felt more than saw the change that had come over Jules. There was a coldness about him that hadn't been there earlier tonight, an icy fury that had nothing to do with the beating. It frightened her almost as much as the note had. "What are you talking about, Jules?"

He released his hold on her. "Sometime when you're short on nightmare material, I'll tell you what I have against Big Tom."

She wasn't sure she wanted that sometime to come. She excused herself and went to the downstairs guest room to pull down the covers and put out fresh towels.

Earlier tonight it had been passion that ignited the space between her and Jules. Now it was something darker, but no less intense. Something seemed to bind them together with ropes that cut deep into her heart, into her very soul. Had one night of making love in the swamp done this, or had fate just played a horrible trick on her? Drawn her inexplicably and inescapably to a man who'd never let himself do more than settle for fleeting passion?

No matter how badly she wanted to be with him, to feel his body wrap around hers, to have him possess her totally, the way he had the one glorious moment that would always live in her memory, she wouldn't give in to the need again.

Not to a man she couldn't begin to understand. One who would disappear from her life as quickly as he'd stepped into it the other night in the moonlight.

JULES WOKE UP and rolled over to an explosion of pain. His head, his shoulders, his stomach. It had been a long time since he'd taken a beating like that. He slung his feet to the floor, swallowing back a moan.

He'd tossed and turned all night, trying to find a pattern, something that would tie Reynard's death to James Trosclair's. And for some reason, Paul's death kept sliding into the equation, as well. Three deaths, two of them connected to him and to Nick Ryan. Could this have to do with them somehow? Could something he and Nick had done in the past set a killer on their trail, caused the death of their closest kin?

But who? And why? If the murders were connected to Nick's business, they wouldn't have anything to do with him. If they were connected to what he knew about certain cops on the NOPD, they wouldn't apply to Nick. The only trouble that applied to both of them had happened years ago at Peltier Point.

Boyce Sincard had vowed he'd get them all one day. Nick, Tyler and Jules. Pay them back for testifying against him in the murder of their friend Dave Lanier. But Boyce Sincard was sleeping with the fish.

So he had to find something else. But nothing he came up with tied Reynard to James Trosclair or to the altered report that Reynard had called Adrienne about. But there were always answers. A good detective had to keep looking until he found them. Only, now he had Adrienne's safety to worry about, as well.

Adrienne. Just the thought of her made his body hard. The house was dark and quiet. He wondered what would happen if he tiptoed up the stairs and crawled into bed beside her. Would she reach out to him in her sleep, welcome him into her arms?

He stood and pain stabbed through his back and up his neck. As much as he hurt now, it would be nothing compared to the way he'd suffer if he let the princess back in his heart and mind. He dressed, thankful that LeBlanc had one of his cooks follow them to Adrienne's last night in his car.

Then, as silently as a snake skimming the waters of the bayou, he crept out of the house and into the sticky grayness of predawn in the swamp.

He had a date with a killer, whoever it might be.

Chapter Five

Adrienne heard the footsteps downstairs. Sliding from her bed, she walked to the window and stared at the shadowy figure crossing the carport toward the Honda.

Jules, sneaking away before the sun cleared the horizon and he was forced to face her in the bright light of day. It was better this way, and yet she felt a strange sense of rejection. He'd let LeBlanc bring him here when he had nowhere else to go, but he would stay no longer than he had to.

She knew where he was going. He was in search of the man who had walked into her house and into this very room. Something cold crawled over her skin at the thought. If a man could walk into the house in broad daylight, he could return in the blackness of night or the grayness of early morning.

The back door couldn't be locked if Jules had left through it. The house creaked and groaned beneath her steps. She passed closed doors, empty rooms, as the same terrifying possibilities that had robbed of her of sleep in the night came back to haunt her.

It was easy to believe Big Tom was guilty of intimidation and greed. But as freewheeling as he was with his interpretation of the law, she couldn't see him shooting two men in the back and dropping them in the bayou.

But someone had. Now that someone was determined that no one delve too deeply into the reasons. She'd only gotten a warning note. Jules had been attacked by three men and severely beaten. But she knew Jules too well to believe that a beating would stop him.

Jules Duquette, a fiery blast from her past. He'd worked for her father the year she'd turned fourteen, spent his vacation at the docks, weighing and loading shrimp. Her father bought the shellfish from the shrimpers and then resold them to restaurants and markets in New Orleans.

He had talked her into tagging along with him one sunny afternoon. She'd hated the blistering heat and the stifling humidity, hated the way her clothes had stuck to her body. Dreaded the banality of her father's dickering over price with the fishermen. And then she'd spied Jules.

The memories overtook her, and she reeled from the images that played in her mind. Jules tanned to a deep brown, shirtless, his muscles rippling. His youthful swagger, his cocky half smile. She could feel the heat on her back and the pangs of sensual awareness that had swelled inside her.

The year she'd first noticed the womanly changes to her body. The summer she'd first really noticed boys. The time of puppy love and Jules Duquette.

After that she'd gone with her father every chance she got. She'd lived for the few teasing words Jules threw her way. And then one day she'd followed him onto one of the shrimp boats. He'd jumped from behind a barrel to frighten her. She'd dived right into his arms. He'd held her close for just a minute and then he'd kissed her—one quick smack on the lips.

The boat owner had caught them like that and had gone back to the others, laughing about catching T.L.'s daughter smooching with the hired help. She'd almost died of embarrassment, but still, she hadn't washed her face for days.

Her father had never mentioned the incident, but that was the last time he'd invited her to the docks with him.

When she went back to school in the fall, she learned that Jules had spent most of the rest of his summer at Peltier Point, in a military-style boot camp for troubled boys. She'd tried to talk to him when he'd come back to school, but he'd brushed her off. The teasing between them was over. Peltier Point had changed him.

She turned the dead bolt on the back door, then stopped. Something had moved in the shadows just beyond the fence. It had been too quick for her to be certain, and yet she would have almost sworn it was a man darting from behind the trunk of a towering cypress tree to a cluster of palmetto.

It couldn't have been Jules. She'd seen him get in his car and drive away. Her heart raced. There were pistols and rifles in her dad's gun cabinet. She knew how to use them, but she wasn't insane enough to go tramping down to the bayou chasing shadows. Stepping away from the door, she picked up the phone and dialed 911.

TOMMY JOE GAUBERT sat at Adrienne's kitchen table nursing a cup of black coffee. The room was cozy, comfortable, especially with Adrienne sashaying about in a loose robe.

"We checked all around the house and the area clear down to the bayou," he said. "If there's anyone out there, I didn't see him. But if you're worried, I could stay out here at night for a while."

"I'm sure that's not necessary."

Right, 'cause she had that swamp rat hanging around. But Jules wouldn't be hanging around long. He'd be dead, and if Adrienne wasn't careful, she'd be dragged into the grave with him. "I noticed your pirogue tied up down at the bayou. I wouldn't be taking it out right now if I were you, not until we arrest the man responsible for the killings."

"I won't."

"And I wouldn't get involved with Jules Duquette, either. The man's got a bad streak in him. Always has."

"I have no intention of getting involved with anyone."

"That's not the way I hear it."

She thrust her hands into the pockets of her robe. "I don't know what you're talking about."

"Breauxville's a small town. A man spends the night at Adrienne Breaux's house, you might as well take out an ad in the Sunday paper."

"I forget how gossip travels around here." She walked over and took the chair across the kitchen table from him. "Three men attacked Jules at Dennis LeBlanc's bar last night. Dennis brought him here for me to tend his wounds."

"Adrienne Nightingale?" Tommy Joe took a long sip of his coffee. "If your dad was still alive, he'd throw Jules Duquette off the property. If you're smart, you'll do the same the next time he shows up. Trouble hangs on him like a burr stuck on your pants leg."

"Jules didn't start that fight last night, Tommy Joe. He was minding his own business."

"Is that what he told you?"

"Yes, and it's what Dennis said, as well. All he's doing is trying to find out who killed his cousin. I can't fault him for that."

She spread her manicured hands on the table. Tommy Joe could imagine them stroking his back. And he could imagine them doing the same to Jules Duquette. The thought sickened him.

"My dad's handling the murder investigation, Adrienne. He doesn't need Jules's interference."

"But no one's been arrested, and now James Trosclair has been killed."

"Big Tom knows stuff about the murder. Don't ever think he doesn't. He just don't go blowing off what he knows until it's time."

She stood and walked to the window, her back to him. "Ask your dad to drop by later. I have a few questions I'd like answered."

Tommy Joe finished his coffee. He'd been bluffing. His dad didn't have a clue about the storm brewing in the swamp. Didn't know about the madman who would stop at nothing to get what he wanted.

Adrienne thanked him for coming and ushered him out the door. She could have been a lot friendlier, what with her grandmother still sleeping. It wasn't as if she had anything else going on. She was practically an old maid by Breaux-ville standards, and he was a better catch than Jules Duquette. He had a job and money in the bank. In a few days he'd have a lot more, if everything went according to plan.

He stopped at the door. "All work and no play isn't good for anyone. There's a live band at LeBlanc's tomorrow night. What you say I buy your dinner and then we catch a few sets? *Laissez les bon temps rouler.*"

"Not this week, Tommy Joe, but thanks for the invitation. I'm not much in the mood for letting the good times roll."

"Then you just take care of yourself, and if you need anything at all, you call me. Anytime."

"Thanks."

He walked back to his car. She wasn't going to call him, not with Jules Duquette back in the picture. Only Jules wouldn't be in the picture much longer. He knew that for a fact.

ADRIENNE LOOKED UP as Mims stepped into the kitchen, a bouquet of daisies cradled in the basket hung over her arm. "I'm glad you came in. It's too hot to be out in that garden."

"I like the heat. It stirs my tired blood. Besides, it's you who work too much."

Adrienne looked up from the folders and notes she had

spread across the kitchen table and glanced at the kitchen clock. Two in the afternoon and she still hadn't heard from Big Tom.

As Mims rummaged in the cabinet for a vase for her flowers, Adrienne went back to her notes, determined to find some link between what she knew and who had killed Jules's cousin.

She wished she'd asked more questions on the phone when Reynard had called her, found out more about the stranger he'd mentioned.

The phone rang. She jumped at the sound and realized how rattled her nerves had become over the past few days. She grabbed the receiver. "The Breaux residence. May I help you?"

"Hello, Adrienne. This is Chief Gaubert. Tommy Joe said he took a 911 call out at your place this morning and that you wanted to talk to me."

"I was hoping you could come out here so that we could talk in person."

"Yeah, and I was planning to, but something's come up. We have our first real lead in the Duquette and Trosclair murders."

"Does it have to do with the altered geological report I told you about?"

"No. Like I told you before, that's probably just coincidence."

"Then what kind of lead do you have?"

"I'm not at liberty to discuss it, but I can tell you that when it all comes out in the open, no one in this town will be surprised. And if I were you, I'd stay away from Jules Duquette. He's…dangerous."

"Are you suggesting that Jules is connected to the murder of James Trosclair or of his own cousin?"

"I'm not suggesting anything but that you stay away from him. You might be interested in why Reynard was in town the day he was killed. He was showing his grandparents' property to some man from New Orleans looking to build a fancy fishing and hunting camp.''

''How could Reynard sell the land without Jules's signature?''

''Seems he was the sole owner of that property. I don't imagine that set too well with Jules. Fact is, if Reynard hadn't been killed when he was, that land Jules is sitting on right now wouldn't belong to him. Neither would any of the money Reynard would have gotten from the sale, and we're talking about a big chunk of wetland.''

Her lungs constricted. This smelled like a setup. ''Are you planning to arrest Jules?''

''I'll do whatever needs doing.''

''Jules didn't kill Reynard. He's here to find the killer.''

''Just stay out of this, Adrienne. It's police business, and there's no cause for you to go making trouble for yourself.''

''Stay out of this or else I'll wind up floating in the bayou the way Reynard and James Trosclair did?''

''Don't go putting words in my mouth. All I'm—''

She hung up the phone, her hands shaking so that she could barely get the receiver back in its cradle. ''I'm going to have to go out for a while, Mims. I'll call Maggie to come and stay with you.''

''I can stay by myself.''

''I know.'' But she was going to call Maggie and then she was going to take the boat and pay a visit to Jules. Down the bayou, to the spot where she and Jules had made love so many years ago. To an isolated cabin that haunted her dreams and tortured her memories.

It was the last place she needed to be, but she had no choice. Jules deserved to know what was going on. He wasn't a killer. She'd stake her life on that. In fact, she was about to do just that.

TOMMY JOE POLED the pirogue through the shallow waters. Another meeting with the stranger, and every time he had to see the man, he dreaded it more. He'd seen evil in a man's eyes before. Hatred, greed. Hell, he was no saint himself, but he'd never seen a man like this.

No doubt about it, Tommy Joe had sold out to the devil himself. A demon who walked around on two feet and carried a wad of cash in his back pocket.

He'd flashed it in Tommy Joe's face as if he'd known how badly he hated being poor. He'd always wanted the kind of money Nick Ryan had. Wanted the fancy cars, nice clothes. That was what it took to get the kind of women he deserved. Women like Caroline Donovan and Adrienne Breaux.

Money could make his dreams come true. That was what he'd told himself for years. Only, Jules Duquette didn't need money. He just waltzed into town and Adrienne Breaux let him sleep in her bed.

So maybe he didn't dread this meeting tonight, after all. Maybe this time doing what he was paid to do would be pure pleasure.

Chapter Six

Jules slid the sharp point of the knife through the slick skin of the catfish, thoughts of Reynard rumbling through his mind. Ironic that Reynard was the one murdered in the swamp. For a time Reynard had been almost obsessed with Boyce Sincard's vow to make Jules, Tyler and Nick pay for their role in sending him to prison.

Reynard had kept up with every parole hearing, been furious when Sincard was released early. He hadn't really let his anxiety go until he'd heard that Sincard had drowned in a boating accident. Now it was Reynard who'd been murdered and Jules left to find the killer.

So far he'd only pulled in empty nets. But there had to be a pattern he was overlooking, a link between Trosclair's murder and Reynard's. He'd tried to tie the murders to Big Tom Gaubert, but to no avail.

For one thing, there was the matter of Nick's stepbrother. Jules had studied the case against Robelot. Big Tom considered Paul's murder an open-and-shut case, but Jules was not so certain. He didn't have proof, just a gnawing feeling that things were not as clear-cut as they seemed. A gut feeling. Instinct. Whatever, it had worked well for him as a detective and he wasn't about to ignore it now.

Suddenly Jules had the sensation he was being watched. He looked up from the fish he was gutting to find Pierre

Trosclair standing just inside the clearing that surrounded the cabin. He'd sneaked up as silently as a scorpion crawling through the quagmire of mud and muck.

"Good to see you, Pierre. Are you looking for me?"

He nodded. "I gotta…" Sweat beaded his forehead. He swiped at it with the sleeve of his shirt. "Gotta tell you."

Those were the most words he'd ever heard Pierre string together. He dropped the half-cleaned fish to the worktable. "What's wrong? What have you got to tell me?"

Pierre's face was white, his eyes wide and dark with fear. "Coming to get me."

"Who? Who's coming to get you?"

Pierre sucked his bottom lip into his mouth. "Killer. Coming to get me."

"Did you see your father get shot, Pierre?"

He nodded, still avoiding eye contact.

"Listen, Pierre, I can help you, but I need you to tell me who killed him. A name. I need a name."

"No. Kill me." Pierre glanced back into the overgrowth behind him.

"I won't let him hurt you. You tell me his name and I'll make sure he goes to jail so he can't kill anyone else."

"Can't tell you… A stranger."

"Then tell me what he looks like."

"No. Kill me." He pointed his index finger at Jules. "Kill you."

"He's not going to kill anyone. We won't let him, not if you help me. Was it Big Tom Gaubert you saw kill your dad, Pierre?"

Pierre shook his head, but his breath came in short choppy gasps and he chewed frantically on his bottom lip.

"Do you know who Big Tom is?"

Pierre nodded and stepped backward.

"I want you to stay with me, Pierre. I'll take care of you. I won't let the man kill you."

Pierre continued to stare at the ground.

"Let me finish here, and we'll go inside and talk."

Pierre sat down on a stump.

Jules turned back to the fish. Pierre was scared senseless. Scared enough to talk. Now Jules had to find a way to convince him to tell everything he knew.

He finished cleaning the fish and tossed it into the pail of ice water. "All finished. Are you hungry?" But when he turned around, Pierre was gone, disappeared as silently as he'd appeared a few minutes ago.

Damn. He should have expected this. Now he had no choice but to go into the swamp to find him. It wouldn't be easy, not if Pierre didn't want to be found. The swamp was his home.

IT WAS LATE AFTERNOON by the time Adrienne was able to connect with Maggie. At first the housekeeper had been reluctant to drive out so late in the day, even though she'd worked for the Breaux family for years. She'd acquiesced quickly enough, however, when Adrienne had suggested she bring her husband along.

The whole town was nervous about the murders. Maggie was no exception, and Adrienne was sure her phone call last night to see if the trusted housekeeper had noticed a man slipping into their house and leaving a note hadn't helped the situation any. Or maybe they had all heard that the suspected murderer had spent the night at her house. Adrienne wondered what people would say if they knew how she really felt about Jules and that she couldn't wait to see him again.

The Duquette cabin was less than a mile away as the crow flies, but it couldn't be reached by land. She'd have to follow the narrow waterway behind her place, row past LeBlanc's. After that, she'd turn into a more shallow bayou, one where the cypress grew so thick that it was dark and tenebrous even when the sun was high in the sky. Now the sun was setting, and the shadows were already lengthening.

A crow mocked her as she walked beneath the cobweb canopy of Spanish moss, and something slithered through the grass in front of her. But it was the heat and overwhelming humidity that stole her breath away and clogged her lungs.

Still, she shuddered at the cool sharpness of dread churning inside her. Reynard Duquette and James Trosclair. Two men, as different as men could be, and they had both met the same fate, been killed and dropped into the bayou. Jules was not the killer, but someone was. And she was about to go trespassing on his killing fields.

She had no alternative. Jules had to be warned that Big Tom might be setting him up to take the blame for murders he hadn't committed. She walked to the water's edge and unlocked the chain that secured the pirogue to the cypress tree. A few minutes later she was dipping the oars rhythmically beneath the surface and gliding soundlessly through a dark passageway where turtles, snakes and alligators were the natural denizens and she was the intruder. Down the gray waters of the bayou to Jules Duquette.

EXHAUSTED AND IRRITATED with himself for not being able to track down Pierre, Jules sat in a rickety rocker on the porch of the cabin and stared into the gathering darkness. He noticed the pirogue approaching as soon as it rounded the bend—a shadow at first, then taking form.

He craned his neck and made out the female figure doing the rowing. A rush of feelings swept through him, heated, so intense they seemed to turn him inside out.

But the anticipation washed away in a surge of adrenaline as the reality of the situation sank in. It wasn't likely that Adrienne had made the trip down the bayou to pay a social call. Something had to be wrong.

Swinging off the end of the porch, he strode across the boggy earth and through the tangled web of vines and undergrowth, not stopping until he reached the clearing where his own boat was tied. He was waiting as she pushed the nose of the pirogue onto the land.

"What's wrong?" he asked, taking her hand as she stepped from the boat.

"Does there have to be something wrong? Maybe I just wanted to check on my patient."

"You don't lie so well, princess. Are you sure you're a lawyer?"

"I'm not sure of anything right now."

Her voice gave her away, shaky and strained, but still with the power to cut into him and strip the flesh from old wounds. Half the bad things in his life he connected somehow to Adrienne Breaux and her dad. Half the bad and all the good. He led her up the overgrown path, clearing the way as best he could.

"It's not much," he said as they drew close to the cabin, "but it's home. Of course it wouldn't be if Reynard hadn't been shot before he could sell it."

"When did you find that out?"

"This morning. Not that it matters. I'd never planned on coming back here. That was the reason I'd turned it over to Reynard in the first place. It was his to sell." He touched a hand to the small of her back as she stepped onto the porch. "This is a long way off the beaten path. How did you find me?"

"I've been here before. Remember?"

"Yeah. I remember." Remembered it as if it was yesterday. Remembered every excruciating detail. They'd slipped away from her birthday party, the one he'd crashed. His grandmother had been in the hospital recovering from her first heart attack. His grandfather had been at her bedside.

The cabin had been all theirs. "I remember that it was a long, long time ago."

A mosquito buzzed her head. She slapped it away. "Are you going to invite me in?"

"Yeah, sure. If you're brave enough to come slumming, you might as well get the full treatment." He held the screen door open while she stepped inside.

The cabin had been sparsely furnished but functional and comfortable when his grandparents were alive. Fishing nets had always been stretched over the front and back porches to dry. Likely as not, a pot of gumbo would be simmering on the back of the old range, and one of his grandma's pies would be cooling on the sideboard his grandpa had fashioned from a cypress log.

But now the place had fallen into serious disrepair. The roof leaked. Spiderwebs hung in the corners of the ceiling like borders of lace. There were no pots of gumbo or boiling crabs. He'd mostly eaten at LeBlanc's since he'd been back in town, and the cabin smelled more of mildew than of spices.

Only, now Adrienne was in the cabin. It would be her fragrance that haunted him when she left, her face, the way it looked right now—soft yet determined, a woman with a mission. But he wasn't certain he wanted to know what the mission entailed. "Would you like some coffee?" he asked, feeling the need to do something besides stare at her.

"Coffee would be good."

He rinsed the morning dregs from the drip pot and refilled it with springwater from a bottle while the old memories sucked away his control. He couldn't go on like this much longer, staying a polite distance from Adrienne when all he wanted to do was take her in his arms and carry her to the bedroom. He wanted her, now, wanted her so desperately that he could barely force his mind and hands to function with any semblance of rationality.

"We can make small talk all night," he said, knowing he couldn't. "Or you can tell me what you came out here to say."

"I had a call from Big Tom this afternoon."

"Big Tom, on top of everything except finding my cousin's killer. Did he tell you to stay away from the likes of me?"

"Among other things." She walked over to stand beside him—too close. His body reacted in a strangling swell of desire.

"You should listen to him." He touched a finger to her cheek and then trailed it down to her chin. "I'm trouble, *chère*. Can't you feel it?"

"You may be trouble. You're not a killer."

He backed away so that he could study her expression. "Surely he didn't accuse me of killing my own cousin. Even Big Tom has to have more sense than that. But then, it wouldn't be the first time the man framed me when he knew damn well I was innocent."

"He didn't accuse you, but he did tell me that Reynard had planned to sell the property. Then he said he had a lead in the murder case and that no one in town would be surprised when he made the arrest."

"And you think I'm the one he's planning to slap behind bars?"

"Why else would he warn me to stay away from you, insist that you're dangerous?"

"He warned you to stay away, yet here you are. Why is that, Adrienne? Do you need a little excitement in your life?" He circled her waist with his hands and fought his hunger for her. "Or do you just like the thrill of danger, the way you did eleven years ago when you defied your father and ran off with me? Sexy rich girl out for a night of fun and games with the bad boy from the swamp."

She jerked away from him. "Is that how you remember that night?"

"What else was there to remember?"

"Nothing, I guess." Her shoulders slumped and she crossed her arms protectively. "I've told you what I know, Jules. I have to go now."

The hurt in her voice, the moisture that welled up in her dark eyes, broke his final vestiges of control. Jules reached for her and pulled her close. "I lied, princess. That's not all I remember." His mouth found hers, and all the years of wanting and needing her burst free and shook him to his very soul.

"I've remembered everything about you every day of my life," he said.

"Then make love with me, Jules. Not for the past, but for now. For me and for you."

"If I do, you won't be able to get rid of me so easily this time. You may never get rid of me at all."

She answered him with a kiss. He scooped her up in his arms and carried her to his bed.

Chapter Seven

Adrienne lay atop the handmade bed, lost in the dream. How many nights had she been here, with Jules lying next to her, looking at her the way he was right now? His gaze washed over her, a silken spray of heated passion.

"I can't believe this is happening," he whispered. "I promised myself I'd never give in to this craving again, not with you." He feathered her face with kisses—her forehead, her eyelids, her nose. "But here I am."

She found his lips with hers. The kiss was delicious, breathtaking. She couldn't get enough. Parting her lips, she felt the warm probing of his tongue. The kiss deepened.

When Jules finally pulled away, it was only to roam her flesh with his lips as his fingers tangled with the buttons of her blouse. His thumbs massaged her nipples as he worked, and she was thankful she'd gone braless in the summer heat.

The fabric fell open. He moaned deliriously as her breasts were bared. Fondling, nuzzling, stroking, he aroused first one and then the other until she arched toward him, the ache inside her hot and excruciating.

And then he moved lower, his mouth searing her flesh as he tore open the snap at her waist and tugged her shorts lower. His hands were masterful. She reacted to every touch, moving in rhythm, meeting his lips and then pulling away. "You've learned a lot in eleven years," she whispered.

"So have you."

So she had. They had both had other lives. But no one had ever made her feel the way Jules did. The first time he'd been bumbling, moving much too fast, but it hadn't mattered. It was his passion that had embedded itself in her. It still was.

He slipped her shorts down her long legs and threw them to the floor. Then his fingers worked their way inside her panties, the sexy red ones she'd bought on sale in a weak moment and never wore—until today. At some level, she knew they would end up making love....

Jules's fingers dipped inside her, and she writhed in ecstasy. "It's not fair for only one of us to be naked," she whispered.

"You're right. Care to help?"

"Oh, yes."

He slid from the bed and stood at its edge. She climbed onto her knees and began working on the buttons of his shirt. The sensual stroking of his hands on her body made it hard for her to function, but somehow she managed to tear the shirt from his chest and slip it down his arms.

For a moment she only stared, struck by the sheer power of his masculinity, the way she had been when she'd nursed his wounds. Muscled, his Cajun flesh tanned to an even brown, the dark hairs sprinkled liberally over his chest and narrowing to creep down his abdomen.

Her breasts brushed his chest as she unsnapped his jeans. He peeled the denim over his hips and let it fall with his briefs to the floor. He stood naked in front of her, his body still bearing the bruises of the attack, his desire obvious. He touched her hand to himself.

Her breath caught as she gave way to a need stronger than she'd ever imagined existed. Jules was no longer the boy who'd kissed her at fourteen. No longer the young man who'd made love to her eleven years ago.

He had changed, and she wanted him in a way she'd never wanted any man. But it wasn't just his body she craved. It was him. Jules Duquette, the man. She slid into his arms and their bodies melded.

"Princess. Sweetheart." He moaned and she felt the shudder that shook his body. "I've dreamed of this so long."

Tears clouded her eyes. "Me, too," she whispered. "We should have been dreaming together."

The next movements were swift, strong, voracious. She lay beneath him as he fit himself inside her. And then they were no longer separate, but one. Flying over the top. Together. Finally together, after all these years.

"I love you," she whispered.

He didn't answer. He didn't have to. Whether he said it, whether he knew it, she was certain that he loved her, too. How else could it have been so perfect?

"ARE YOU HUNGRY?" Jules asked when she finally stirred beside him in bed.

"Famished. How about you?"

"I could eat. Or I could do other things," he teased.

"You did. Twice."

He stroked her stomach. "Who's counting?"

"Not me. But I need food. Then we'll have the rest of the night together."

"I don't have much in the way of menu choices. But I could fry the catfish I caught this afternoon."

"That sounds wonderful. I'll help."

"You're on." He slid off the bed and pulled on his jeans.

She slipped on her panties and started to stick a foot into a leg of her shorts. He caught her hand. "Let's just leave those off. I like you in red." He bent over and kissed her.

"We better start cooking," she said, smiling, "before we don't make it to the kitchen."

"Worse things could happen." But he left her and padded barefoot and shirtless out of the bedroom.

She pulled on her cotton blouse but didn't bother with the buttons. She followed him into the kitchen, still basking in the afterglow but already thinking about Big Tom and his intimation that Jules was about to be arrested and charged with murder. And a chill sneaked inside her and pricked away at the warmth making love had left there.

WHILE HE BATTERED the fish, Jules told Adrienne about his visit from Pierre Trosclair. Adrienne listened, only interrupting to ask a question. Now she was standing nearby, looking so sexy it was all he could do to keep his hands off her. But her mood had changed, and her brows were pulled close over her gorgeous eyes. She saw him watching her and managed a smile.

He dropped one of the battered fillets into the hot oil. "I hope that pained look is not due to something I've done."

"No, I was just thinking. You said earlier that if Big Tom arrested you, it wouldn't be the first time he'd framed you for something you didn't do."

"Did I say that?"

"Don't start playing games again, Jules. You know you said it, and we both know you don't say anything you don't mean. So what were you talking about?"

She didn't want games, but in this case she wouldn't like the truth any better. Even dead, her dad would stand between them. T.L. would love that.

"Were you referring to the summer you spent at Peltier Point?" she asked, stepping closer.

He studied her, knew she wouldn't let go of this until it was out in the open. Besides, if they were going to have a chance at a life together, he couldn't keep secrets from her.

A life together? It was amazing how making love could

addle the brain. Make a man forget that some bayous couldn't be crossed.

"It is about Peltier Point, isn't it?" she insisted.

"Yeah. But that was a long time ago. Let it lie. Even a dead skunk can stink up a place if you mess with it."

She sighed, but kept her gaze pinned on him. "Tell me, Jules. I need to know. What happened that summer?"

He gave up. "What happened? You, princess. You stepped—or was it fell—into my life and I made the wrong move. At fifteen, I should have known better than to touch T.L.'s daughter."

"What are you saying? All you did was kiss me, and I was as guilty of that as you were. I certainly didn't object. It was just as much my fault."

"You must be mistaken. It couldn't have been *your* fault. I didn't see *you* out there with me that summer, sleeping with the snakes and spiders, being barked at from morning until night, knocked around if you dared protest anything, afraid to sleep because you couldn't watch your back with your eyes closed."

"Peltier Point was a detention camp to help boys mature, not a prison."

"You're right. It wasn't a prison, more like a sweaty bug-infested hell."

She pressed the heels of her hands together. "But you must have done *some*thing to get you sent to a place like that. You surely aren't saying you were sent to Peltier Point just because you kissed me."

"Oh, no. Big Tom and your dad were far more creative than that. Supposedly I stole from the cash box your dad kept on the docks to pay the fishermen a piddling sum for their day's catch. No trial. No proof. Just accusations and a free vacation."

Adrienne turned away, but not before he saw the pain in her face. No matter what T.L. had done, he'd been her father. But then, there had always been impassable barriers between them. One evening of making love couldn't change that. "I'm sorry, princess." And he was. Sorry for everything. What was and what would never be.

She walked to the window and stared out. "I knew my dad was hard, even had doubts about the integrity of some of his business dealings, but this…"

"T.L. took care of his own. He saw me as someone dangerous. One of the swamp rats."

She turned to stare at him. "I never thought of you that way."

"Then you were the exception. Reynard and I knew what the kids in town called us. I'm not saying the name-calling didn't hurt, but we lived with it. Our grandparents took us in when we had nowhere else to go. They loved us and we loved them, and nothing anyone said could make us ashamed of the way they brought us up."

"Still, the summer at Peltier Point changed you. I knew it from your first day back at school. But at least now I know why you stayed away from me."

"I stayed away because you were out of my league. We're different, you and me."

"You didn't think I was so different the night of my eighteenth birthday party."

He wrapped his arms about her waist and touched his lips to her sweet-smelling hair. "Swamp rats and fools do crazy things. Even Peltier Point couldn't change that about me." He let her go and went back to remove the first fish from the simmering oil. "The summer from hell had its moments, though. I made two of the best friends I've ever had while I was at Peltier Point. In that kind of place you learn fast who your friends are."

"And you already knew who your enemies were. My dad and the chief of police."

"I made a few more that summer, one in particular."

"Anyone I know?"

"Not likely." Old memories welled up in Jules's mind like noxious gases. He gulped in a supply of air. "Nick Ryan, Tyler Belton and I saw a boy kill another of our buddies that summer. A snotty rich kid named Boyce Sincard pushed our friend Dave Lanier under the water and held him there until he drowned. Murdered him, like he was nothing."

"How terrible." She walked over and stood beside him. "You must have been horrified."

"Shaking in our boots, but each of us tried to act tougher than the others. We took a blood oath, promised we'd stand by each other no matter what."

"What did you do about the murder?"

"Told what we knew. We had no idea what kind of retaliation we'd face for squealing, but the boy who was killed was our friend, and we couldn't just let him die without making the guilty man pay."

"The same way you're determined to do now with Reynard."

"A man who doesn't stand up for family and friends is not much of a man."

"But you weren't a man then. You were only a boy."

"I grew up fast that summer."

"What happened to the boy who killed your friend?"

"He went to jail, got out a few years ago on a technicality. Evidently some goody-goody judge decided his juvenile rights had been abused at the trial."

Adrienne grabbed his arm. "But this Boyce fellow would have reason to exact revenge on you. Maybe even by killing your cousin. He could be the murderer, Jules. He could be out there now waiting for his chance to shoot you in the back of the head and drop you into the bayou like he did Reynard."

"He could be, if he was alive. In fact, he would have been my first suspect. But I checked out the details of his death again this week. He drowned in a boating accident. Several witnesses said they saw him go under and never come up. The coast guard checked it out and came to the same decision. Even the insurance paid off without a hitch.''

''Died in the same way he murdered your friend. I guess that was justice of a sort.''

''I can't help but wonder if he thought of Dave while he was fighting the water for his own life. Wonder if he ever felt any kind of remorse.''

Adrienne dropped the potato she'd been peeling and threw her hands in the air as if she'd just had a divine revelation. ''Nick Ryan and Tyler Belton. They're your friends, Jules. They can help. Call them.''

''That would be a little hard. Tyler's dead. And there's no cause to pull Nick into this mess. No cause for my trouble to be his. He's had his own share lately. Besides, we're not teenagers anymore.''

He didn't mention that the last time he'd called Nick for help, the call had never been returned. Some hurts were better kept inside.

Adrienne stepped between him and the frying fish. ''But you said yourself that you all promised to be there for the others if you were ever needed. You're about to be arrested on murder charges. You need all the help—''

''Shh.'' Jules quieted her, his ears and mind alert to the drone of a boat motor in the distance. He rushed to the window, peering into the darkness. The motor was cut off.

''Get your clothes on, Adrienne. Someone's coming.''

''What will you do?''

''That all depends on who it is. I need to buy a little more time. I'll hide behind the house. If this is someone I can trust not to harm you, I plan to disappear before I'm stuck behind bars.'' With a flick of his wrist, he turned off the fire under the fish and rushed to the bedroom, stopping only long enough to grab his boots and shirt before he jumped through the back window and disappeared into the boggy jungle he knew so well.

"WHAT THE DEVIL are you doing out here?"

Adrienne smoothed the front of her blouse and shorts and stared at the man who'd just pushed his way through Jules's kitchen door. "I don't believe that's any of your business, Tommy Joe."

His eyes narrowed and she could see the veins in his face and neck. "You said it. It's none of my business who you shack up with. Where's Jules?"

"He's not here."

He crossed the room and stepped inside her space. "I reckon he'll be back soon if you're hanging around. I don't guess you came out here looking to trap yourself a nutria for supper."

"I came to talk to Jules, the same as you."

"Talk? The way you did the night of your birthday party when you ran off with him? Don't look so surprised. If you hadn't been enjoying yourself so much, you'd have seen me following you that night. Heard me outside the window while I watched."

Her stomach turned inside out at the thought of Tommy Joe spying on Jules and her while they'd made love. But this was no time for queasiness, no time to show weakness. "I don't know what your dad told you, but Jules didn't kill Reynard or James Trosclair, Tommy Joe. He's innocent."

"And I suppose you got that gem of information from the swamp rat himself."

"No. Pierre Trosclair knows who killed his dad. He'll be able to identify him."

"Pierre Trosclair? He's crazy. Even if he could talk, no one would believe anything he said."

"He's not crazy, Tommy Joe. He's autistic. No one thinks

he can talk, but he can. He knows it wasn't Jules who killed his dad.''

Tommy Joe grabbed a handful of her hair and yanked her to him, his breath reeking with the odor of garlic and cheap bourbon. ''Of course not. It was the mysterious bayou killer who shot him. The same way he's going to kill you and Jules. You shoulda listened, instead of sticking your nose where it don't belong.''

''So you were the one who left the note.'' She kicked and tried to pull free. But he was too quick and much too strong. He knocked her to the floor, then pressed a knee into her stomach while he held her hands over her head.

''The alligators are hungry tonight, *chère*. They're gonna like you plenty good.''

She tried to scream, but he slapped her hard across the face. Then he yanked out a pair of handcuffs and bound her wrists.

''We'll go down to my boat for a little moonlight trip. I have someone there who's been wanting to meet you.''

''Who? Who's out there with you?''

''An old friend of Jules's. A man from way back in his past. Someone who hates him even more than I do.''

''Boyce Sincard?''

He didn't answer, but she knew by the look on his face that she'd guessed right. So much for the man being dead. ''Boyce Sincard is a killer, Tommy Joe. You can't trust him. He'll only kill you, too.''

''You're smart, Adrienne Breaux, but not smart enough.'' The voice came from a tall slim man standing in the doorway. A jagged scar ran from just under his ear to his neck. His hair was dark and bushy, and his eyes glowed like those of a wildcat about to attack.

He laughed, a raucous taunting cackle that echoed in the

cabin and through her mind. She swung her arms and kicked wildly, connecting with nothing but the stifling air.

The bayou killer was about to strike again, only this time she would be the victim. And she was powerless to stop him.

Chapter Eight

Boyce Sincard made his way down the bayou with Adrienne lying at his feet, her hands and ankles bound, a handkerchief shoved in her mouth. Boyce had waited thirteen long years for the sweet taste of revenge. It had kept him going in that cesspool they called a prison. He'd spent his nights plotting how he'd find and kill first one and then the other of the boys who'd testified against him and stolen what should have been the best years of his life.

In spite of all his plotting, the first two attempts hadn't gone the way he'd planned. Tyler Belton and Nick Ryan had troubles, all right, but they were still alive. But there would be no dalliance this time. Tommy Joe would find Jules and explain that his old nemesis, Boyce Sincard, had his woman and that he was going to kill her. Once Tommy Joe did that, nothing would keep Jules away.

He would kill all three of them, of course. Jules. Adrienne Breaux. The fool cop, Tommy Joe. After that he'd track down and kill Tyler Belton and Nick Ryan. The three friends who thought they were invincible. But soon they'd all be dead, and he would be walking around a free man, safe in the new identity he'd assumed.

His pulse quickened and his heart pounded as the thrill of victory roared in his head. At long last vengeance would be his.

ADRIENNE LAY on her back in the carved-out bottom of the pirogue as Boyce guided it through the narrow passage. The boat motor droned on, but still they moved slowly. She couldn't see where they were going, but his curses and complaints informed her that the bayou in this area was choked with water hyacinths and thick clusters of lilies. He had to turn the motor off frequently and row through the worst of it.

But still they kept moving, away from Jules. Away from help. Away from a chance to survive.

Less than an hour ago she'd lain in Jules's arms, thrilled to the touch of his fingers on her flesh, tingled with each kiss, each move. Making love with him had been even more exciting than she'd dreamed. More joyous. More perfect. More meaningful.

She was sure he'd escaped into the swamp when he'd realized the caller was Tommy Joe. He'd have had no reason to stick around. He'd believed Tommy Joe was irritating and bumbling, but not dangerous.

He wouldn't know what had happened to her until someone dragged what was left of her body from the murky water, the same way they had Reynard's and James Trosclair's.

Squirming as best she could with her wrists and ankles bound, she tried to stretch her legs. They refused to budge, had become lodged between two immovable objects that she couldn't see and couldn't make out by touch. Her cramped legs were growing numb, but she wouldn't give up. She couldn't. Not as long as there was breath in her lungs.

PIERRE TROSCLAIR raced across the boggy ground, his boots, being sucked into the mud, sounding like someone was slurping the last of their soup. The bad man had taken the pretty lady. He would hurt her, the same way he had hurt his dad.

The bad man had tried to hurt Pierre, too, but his dad had

pushed him out of the boat and screamed at him to swim.
He had. After that he'd just run and run and run. As fast as
he could.

He didn't want to talk about it. He didn't like to talk at
all. If you talked, people made you do things you didn't want
to do. Like try to read numbers and make letters on paper.
So he'd just quit talking. Only, sometimes he talked to the
animals that lived in the swamp. And sometimes he'd talked
to his dad.

Before the bad man killed him.

The bad man was in the boat now with the pretty woman.
The bad man would come back, but the pretty woman
wouldn't.

Pierre raced through the swamp, keeping up with the boat
as best he could while keeping himself hidden in the thick
undergrowth. But they were in dangerous territory now,
places where the mud was so thick it sucked you inside it.
He'd have to give up soon.

His foot tangled in a mesh of vines, and he tripped, landing headfirst in the muck. Water splashed into his eyes and
nose. The boat motor droned on. But there was another
sound. And then he saw the red eyes and heard the sloshing
crush of movement. He'd stumbled into a nest of baby alligators, and the mother was rushing toward him.

He shinnied up a tree and waited as the sound of the motor
disappeared. Sweat ran down his face and soaked his
clothes. The world had turned bad.

But he wasn't alone. He heard footsteps coming toward
him. It must be Jules. He tried to scream a warning, but
when he opened his mouth, nothing came out but a guttural
bark.

"Where's Jules Duquette?"

He stared as Tommy Joe Gaubert moved toward him—
and the nest. "If you can talk at all, you better start. I know
Jules Duquette is out here somewhere. Have you seen him?"

The huge mouth of the mother alligator opened and locked around the cop's leg before he even knew what was happening. Pierre closed his eyes. He hated the sight of blood. A second later he slid down the tree and escaped while the momma gator was busy protecting her young.

"I GUESS THIS IS as good a place as any to dump a body," Boyce said, killing the boat motor and turning to face her.

He shoved the metal object away from her legs with the heel of his boot. The boxlike contraption scraped across the bottom of the boat and scratched a layer of skin from her leg. Leaning over, he grabbed Adrienne's arm, yanking her off the floor and pushing her onto the wooden seat.

"Guess it wouldn't hurt to let you talk now." He snatched the damp handkerchief from her mouth and tossed it into the water. "No last meal, but you can have a few last words. Try to make them memorable."

"Why? You'll never tell anyone that you heard them." She swallowed hard a few times, her mind jumping from one possibility to another. There had to be something she could say, something she could do that would keep him from killing her.

She didn't want to die. She wanted to be with Jules. Make love with him. Marry him. Have his children. Tears burned her eyes. "You won't get away with this."

"I will get away with this. I'm a dead man. Dead men can't be arrested for murder. You and Jules will just be two more victims of the bayou killer. Murder cases that will never be solved."

"You hated Jules so much that you faked your own death just so you would be free to kill him? Do you know how sick that is?"

"What do you know about sick? You sit up there in that big house of yours and play lawyer. I was the one who rotted in that jail year after year."

"You murdered an innocent boy. It was the punishment you deserved."

"The boy was stupid. If I hadn't killed him, someone else would have. It's that kind of world."

"It may be your world. It's not mine."

"No? It's the world your friend Tommy Joe Gaubert lives in. He didn't hesitate more than a few seconds at the chance to make a few dollars."

"So that's how you won him to your side. You paid him."

"No, I only *promised* to pay him."

"Tell me, how much does it cost to buy a man to help you murder innocent people?"

"I don't know. In the end it wasn't money that made Tommy Joe cooperate. It was fear. He'd crossed the line, and he knew it was too late to back out. He'd seen what I'd done to Reynard and James Trosclair and even to Paul Marchand. He didn't want to be next."

"But you still don't have Jules. And you didn't kill Nick Ryan or their friend Tyler, either. All you have is me. So it looks like you're still a loser. And Jules will catch you before this is all over and send you back to jail, this time forever."

She spit the words at him, but her attempt at bravery didn't stop the wild pounding of her heart. She was scared, so scared she could barely breathe, but she couldn't give up. As long as she could keep him from putting the bullet in her head the way he had his other victims, there was still a chance for her to get out of this alive.

"I'm not a loser. I'll never be. I've killed the people closest to both Nick and Jules. Now I'll kill the women they love, starting with you. And then I'll kill them." His voice rose in anger, echoed through the quiet bayou. The boat swayed on the water, and for a minute she thought she was going to be sick. She gulped in a huge helping of air.

Her gaze scanned the boat for something she could grab if the madman took off the handcuffs. "You can't kill everybody," she said, stalling for time. "Sooner or later someone will kill you."

"I'm already a dead man, remember?" He reached into the metal container at his feet and pulled out a pistol. "Tommy Joe is on his way to meet me right now, and he'll have Jules with him."

"Jules will never come out here with Tommy Joe."

"Of course he will. You're the bait. In a few days you'll both wash up down the bayou somewhere. Someone will find you, bullets embedded in the back of your skulls. Gator and turtle bites all over your mottled bodies. The fish will nibble, too. Maybe even one of those slimy eels swimming between your legs and over your breasts." His voice slithered across the words. He meant to drive her nuts while she waited for the bullet that would end the nightmare.

He faced her, holding the pistol with his right hand and steadying it with his left. "In fact, there's really no reason for us to wait for Jules. I can shoot you right now and start the fun."

Her body reeled from pure terror, but she couldn't give up. Not yet. "You shot the others in the back of the head. Are you going to change your MO now?"

He smiled. "Too bad I have to kill you. You'd make a great assistant. Now turn around."

She spit at him but didn't turn. He stood, the gun still pointed at her head. If she tried anything, he'd pull the trigger. If she didn't try anything, he'd still pull the trigger.

He moved toward her. She waited until he had one foot in the air and was about to step around her so that he could shoot her in the back of the head. Then, leading with her shoulder, she threw her body into him. The gun went off. The bullet cracked like thunder in the quiet night and Boyce toppled over the edge of the boat and into the dark bayou.

She could hear him splashing and see his hands clutching the side of the pirogue. The boat rocked toward him. She screamed as loud as she could for Jules. He was her only hope. She tried to catch herself, to keep from falling, but the cuffs stole her balance and she fell against the side of the boat just as Boyce threw one leg over.

Everything happened in an instant. One second she was falling into Boyce, the next she was plunging headfirst into the bayou. She tried to swim, managed to somersault under the water, but the ropes cut into her ankles and the cuffs into her wrists. Her feet hit the muddy bottom and sank into it. The water swirled around her breasts, splashing into her mouth. And all the while, the mud sucked her deeper into the watery grave.

Chapter Nine

The sound of gunfire blasted through the swamp. Jules stopped and listened, his heart crashing against the wall of his chest. He'd run across Pierre in the swamp, shaking so that he could barely talk, but somehow he'd gotten out enough to tell Jules that the man who'd killed his dad had taken Adrienne away in a boat. The last time Pierre had seen them, they were heading deeper into the swamp.

Did the gunfire mean that he was too late, that Adrienne had taken a bullet through her head the way Reynard had? No, he couldn't allow himself to accept that. He raced doggedly, not sure he was going in the right direction. Not sure he'd be able to deal with what he might find, only knowing that he couldn't give up.

He'd worried about a thousand foolish things before. Believed that he was too different from Adrienne. Been sure the odds against them having a life together had been too great. Now those problems drowned in insignificance. All that mattered was that she was safe and that he could hold her in his arms again.

A scream cut into his fear. Adrienne, calling his name. She was alive, and he had to find her, had to save her. If she died before he reached her, her blood would be on Jules's hands, and he'd never draw another peaceful breath if he lived to be a hundred.

The screams grew weaker and then stopped altogether. But still they echoed in his brain, firing fear and adrenaline into his bloodstream. He followed the direction the sound had come from, tripping over logs and cypress knees, sometimes running though water up to his thighs. The dangers in the swamp meant nothing now. If he couldn't save Adrienne, he didn't want to live.

Finally he reached a clearing. The moon filtered through the treetops and glinted off the still bayou waters. And then he saw her. Her head bobbed at the top of the water as if she were dancing on tiptoe to keep her face above the surface, but he knew she had to be sinking into the muddy bottom. Otherwise she would have swum or waded to shore. Relief shuddered through him.

"It's okay, Adrienne, I'm here."

"No, Jules, no. Run. Run." Her voice was hoarse from screaming, but still it quaked with fear. "It's Boyce. He'll kill you."

Boyce. The name thundered through his brain. It couldn't be, and yet he knew it was. He reached for his gun. A second too late.

Gunfire cracked in his ears and he felt the torturous burn as a bullet tore through the flesh of his upper arm. Blood gushed from the wound and he threw his left hand over the ripped flesh to stop the flow.

He turned and stared into the face of Boyce Sincard.

"Jules Duquette, hero to the rescue. But it looks like you're too late. Now take your pistol nice and easy and throw it in front of you."

Jules did as Sincard said, his mind fighting to find a way to save Adrienne before the loss of blood affected his power to act and to reason. "I see jail didn't change you," he said, his gaze locking with Sincard's.

"It changed me, all right." Boyce stepped out of the

tangle of underbrush and tree roots. "I learned not to make mistakes, not to leave witnesses."

"But you're still the same old yellow-bellied coward."

"Not me, Jules. I never hid behind my friends. That was you and Tyler and Nick."

"No. You hid behind your dad's money. At least you tried to." Nick stepped toward the bayou, knowing he had to get to Adrienne before her mouth slid beneath the surface and her lungs filled with the murky water. "I'm the one you want, Boyce. Me, and Nick and Tyler, but you don't have the guts to just come gunning for us. Instead, you go for innocent people, decent people who don't expect your kind of evil."

"I have all the guts I need."

Jules had to keep him talking, keep him from firing a bullet through his brain while he thought of some way to save Adrienne. "So why did you kill Paul Marchand? Why did you kill Reynard and James Trosclair?"

"It was all part of the plan. My perfect plan. I spent years drawing it out, deciding how to get you and your buddies from Peltier Point without being caught. I did it brilliantly, don't you think? Faked my own death. Changed my appearance so much that you didn't even recognize me when you saw me at LeBlanc's bar the other night."

The suspicious stranger. It was all starting to make sense. "You're right. I didn't recognize you, but Reynard did. Is that why you killed him?"

"I would have killed him, anyway. I just had to do it sooner than I'd planned. You didn't think I was really going to buy that piece of swampland you live on, did you? That was all just a ruse to get him out here where I could kill him and get away with it."

"You won't get away with this. You can't kill the world and walk away a free man."

"I don't plan to kill the world. When I'm through with

you and your buddies, I'm moving to the Caribbean. I'll be lying on the beach sipping cold beer with some babe in a bikini before you and your lover out there are cold in the grave.''

He moved the pistol so that it pointed at Adrienne's head. ''First her. Then you. You're the easiest of all, Jules. The other two foiled my plans. Not that it matters. I'll get them before this is over. But you walked right into the trap. Came running back to the bayou as soon as you heard Reynard had been killed. You're hardly a challenge at all.''

Boyce stepped around the boat and to the water's edge. He eased in one foot at a time, walking out until he was knee-deep, moving closer to Adrienne. He steadied the pistol with his left hand, his finger resting on the trigger. ''Sorry we didn't get to know each other better, Miss Breaux. But then, I wouldn't want a woman who'd slept with Jules Duquette, no matter how pretty she was.''

''Pig.''

She spit the word at him, and his face twisted in anger, but now his gaze was glued on her.

Now or never. Jules had to make his move, no matter how futile it might be. He only hoped that Adrienne knew how much he loved her.

He dived into the bayou, felt something slimy brush his leg. Gunshots hit the water around him, but Jules kept swimming beneath the murky waters until he could grab Boyce and pull him under. Boyce's legs tightened around Jules's waist like a vise, pulling him under with him until his lungs felt as if they'd explode.

They burst to the surface simultaneously. Jules plowed a fist into Boyce's face, but pain shot through his wounded arm and the hit lost its force. He lunged at Boyce again, this time managing to knock the pistol from his hand. Boyce grabbed Jules's neck and squeezed with his meaty fingers, cutting off his air supply.

The water around him turned red, colored by his blood. But Jules kept hitting, kept pushing, kept struggling for a breath. Adrienne screamed and Boyce's grip loosened. Jules gulped in a helping of oxygen and turned to see what had stolen Boyce's attention.

A half dozen adult gators with glowing eyes had crept to the edge of the water. The first one splashed into the bayou and the others followed, like a hunting party who'd spotted its prey.

Boyce went crazy, splashing, kicking, yelling curses as if he thought the gators could understand his threats. But all the reptiles knew was that something wild had invaded their territory.

Jules moved silently through the water, cautioning Adrienne not to make any sudden moves. He wrapped his arms around her and pulled her to the bank.

"I thought it was all over for us," she whispered.

"So did I, princess. So did I."

He held her for a second as Boyce stumbled from the water, stammering curses. His actions had driven the gators away, but not before one of them had buried its teeth in his leg. But it wouldn't be a gator who took Boyce Sincard down that night. It would be Jules.

Forgetting his own pain, Jules picked up his gun and pointed it at Sincard. Part of him ached to pull the trigger, to kill without mercy the way Sincard had killed Dave so many years before. The way he had killed Paul, Reynard, James and who knew how many others.

But Jules was made of better stuff. His grandparents had seen to that. There would be no murders in the bayou tonight.

"Guess you'll be going back to jail, Boyce. Hopefully this time for the rest of your life."

Jules cut the ropes from Adrienne's ankles and used them to bound Boyce to a tree while he held Adrienne close and readied the boat for their trip up the bayou. "We need to get you home and out of these wet clothes."

"And out of these handcuffs." She closed her eyes and moaned. "I don't think I can stand to be alone after what I've been through. Will you stay with me tonight?"

"Just try and get rid of me."

"Never. I love you, Jules. I think I always have. I know I always will."

"And I love you." He stood and pulled her into his arms. "The swamp rat and the Cajun princess. Who'd have ever thought it?"

Not him, that was for sure. But in his whole life he'd never liked the thought of anything more.

Epilogue

Two weeks later

The engagement celebration was a *fais-dodo* of magnificent proportions, the kind of party that south Louisiana was famous for. Huge pots of crawfish, corn and spicy potatoes cooking over gas burners. Enough seafood gumbo, potato salad and shrimp *étouffée* to feed a small army. And kegs of ice-cold beer to wash everything down.

A fiddler had everyone in the vicinity tapping their toes to a Cajun beat or else swinging their partner around the makeshift dance floor that had been set up beneath century-old oaks.

Jules watched as Adrienne glided from one group of their guests to another, as gracious to the old fishermen and trackers he'd grown up with as she was to the richest people in town. Her long dark hair fell down her back halfway to her waist, and the white sundress showed off her curves to perfection. She spotted him watching her and waved. He smiled and waved back, determined not to let his disappointment spill over and spoil her fun.

He should be in as good a mood as everyone else, anyway. Tommy Joe Gaubert was in the hospital recovering from the alligator attack. When he did, he'd be going to jail for his role in helping Boyce Sincard. Big Tom had voluntarily stepped down from the post of police chief now that the news was out about his conning his neighbors out of their land for prices far below their worth.

The district attorney was currently investigating some geological reports that had been altered to make it look as if there was a large supply of oil in the area. It hadn't been proved, but the evidence pointed to Big Tom as the one responsible for the alterations. Evidently Reynard had turned up one of them when he was considering selling his land to Boyce.

And best of all, Boyce Sincard was back behind bars. Everything had come full circle, and yet the circle seemed broken beyond repair. Tyler wasn't dead the way he'd thought. He'd found that out through evidence the district attorney had collected about Sincard's activities over the past few weeks. Tyler wasn't dead, but he'd made no move to get in touch with Jules. Neither had Nick Ryan, though Jules had called and left messages that he wanted to see him whenever he surfaced again.

He couldn't blame them any more than he blamed himself for their drifting apart. He'd let life come between them. They all had. But that was not the way it should have been. His thoughts drifted into the past, to three boys in a swamp, scared half to death. One at a time, they'd taken the sharp pocket knife and slit their flesh, letting the blood run and then mingling the sticky crimson flow.

Blood brothers. For always.

But always had come to an end.

Adrienne waltzed up behind him and wrapped her arms around his waist. "You look glum, husband-to-be. You're not getting cold feet, are you?"

He grabbed her and held her close. "Nothing about me is ever cold when I'm around you."

"I like the way you talk."

"And talking is *not* what I do best."

She raised on tiptoe and kissed him. "Are you disappointed because your friends didn't show up?"

"No," he lied. "It would have been nice to see them, but I didn't really expect them. We can't even be sure the invitations reached them."

"Well, you better start expecting," she said, her eyes dancing, "because a car just drove up in front of the house with four people I've never seen before."

Jules turned. Son of a gun if Tyler Belton and Nick Ryan weren't crossing the lawn, smiling from ear to ear, each with a gorgeous woman on his arm. He started toward them, feeling younger than he had in thirteen years.

"MAN, I'D LIKE to have been there to see Boyce Sincard trying to scare off those alligators." Tyler Belton took a long swig of his beer and stretched his legs in front of him. "Too bad we don't have it on video."

Jules rubbed the bandage on his right arm. "Yeah, well, I wasn't exactly in a position to be making a movie at that point. But if I'd known you were alive, I might have invited you to the swim meet."

"Like I said, I was mad enough to chew nails when I found out about that FBI stunt. I never dreamed they'd tell you two I was dead. But, all's well that ends well, and it looks like this is the end of the reincarnation of Boyce Sincard. Now he probably wishes he'd really died in that fake boating accident."

"I just wish we'd figured out what he was up to in time to save Paul and Reynard," Nick said. "James Trosclair, too. Sincard has to have one twisted mind to come up with what he did."

"We still wouldn't know just how twisted if the DA hadn't finally got him to talk. Apparently our boy Boyce is afraid of something. He's afraid of spending the rest of his life in jail, and he thinks cooperating now might help his cause.'' Jules slipped out of his shoes and shoved his stocking feet into the thick carpet of grass.

"Still don't like to wear shoes, uh, Duquette?'' Nick asked.

"Not if I can help it.''

Nick stood and walked over to lean against the trunk of a giant oak tree. "You know, guys, as much as I'd like to get back to those three gorgeous women who are undoubtedly comparing notes about us that could get us into hot water, I'd still like to know how Sincard figured into the deal with Framingham.''

"I can help you out there,'' Tyler said. "As I understand it, he hired Framingham to burglarize the Blankenship Corporation to get information on your property. He directed Framingham to hire me for the job. Framingham's henchmen were supposed to kill me and pin the burglary on me. I'd be an FBI agent gone bad.''

"Only, the real FBI agent gone bad was the one Sincard paid off,'' Jules threw in. "I've always said money is power, and Sincard had unlimited funds.''

"Then Sincard ordered the hits on Paul and Caroline,'' Nick said. "Robelot was supposed to take care of me, as well.''

Tyler shook his head as if he still couldn't believe the way things had turned out. "Boyce Sincard, the teenage killer from Peltier Point. Complex, filthy rich and evil to the core. Do you think life would have turned out differently for him if we'd been too scared to squeal on him back when he killed Dave?''

"He'd have probably killed even more people. Destroyed more lives,'' Jules answered. "Too bad a man that smart chose to use his brains for evil.''

"He was smart, all right,'' Nick added. "He knew the only way he'd have a chance against us was to keep us separated. That's why he went so far as to have Jules's phone bugged. At least that's what I figure he did. Otherwise I would have gotten your calls when you resigned under duress from the NOPD."

"But Boyce didn't win," Tyler said. "We did. Or maybe good just triumphed over evil. I still believe that what a man does can make a difference. That's why I'm going back to the FBI. What about you, Jules?"

"I haven't decided what I'm going to do yet, other than marry the princess. But the Breauxville Town Council offered me the recently vacated job of chief of police. They say they're ready for a turnaround and that I can run a tight ship. I do have an itch to pin on a badge again."

A waiter in a white shirt stopped by the trio of men and refilled their beer mugs. "One more drink," Jules said, "and then we really should go find the three prettiest women at the gala before some hot-blooded Cajun guys steal them out from under our noses."

"First a toast," Tyler said. "To friendship."

"To ridding our lives of Boyce Sincard, we trust for the last time," Nick added. "And to knowing what's important in life. Like friends and the love of the right woman."

Jules leaned in closer. "To letting nothing come between us ever again."

"Shall we take a blood oath on that?" Nick asked.

"We don't need it," Tyler said, raising his glass. "Our blood is already mingled forever."

They tapped their mugs together, sloshing foam onto the ground at their feet. The day was hot and the beer was cold. The women they loved were nearby. And the bayou blood brothers were together again.

Laissez les bon temps rouler.

INDULGE IN A QUIET MOMENT
WITH HARLEQUIN

Get a FREE
Quiet Moments Bath Spa

with just two proofs of purchase from any of our four special collector's editions in May.

Harlequin® is sure to make your time special this Mother's Day with four special collector's editions featuring a short story *PLUS* a complete novel packaged together in one volume!

Collection #1 Intrigue abounds in a collection featuring *New York Times* bestselling author Barbara Delinsky and Kelsey Roberts.

Collection #2 Relationships? Weddings? Children? = *New York Times* bestselling author Debbie Macomber and Tara Taylor Quinn at their best!

Collection #3 Escape to the past with *New York Times* bestselling author Heather Graham and Gayle Wilson.

Collection #4 Go West! With *New York Times* bestselling author Joan Johnston and Vicki Lewis Thompson!

Plus Special Consumer Campaign!
Each of these four collector's editions will feature a
"FREE QUIET MOMENTS BATH SPA" offer.
See inside book in May for details.
Only from

HARLEQUIN®
Makes any time special ®

Don't miss out! Look for this exciting promotion on sale in May 2001, at your favorite retail outlet.

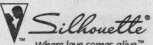

HARLEQUIN®
INTRIGUE
opens the case files on:

TOP SECRET BABIES

Unwrap the mystery!

January 2001
#597 THE BODYGUARD'S BABY
Debra Webb

February 2001
#601 SAVING HIS SON
Rita Herron

March 2001
#605 THE HUNT FOR HAWKE'S DAUGHTER
Jean Barrett

April 2001
#609 UNDERCOVER BABY
Adrianne Lee

May 2001
#613 CONCEPTION COVER-UP
Karen Lawton Barrett

Follow the clues to your favorite retail outlet.

HARLEQUIN®
Makes any time special ™